Chantepleure

chanter *Verb, intransitive* (a) to sing

pleurer *Verb, intransitive* (a) to cry, weep

chantpleure [sic] (*Archaic*) 1. to sing and cry at the same time

A Novel

by Linda Robinson

Chantepleure

Library of Congress Cataloging-in-Publication Data
Chantepleure / Linda Robinson

ISBN 979-8-9859915-0-5

Book design by Rebecca C. Raupp
Cover art and design by Linda Robinson

For the women who have gone before

"We don't see things as they are, we see them as we are." ~ Anais Nin

Chapter 1

Monsieur Lavoisiere walked slowly through the early morning light and the carpet of strewn autumn leaves. The air was full of dancing foliage, like bats waltzing in the dim. M Lavoisiere put one foot into the center of a leaf vortex that was spinning into oblivion on the sidewalk, and his figure became briefly the center of the maelstrom.

His mind was elsewhere long ago.

The streetlights, still lit in the present early day, became gaslight in his mind, and wafting on the breeze the smells of rolls baking in a wood fire, and thick, sweet coffee and cigar smoke mingled with the smell of trash in the gutter and too-sweet perfume from the bordello across the road. The bract toddled ghoulishly in giant macabre shadows on the storefront bricks as the trees tossed broken blades with twiggy fingers into the air.

In his mind he unlocked the door to his shop and was greeted by the big orange cat with as cordial a greeting as the cat ever delivered - a long stretch of her forepaws on the wood floor, then back paws, a shake of the head, and the cat turned away to saunter into the back of the store, which would soon be warmer when Monsieur Lavoisiere lit the small fireplace in his office.

Fire kindled, tea water set to boil, Lavoisiere would roll his stiff white sleeves to mid-elbow, stumble his apron over his head, and tie it to the side. His arms no longer reached the back, and the bow in the front could be tangled in his work, so the side was his only choice. He made do as the years shortened the list of his abilities. Each year more tasks were added to the trash bin of history.

M Lavoisiere sighed, closed his eyes, dragged a heavy breath of ink and raw paper and machine oil into his nostrils, remembering the special aromas of his favorite time of day. The stories that would be set in type would be on his desk, expertly scripted on second sheets, tidily stacked and edged in the box marked "Set" by the youngster apprenticed to him. The boy was careful, if gawky, and with a gentle poke around his edges, might be a fine letterform foundryman in a dozen years.

Where was the boy now? wondered the current M Lavoisiere, his aged gait jockeyed by decades past. He slowly neared the glow emanating from the bakery. The apprentice would be a middle-aged man now. No way to know, no way to find out. Lavoisiere sighed again. The bakery's light brought color back into the world. The leaves swirling dizzyingly in front of the store were gold, copper, brown, yellow, red; colors still muted by the dark's reluctance to bow to the light.

The bell over the bakery door tinkled.

"Up early again, Antoine," observed Joseph the Baker himself, as he dematerialized from the lit shop into the dusk of the nascent day, the words wrapped in the flaky smell of dough ingredients newly mingled, crossed arms woven into his floured apron front like a braided pastry.

Antoine Lavoisiere continued on his way with his slow, deliberate gait. "Work," he mumbled.

"Work where?" Joseph's face hinted a smile.

M Lavoisiere glanced up from his careful study of the sidewalk with a barely perceptible nod, still moving, he passed Joseph's bakery without pause or answer.

"Was that Mr. Lavoisiere again?" asked Mrs. Joseph, as she pummeled an enormous ball of dough with her knuckles, sending flour dust billowing.

"Yes," Joseph answered, wrestling another dough ball out of the wooden bowl and slapping it onto the butcher table. "He said he's going to work."

"Poor old man," sniffed his wife. "His brain has gone back to Prague a hundred years ago. Do you think we should call someone? Does he have family?"

"I don't know. He seems harmless. Three hours from now he'll be back from wherever he went, stop for a coffee and a day-old roll, and do it all over again tomorrow."

"Maybe you should follow him one morning. See where he goes?"

"I'm busy - he must have people. He's got money to buy food, and I don't think he's sleeping on the street. Leave well enough alone. A man needs to have work to do, even if it's imaginary -- let him work, I say."

M Lavoisiere stepped carefully around the corner, away from the streetlights and glanced up at the pinking sky. Purple gray clouds morphed out of the leftover night and orange sherbet jet trails scarred the lightened sky. He stepped into the alcove of a recessed door, worked patiently to organize his shaking hand to fit the key in the lock, turned the key and the knob and stepped into the shop.

The bell over the door tinkled.

The woman seated behind the glass counter glanced up over her half-eye glasses, set the newspaper she was reading down, and gestured toward the back of the shop, the motion carried in shadow tenfold to the wall, brought to life by the reading lamp at her elbow.

"Good morning to you, Mr. Lavoisiere. You're always right on time, aren't you? The fire's set and the kettle, too, as always. Well, and look who's here to wish you a good morning…pretty old kitty." This she purred to the orange cat who was stretching front paws on the wood floor.

Monsieur Lavoisiere did not answer, nodded as he tipped finger to hat brim, turned and heavily removed his top coat, settled it on the coat rack, and brushed the fabric into straightness. His felt hat he lowered from his head to his fist, brushed it lightly with the back of his hand, and set it on the hook next to his coat. One small leaf fragment jittered to the floor. He bent to pick up his tote with the sparkling fish on the sides, turned, nodded to the woman again, and walked slowly toward the curtains separating the front of the shop from the back room, his footfalls creaking the wood boards of the floor.

The woman behind the counter, eyes following each step the old man made as though she, not he, was conducting his feet, smiled as he shuffled the curtains aside, then she readjusted her spine on the thin-backed stool, flipped her long gray braid to the rear, and snapped the paper to her attention once more.

The bell over the door tinkled.

A man swept in, the door banged against the jamb, the wind swirling maple, birch, and pin cherry leaves in and over the red oak floor, accompanying his hat careening to the back of the building; hop, tumble, hop.

"Goodness, the wind," he turned to push the door closed. "Sorry, it's very windy. Rain soon. My." He brushed leaves from his shoulders, arms. "Umbrella won't do, um. Sorry." He gestured, palms out and upward, eyes apologetic. "I wonder…" he stopped, turned in a slow circle, head back, gazing rapt at the ceiling. "What's that smell? Oh my." He smiled and closed his eyes. "Like, like, angel chime candles. Is that it? Did they have a smell? Reminds me of Christmas at home when I was a boy. Remember? The candles would burn and the angels would go round and round." He smiled, finished.

The woman seated behind the glassed counter watched him, peering over her glasses. She said nothing.

"Um, yes, well. I'm looking for today's paper. I meant to go to the drugstore, but, it's too early, not open, yes, here I am. Would you have the paper please?"

The woman picked up the paper in front of her and silently handed it to the man.

He brushed more leaves from his jacket, shuffled an umbrella from arm to arm, and lifted the paper to read. "Um. This is in Finnish. Is it? I actually wanted the paper to look at the want ads. You see, I lost my job, I need a job. Would this be local? I mean to say, it wouldn't have jobs in Finland, would it? I need a job, well. Here." He put the newspaper back on the counter. "I'll just try the drugstore later. I'll go now. Into the wind again. They say maybe rain later. Um, bye now. Thank you.”

The woman picked up the paper and began to read.

The bell over the door tinkled.

“Honestly, Frasier, don’t be daft. It’s not like we’re taking food out of anyone’s mouth. These people are filthy rich. Oh.” the stylish woman paused, looked accusingly at the newspaper and the woman. “This isn’t the restaurant. It must be the next door down. What is that fragrance? Is it caraway? Oh my goodness.” She spun on one high heel. “Must be from the bakery. Frasier, for heaven’s sake, turn around,” and her hand reached into the street to push the hidden man. “Go!”

The door had just touched the wood shut and it swooshed open again; more leaves and the man with the umbrella. “My hat. Must have blown off somewhere, I hope in here. It was on my head, I think...” as he walked quickly, bent over, head swaying left right. “Did you see it? It’s gray. I think. Or no, brown. Ah, here it is.” He straightened triumphantly, jamming the wandering hat solidly on his crown. “Now then. Well. I seem to be back here again. You wouldn’t know of any jobs around, would you? Something, um, well, that pays? Money?”

The woman flicked a yellow leaf from the glass counter with her finger and removed her glasses, set them gently down on the space left vacant. She looked up at the tall stranger, standing expectantly with his umbrella tucked under his arm, his hands clasped together as though praying for a positive answer. The woman folded her arms, still watching the man. "Monsieur Lavoisiere?" she called loudly.

The young man started. "No, actually. Um, Edgar. Some people call me Ed," he barked a laugh, cut it in half. "But generally I stop them. I don't mind Edgar, and well, prefer it." He stopped, looked at the woman, who smiled.

"Monsieur Lavoisiere is in the back room," she smiled more. "He may know of some work for you to do."

"Oh! Well, wonderful." Edgar sighed. He turned his body in a pirouette, and waited, watching the curtains at the back of the shop for the Monsieur Lavoisiere to appear.

The old man who pushed the curtains aside in a grand gesture, either aware of the grandiose stroke, or rigid with shoulder pain, was elderly and compact. The eyes, ringed with wrinkles, and pinked by age at the edges were a shocking blue; blue as the sky in early October when the autumn winds sweep the sky. They blinked as slowly as his arms had moved the curtains, and he swept them unhurriedly from their brief study of Edgar to the woman behind the counter. He wore gold-rimmed spectacles that perched on his forehead; the metal as thin as the hairs carefully combed on his head.

He moved no further into the room, but stood, large hands calm at his sides, back bent from the base of his neck, as though it was only with great effort that his head remained erect. He wore a heavy apron tied with an untidy bow at his side. His white shirtsleeves were rolled up to each elbow, and his shoes were shined so brightly that Edgar could see the glimmer of a reflection from the light on the counter on their leather buffed tops.

"Yes, Saima?" the soft old voice queried gently.

"Antoine, this young man is looking for work. His name is Edgar. Perhaps you might spend a minute or two in conversation and maybe something will come to mind that will benefit both of you. Would that be fine with you, Antoine?"

Edgar waited stiffly while Monsieur Lavoisiere stared at Saima first, and then at him. Antoine Lavoisiere turned in s flurry of little steps, like a heavy block of wood being rotated by a machine. Edgar let out his breath and dropped his shoulders, the brief bubble of excitement popped, abandoned.

Lavoisiere moved the curtains with the same slow, majestic sweep and turned his head to the left. "Please come this way," he said to the wall he was facing.

Edgar bounded to retrieve the curtain from the old man's hand, and held it while M Lavoisiere shuffled into the back.

Saima smiled again, and picking up her glasses, parking them on her nose, once more returned to reading the newspaper.

Edgar peeked around the bundled curtain in his hand, ducking to escape the drape caused by his hand still holding it aside, and was surprised by the room hidden behind. He had expected what one would ordinarily find in the back of a shop: cartons, shelves, cleaning equipment, an untidy toilet and industrial sink.

The small fire burning in the little fireplace glowed on the polished wooden surface of a very old desk to Edgar's left, its sheen clearly accomplished by the same old man who burnished his shoes. The wood was lustrous, and the flames danced on the wooden floor as well. Two Queen Anne chairs faced the fireplace on the right, arranged with a doily-covered occasional table between. On the table was a book with a piece of paper marking the reader's spot. A china cup with a bird pattern sat in its saucer, half full of tea. A ceramic teapot rested ready to pour nearby. The lamp was chimneyed of rose glass and added its color to the warmth of the room.

The walls were shelved and cubbied, and every niche was stuffed with books, rolled manuscripts, and papers piled in alcoves. Straight ahead was a long table. At the back of the table were bins, three rows high, tipped toward the middle of the room. Scattered around the table were metal disks, files, large pieces of what appeared to be handmade paper.

Facing Edgar behind the long table was a cabinet, wide with narrow drawers. Edgar thought perhaps it was an architect's file cabinet; the three-inch high drawers able to handle long blueprints. He had seen one such at a jewelry store, one drawer for each artist, the creations pinned to a felt liner.

M Lavoisiere had arrived at his chair, and settled slowly to its seat, hands on the arms to keep himself in transit to the cushion without falling. He sighed when he was seated safely. He closed his eyes in silent appreciation. "Please. Do sit down."

Edgar took a moment to realize it was he who was to sit, and moved quickly around the back of the more distant chair and sat stiffly, removing his hat, and holding it in both hands as though it were his homework about to be delivered incomplete to his expectant and disapproving tutor.

"Would you care for some tea?" asked the old man. "There is another cup on the mantel of the fireplace, if you would be kind enough to retrieve it."

"No thank you, Monsieur Lavoisiere. I had my coffee with breakfast earlier."

"Well, then. Edgar, is it?" Lavoisiere inquired, nodding when Edgar assented. "What sort of work are you accustomed to doing?"

"I will do any sort of work, sir," Edgar leaned forward eagerly, still offering his hat to the room. "I am most eager and diligent, sir, and um…well, I need to work, sir, and as soon as possible."

"But what type of work have you done?"

"I worked at the university lithographer, sir. In the IT department. I was responsible for maintaining and supporting the company's computer network, and had been in the university's employ for eight years." Edgar's face was crestfallen. M Lavoisiere waited

11

quietly. "Most of these functions have been transferred overseas, sir. All of it is handled electronically, of course, most of the paper has been eliminated, and a center in Asia can handle the job I used to do, along with most of the other such functions at the plant. There are several of us out of a job. This isn't the only type of company that is impacted this way. Most technical support is outside the country. Cheaper labor, fewer taxes to pay.

"I don't resent the corporate decisions made: if I were a company owner, I'd examine an offshore relationship for work that doesn't require a body in a cubicle on site. But I'm out of work nonetheless. I try to think of my foreign counterpart enjoying a lifestyle to which I had become accustomed, but there you are... I was accustomed to having one."

"Did you enjoy this work?" M. Lavoisiere leaned to the side, picked up his teacup and cradling it in both hands, brought it to his lips, tipped the delicate bowl and sipped the steaming liquid, once, twice, then returned it shakily to its saucer. He glanced up quickly at Edgar, moved his gaze to the fire.

"I did, yes, sir, um, well, actually what I enjoyed was being around books and printing, Monsieur Lavoisiere. That is what I truly enjoyed." Edgar looked longingly at Antoine, peering for understanding in the lined, ruddy cheeks facing him.

"So it wasn't the work you did that you enjoyed; it was the end result, yes? The books that went out into the world as a result of your work." Lavoisiere asked softly.

"I don't understand...oh yes, I see, well, yes. Oh! So the satisfaction I got...more than the paycheck and what I did exactly - it was knowing books were being produced, and people were reading and learning, yes. Yes. That's what I enjoyed." Edgar sighed and sat back, resting his hat on his lap, still clasping it with both hands.

"I love books, sir. I do. I like to read, of course. Nonfiction books about subjects I find interesting. Fiction that is well-written. I like paper, too, sir: the texture, the shades of white. There was a time when I collected first editions, or rather, I saved first editions that I had acquired whether through diligent search or by accident." Edgar bent forward suddenly as though confronting the fire's previous inattention to his words.

"But, Monsieur Lavoisiere," Edgar was intense, his eyes darting with the power of his thoughts, "Monsieur Lavoisiere, what I now find I love most is the story behind the story. The people who brought the book to my hands. My hands..." Edgar let loose his hat and turned his hands in front of his eyes, this way, that way, finally holding them, fingers spread, palms out like the wings of a startled heron launching into the sky. He looked at Antoine with excited realization. "Someone thought that the story needed to be told. Another person had the skills to put the words on paper, bind the pages together, take the story to market. Someone else worked hard at a business that stored the books, waiting to be sold to me." Edgar paused, slumped back in his chair, his hat tumbled unattended to the floor.

"My little job did not need my hands to accomplish any of this. Now I see why it wasn't necessary for me to have that job. Another person can do it somewhere else just as easily. I suppose I shouldn't be sorry the work is gone. There was no...."

"Self," Monsieur Lavoisiere finished for Edgar.

Edgar sighed and closed his eyes tightly. "Self. Yes. Me. My joy. None of it." Edgar's mouth tipped precariously down at the corners, and Antoine gave a small, throaty "ahem" to remind Edgar he was not alone. Edgar opened his eyes, their rich brown muted by disappointment. He looked at M Lavoisiere for a moment before speaking. "I have on my desk a little woodcut that my sister gave to me. It reads 'Work With Joy.' Perhaps she knew something I didn't. I have not worked with joy. Maybe she was telling me to find that." Edgar sighed once more. "It would be grand to work with joy."

M Lavoisiere ahem'ed again, delicately bringing his fist to his mouth. "What do you love, Edgar?"

"Pardon?" Edgar, startled as a baby bird, stretched his neck in attention. "Love? Well, my, um. I don't know. Books I suppose. What sort of love?" Edgar asked suspiciously. "Just love? Just like that?"

Antoine smiled so that the corners of his eyes crinkled like a Chinese fan. "Yes. Just like that. If I may give you an example, I love tea. And a warm fire. And conversation with interesting people."

Edgar smiled with his eyes, while his mouth still thought about it. "All right then. I love my sister, and my parents still, even though they are both passed. I love good food, and time with friends." He turned fully to Antoine and leaned toward him, hands rising slightly as though to offer his sincerity as a gift. He scooted forward on the chair, positioning his face in the radiance of the reading lamp so that he was aglow with animated warmth.

"But, Monsieur Lavoisiere, I love language, too. Words and the thoughts they represent. The careful selection of each phrase so as to convey meaning fully to the listener. Or the reader. I love the surprise of humor, and the longing of grief, the struggle of despair.

"I think sometimes about a writer, alone in a cold room with a sputtering candle - maybe his last - hurrying to put his heart on the paper before the light goes out. I think of a writer, so full of the words that he grows impatient with his hand and begins to speak aloud, racing to spill the emotion out before it consumes him. Imagine a writer, so overheated with the life of his characters, that he has to run down the stairs and stand in the snow with his face upturned to the sky to put out the fire in his soul."

Edgar collapsed against the chair back. M Lavoisiere watched the young man, his eyes pooled with the emotion Edgar had drawn.

15

"Just so, Edgar. You understand in your heart. The writer's words, carved when language began, then etched, inked, stamped, printed; now computerized. The beautiful long, rich history of words and paper. My history specialty lives in the 1500s. Ah, the passion and pathos of the early printing houses!

"Martin Luther's 95 Theses, nailed to the Castle Church door in Wittenberg, were printed on a press, as was the copy he mailed to Albert, Archbishop of Mainz, signaling the beginning of The Reformation in 1517.

"The subsequent eager adoption of the printing press, while making religious tracts widely available, and enhancing the ability of the church to fortify its parishioners with single page devotionals, brought with its invention the twin ability to easily distribute oppositional thought. Publishers with patrons gained commissions for favored tomes, and printing job shops could make money both from the establishment and its acceptable and condoned manuscripts, and also quick one-offs for the functionally literate.

"In 1539, Robert Estienne was granted permission to add the bookplate credit awarded by Charles V - "Printer in Greek to the King" - but despite the honorarium from the monarch, and the enterprise granted him by several repeat clients; being persecuted by court favor-seekers, he fled to Geneva in 1550.

"By 1540, Paris was a dangerous place for anyone connected with printing. In an attempt to halt the spread of the heresy of the

Reformation, King Henri II, ascending to the throne in 1547, decreed severe penalties against anyone producing subversive literature. At least one printer was burned at the stake, and others fled the city or were banished.

"Publishers, calligraphers, punch-cutters, woodcut artists, printers who could afford to leave Paris did so in the following volatile decades. Christoffel Plantijn moved to Antwerp and established his successful venture there. By 1562, however, accused of heresy in his adopted homeland, he fled back to France for two years."

The old man started from his reverie; his eyes, wandering in Europe of long ago, returned to the room, and the young man leaning intently toward him, his young mouth open as though he had been eating Lavoisiere's words.

"Forgive me, Edgar," Antoine Lavoisiere whispered. "I talk too much. I am an old man who does not remember that young people live in the now."

"Please, Monsieur Lavoisiere, I am eager to hear your words. I... if I may, I seem to remember that the 'one-offs' of which you speak would have been popular pieces that we would recognize even today. Yes? Recipes and horoscopes and schemes to get rich quick. Is that so? Hawkers would sell them on the street for small change, and the sellers would flee if questioned by a suspected representative of the church or king."

The smile that overtook Lavoisiere's face surprised Edgar. "Ah, how delightful that you have studied this, Edgar! A kindred soul. Edgar. What is your surname, Edgar?"

"Pavelka." Edgar murmured back.

Lavoisiere started. "Pavelka? Where was your father from?"

Edgar picked his head up and looked curiously at Antoine.

"Czechoslovakia. Now the Czech Republic. Why?"

Antoine Lavoisiere fainted.

Chapter 2

Margo Sawyer sat quietly in her chair in the noisy restaurant, wanting first, a cigarette and second, to throttle the two people sitting across the breakfast table: the one activity she hadn't done in fifteen years, the second unlikely she'd ever do, but both beckoned desperately at this moment. The woman of the twosome was droning on in an annoying, nasal voice that probably triggered whatever chemical process now fouled Margo's blood with acidic distaste.

Margo readjusted the focus in her head to mute the clatter and clink of dishes being delivered and removed, and tried to concentrate on the woman's words.

"We have our budgets set, of course, by our Board early in the spring - April actually - and as this is October, we have no discretionary funds to use in the manner you propose. Certainly we can discuss your proposal again in say, March, as we enter the budget process, but it's just not remotely possible this quarter. Not at all. If you could prepare a document outlining what we've just discussed, I'll look at it sometime in the next two months gladly. For now, I'm getting situated in the job, and have my hands quite full." The woman, crossing her legs, kicked Margo in the shin, said "excuse me," folded her arms, and glanced triumphantly at the man seated next to her. Margo envisioned mental high fives being smacked between the two.

The man glanced at his watch, set his napkin on the table, adjusted the lapels of his suit; having let the woman deliver the bad news, he was preparing to leave. He stilled as she glanced up at Margo, the half smile collapsing like a poorly constructed bridge.

Margo wiggled imperceptibly as she savored the word pummeling she was about to deliver to these two. The man didn't matter: he was one of those recent college graduates, probably an engineering student, who had taken a job in the marketing department of an insignificant manufacturing company, afraid to wait out the hiring decision of the important firm where he had interned. Not top of his class; not touted by his advisor, not having made a valuable first impression on his supervisor at the Big Company. He wore an ill-fitting suit that showed signs of being dry cleaned too often; its sheen on the creases outshined his performance at this meeting.

It was the woman that made Margo squirm with anticipation. She was topnotch and would make an interesting crop circle in whatever field she grazed pursuing her career. She was young, smart, self-assured and her suit fit her like a second personality. Shawl collar and one button in an unusual color for business Margo thought of as 100 year old cognac, the choice told the world she would wear exactly what she wanted, and what she knew everyone who saw her would want to wear; not realizing that it wasn't the suit, but her assurance of winning unrelentingly that made the clothes look good. Her shoes cost more than her weekly salary, Margo knew. Here was the flaw that Margo would wheedle a doubt into: no one with absolute belief in herself would have bought those shoes so early in her career.

"I know when your budgets are set, Karen. I was at the budget meeting in March. I'm on the Board. Frasier and Walter are law school roommates." Margo sighed dramatically as she set her napkin slowly on the tablecloth. She treated herself to a tiny flurry of eyelash batting before she sighed again and continued.

"Quite frankly, it's a little surprising that you two haven't done more homework in preparation for this meeting, especially as you're new. I assure you this breakfast was a courtesy only - I hoped we could get acquainted, finalize the table arrangements for the dinner, perhaps discuss the level of your company's participation in our Valentine's Day event in February. I'd rather not bother Walter at this late date about what should be just last-minute details. Quite tiny details, really, as all the planning is done already, and a company president should expect the minutiae to be handled without his attention. But it seems I should give him a call. Unless you can assure me it's not quite necessary?"

She reached sideways for her handbag, eyes bouncing between the two uncomfortable people, knowing they were scrambling for a way to save face, but primarily, to keep her from flipping open her slick black cellphone to call their boss.

Frasier, stifling a laugh, coughed lightly into his table napkin, as the two rookies, hands gesturing and words tumbling, tried to tap dance around their misstep.

On the leaf-blown sidewalk, Margo paused a moment with her back to the wind, turned her phone on, waiting a minute for voicemail to sound, and tossed it back in her handbag. She glanced at the lowering clouds, put her bag back on her shoulder, and turned to Frasier standing with his hands in his pockets, watching the clouds moving east like an armada set on speedily conquering the horizon.

"I know you need to get back to your office, Frasier. Take the car; I want to look at the shop we stumbled into next door. I'll catch up with you later. Expect a call from Walter - those kids will want to cover their butts by telling him in their own way what went on this morning. Be generous with them. Bye." Margo spun on her heel 180 degrees and crunched along the fallen leaves toward the recessed door.

The bell over the door tinkled.

The woman with the braid wasn't on the stool she had been sitting upon when they'd opened the door this morning. Margo glanced up at the bell that had signaled the opening door, but didn't bring the woman from where she had gone. It was darkened with age, its surface scrolled but illegible. Glancing down at the leaves dashing into the store like late Christmas shoppers, Margo hurried to put the door back into its frame. She turned to examine the shop.

The counter where the woman had been sitting was solidly antique, the beveled edges of the glass signifying thickness not found in contemporary displays. The top shelf was glass, perched on ornate brass brackets, screwed into the exterior glass. The bottom was wood, polished to reflect the small number of items displayed within. Margo wanted to take her time looking at all of them later.

The register was a keyed monstrosity that would indicate the total sale on placards elevated by the mechanism inside, as the door tinged open to accept the cash tendered.

An elaborate glass chandelier dangled from the middle of the tin-pressed ceiling but wasn't lit. Bureaus, chifforobes of indeterminate vintage, one box Margo recognized as a music cabinet, were arranged in no discernible order throughout the small room. Another two glass counters were at the back, one next to a curtained doorway, and one to the left against the wall. The floor was etched with decades of foot scrapes and furniture drags, but clean and polished. The yellow leaf nearest Margo's foot was reflected in the glass on the counter face and in the floor on which it rested. The light on the counter was a green-glassed reading light by which the woman had been reading the newspaper that lay partly on the counter, the balance on the floor behind. She'd left in a hurry. Bathroom?

"Hello," Margo called, stepping further into the store. "Hello?" No answer. Margo frowned, moved toward the curtained doorway. She reached for the space in the middle, lit from within, just as the curtain was swept aside and Margo found herself face-to-face, too close to the woman from the stool.

"Oh! Hello," Margo said, one quick step backward almost upending her completely. "I'm sorry, I saw the newspaper on the floor and wondered if all is well?" Over the woman's shoulder, Margo saw a small man slumped in a winged chair; a younger man knelt hovering at his side, his focus concernedly on the unconscious old man, a cloth stroking the wrinkled forehead. "Doesn't look as if all's well at all. Is he all right? Can I call someone?"

"He's recovering, just fainted," the woman smiled. "Can I help you with something?"

Margo looked at her, confused. "Sorry?"

"You came into the shop. You were looking for something in particular?"

"No. I...I don't know why I came in actually. Are you sure he's going to be okay? Have you checked his pulse?" Margo walked to the chair, picked up the man's wrist and turned her head slightly to the fire as she felt for evidence of normal heart action.

"Really, he's going to be fine."

The young man was agitated and stroked his own knee with his other hand as he mopped randomly at the limp man's head with a handkerchief. "It was so sudden. We were talking and then he just slumped over as though the bones had left his body. Remarkable. Um, well, he fainted. At my last name. Odd really. He broke his cup. His hand hit it and knocked it to the floor. I should clean it up before someone steps in it." He awkwardly got to his feet, bent over, began picking up teacup pieces. "It's irreparable. Shame. Lovely design. Is that a pheasant?"

Margo had her eyes shut, listening to the blood work through the old man's body. Yes, he was alive. Weak pulse, but he was stirring. She opened her eyes to look at the broken cup the young man was putting in his handkerchief. Margo stared at the shards, then her eyes darted to the table and the teapot. Her own heart fluttered lightly. "Yes, it's a pheasant. A golden pheasant. My mother had the same design on dessert plates. That's strange. I've never seen the design other than on those plates. I don't know if they were hers or my grandmother's. I only found them in a cupboard after she died. The mark is from Czechoslovakia."

Margo straightened and looked at the tall man as he stood with the cup pieces. And at the woman with the braid who stood watching her quietly.

"What is this place?" Margo asked the woman softly. "Who are you please?"

"Pavel," mumbled the old man, his hand lifting to his brow. "Pavel."

Three pair of hands reached to settle him back in his chair as he flapped his arms and moved his legs as though he were drowning. He slumped into the cushions once more, blinking dazedly at the faces gathered around his chair.

"What has happened?" he asked, looking from one face to the next.

"You fainted, Monsieur," said Saima. "Perhaps the warmth of the room, maybe the excitement of your conversation. But you're fine. Just rest and recover, M Lavoisiere. I'll get another cup for your tea."

Antoine settled more comfortably in his chair and crossed his right leg over his left, tented his hands, and brought the fingertips to his lips. He looked like a wizened monk praying, eyes shining with reflected firelight.

Antoine reached with both palms outstretched like a street urchin reaching to a benefactor and received the steaming teacup being offered by Saima. He nodded his appreciation regally and continued where he had left the discussion, the reason why he had fainted momentarily forgotten.

"Yes, let me see, yes, Christoffel Plantijn moved to Antwerp, but moved back to Paris in 1562 to avoid a heresy trial that surely would have ended his life."

Antoine Lavoisiere sighed into his tea, sending a tiny swirl of steam undulating into the air, its ascent ended by the heat from the fire. "My family came to Antwerp in those years from Paris, reversing Plantijn's flight then, although we would return to the East later in the century, for reasons other than fear of prosecution. One of my ancestors became a punch-cutter to the firm of Phallèse and Bellère, and there begins the love of letters and words that has flowed in my family's veins for centuries."

Margo turned the key in the lock, moving quietly so as not to wake her husband, opened the door holding the doorknob tight with one hand, pushing down to keep the hinges from creaking, stepped into the house, turned and pushed the door with her other hand until her palm was flush with the jamb. The house was quiet. She leaned her forehead against the wood and listened to her Honda sportster ticking in the garage. The garage door settled softly to the cement.

She rolled her forehead to the right. The light over the stove was on in the kitchen, but that didn't mean Frasier was in bed. Could mean he wasn't home. It would be nice if he wasn't home. She picked her head up, shrugged her coat off, left it on the chair in the hall, and walked into the living room to the bar.

The Haut-Médoc was gone, but there was no pink-tinged glass left on the bar, so he took the bottle with him unopened, and wasn't in the house. Margo would have liked a martini, but it was easier to open a bottle of wine. As she reached for the Shiraz, she thought, oh hell, a martini would do fine. Especially as she'd bought blue cheese stuffed olives on Wednesday. She bent and retrieved a frosted glass from the tiny freezer, tipped Grey Goose, dribbled vermouth, splashed olive liquid in the shaker and poured the compound joy juice into her glass. Dirty fishbowl. Lovely. One olive. Ah, phooey. Two.

She kicked off her shoes, and melted into the copper leather couch, examining the glass with her connoisseur's eye. Clean, modern design, Manhattan-esque, skyline represented by the geometrically-aligned shapes that traversed the corners. Frasier had picked them out for the designer's name. Good design indeed, but a square glass just didn't feel right. *Barware designers should be serious drinkers*, critiqued Margo's brain, in a jaunty advertising agency mood. Happily, the stuff the glass contained was divinely perfect.

"'I love to have a martini. Two at the very most. Three I'm under the table, four I'm under the host.' Cheers, Dorothy Parker. Wish you were here." Margo smiled, raised her glass, brought the chilly rim to her lips and sipped loudly. "Ah." She fished the glass cocktail pick from the shallows and pulled one big olive into her mouth with her teeth. So this is how the other half lives, she thought, decades later, still uneasy in her denial of the litany of indulgences that sent a young girl from the big city down the road to hell, followed by an early demise, according to her mother. Ah, gee. One blue cheese olive without the mom tape playing in the background would be nice.

Margo banished her mother's voice with the olive pick, waving it in a circle, twice to be sure. "Be gone. I bought the olives with my own money. And I love it." To kill the aftertaste of sour note, Margo ate the other olive.

"Music," she offered herself brightly, and walking silly in her stockinged feet, draped Mozart's 14th Symphony in A Minor over the living room, into the library and halfway up the stairs. She sat on the chaise on her return, setting her drink on the floor, noted the fabric in the weak light from the kitchen, and recalled it was copied from an Iznik tile pattern she had admired obsessively on a trip to Istanbul. It had taken her most of a year to find the fabric in Turkey, have it delivered along with its U.S. custom forms, and she'd had the chaise and a matching wing chair covered in its extravagant beauty.

A frisson of recognition from the extraordinary experience today at the shop tapped her chillingly on the neck.

Lavoisiere mentioned Istanbul today. Suleiman. Art. The Golden Age. Margo stared at the pattern, remembering the old man's face, firelight dancing in his eyes as he described what the capital would have been like, people working in the Sultan's atelier, candlelit joy reflecting his antiquarian face into Margo's vision of a workshop filled with artisans doing work they loved for a man they respected.

And Edgar. Edgar who? Pavelka. His father's memories of Prague as he relayed the stories to those listening in the unusual shop: his voice, subtly strident with feeling, drenching her ears like this Mozart symphony engulfed other millions of ears over the centuries: tympanic membranes a seashore, awash in the ocean's magnificent obsession; continually and unrelentingly touching auditory landfall; retreating, touching again.

She laid back on the chaise, having eaten the olives from the martini, it had served its purpose. Her sister called martinis for Margo "an olive delivery system" and Margo had to agree. What dredge remained after the purpose was gone must be abandoned without thought or remorse. And isn't that how it should be? No. No "should." Must. From Old English mōste to be allowed to, have to. To be presumably certain to. Not *should*. A listless, damaged word grown in the societal predilection to control. As useless as the English literature undergraduate degree Margo kept stapled to her wall in the home office, with its obligatory cheap document frame, as useless when she bought the frame in 1979 as the degree was now.

Chantepleure

Margo draped her forearm across her forehead, let her other hand dangle to the floor. *What remains after purpose is gone should be abandoned.* Objective achieved, target pierced center. Then what? What had her mother's aspiration been? She was a beautiful sapling withered before her potential was realized. What would accomplishment have meant to her? What of her would have been revealed? Where would she have gone with money, freedom, an uncrumpled childhood and zero rather than eight children? Would she have taken her brilliant Czechoslovakian Golden Pheasant dessert plates with her?

Margo sat up, nestled her head in her palms. She pulled her face upright, looked at her palms. Here it is. Her mother's life had gone off the tracks because she didn't work with her hands. So simple and so true, but each time she said it out loud over the years - more often lately - some new person in Margo's life checked the box marked "bonkers." She'd done it again last weekend at the club meeting.

We work with our brains into our 20s and after that, we work with what mushes those brains into submission, unless we see the results of our labors before us. We don't know who makes our tools; hell, a good percentage of us don't ever use tools of any kind. We used to know how to make what we needed to survive, and if we didn't know how, we knew the person who could make the tool for us. Or could grow the seed. Or watch the children while we went elsewhere to find what we needed and we could return, mission accomplished, and expect to find the caregiver still there, and return the supervision when needed. And someone in our circle would tell the stories; and someone—with their hands—would draw the art that sustained us. Someone would sing the songs and each generation following would sing again and again. New songs would twill in the weave of the fabric that was the tribe.

This day's generation will go out into the world without having ever held a child, had someone else rely on them for sustenance and care, or been called upon to succor an elder in need; and done so, whether reluctantly or imbued with duty. The new generation will give birth to another generation who may very well have to know things their parents cannot tell them, show them, or instruct them how to find.

Enough, Margo thought. She closed her eyes, laid back on the chaise and once more, draping her hand on the floor, imagined herself in the Sultan's harem, the gleam of Iznik tiles and the tactile pleasure of fabulous, sumptuous fabrics, the pungent smoke of Persian incense - myrrh, frankincense, cedar, saffron. The music flew her north: arms flung, she drifted in the vision of airborne bliss, out of body, diaphanous gown parachute silk wide, stuttering on her bare feet, north in the klieg light night to moon-bright Prague and the beautiful Vltava River: the river's own watery dress bowed center city, and - water nymph and trickstress - as she turned her silken back on the Strahov Monastery and its illuminated manuscripts, she became the Danube.

And Mozart.

Oh, weird.

What CD was this? Who's playing? Margo jumped up, knocking the remains of her martini to the floor, the glass bouncing unbroken on the carpet, designer city secure, rolling through its spent liquid to a stop.

She hurried to the CD player, turned the light on over the electronics and picked up the Mozart jewel case.

Sir Charles Mackerras. Conducting the Prague Chamber Orchestra.

"Frasier." Margo began, early the following morning. Her handsome spouse looked up from spitting his toothpaste out and narrowed his eyes at Margo in the mirror. Margo kept her eyes on his hazel eyes while continuing to organize her hair. "Would you recognize yourself if you bumped into another one of you on the street? Or maybe in a meeting. Yeah, in a meeting, across the conference table from you. Maybe opposing counsel. Hmm? Would you recognize someone just like you?"

Frasier straightened his back and crooked his mouth; his face composing into the sneering demeanor signifying his distaste; a look with which his wife was too familiar.

"Margo, I have no idea what you mean and I wouldn't answer a question like that if I had an inkling. What's going on with you this week?" He set his toothbrush on the counter and twisted the cap back on the toothpaste viciously, then picked up his hairbrush.

The tall woman next to him smiled, set her brush down just as quietly as he'd picked up his, rotated her upper body to face the man she married. "Frasier, you keep treating me like a mildly curious but psychotic zoo exhibit, and one of these days I'm going to start acting like what you believe me to be." She smiled widely. "I doubt you'd survive." She brushed past him closely and with vigor so that he had to put his hand on the counter to keep from slopping into it. "Margo! What's gotten into you?"

"I believe it's more about what's gotten into someone else, Frasier." She felt rather than heard his hairbrush bounce off the granite countertop.

"What the hell are you talking about? What is it you think you know? Stop being so cryptic and sullen and come out with it." Frasier followed her to the double closet doors and arrived just as Margo flung the bifold open on the side where Frasier now scrutinized her face, tight-lipped, arms folded, almost clipping him on the ear with the door edge.

"No, Frasier. I don't think I will tell you what I'm talking about." She turned to face him, folding her own arms as she moved her feet closer to his wingtips. "You see - that dance is over. You ask me what I think I know or feel or wonder, and then you tell me how wrong I am. From now on - and I mean till death do us part, Frasier - my feelings, thoughts and wonder are my own. Not subject to debate, discussion or derision. Understood?" Not waiting for an answer, she turned and pulled a suit out of the closet, threw it on the unmade bed and bent to pick up a box of shoes. She was smiling.

Frasier said nothing but she could see his expensively shod feet heading for the bedroom door. Well, thought Margo happily, that felt so good I think I'll take on that global warming issue today. Who can I call to get that little thing organized? She thought another second, returned the black suit she had chosen to the closet, and pulled out the emerald green. Oh yeah. It's a jewel tone day, she congratulated the sky on the way by the window, spun around, billowing the plastic bag and did it once more. Just for fun.

She was humming when she pulled into her parking place in the garage, and still humming when she pushed open the glass doors to her office. "Good morning, Julie. Hi, Marion. Yes, Bob, I'll be in there in just a few minutes. Let me put my bags down and grab some coffee. Is Trish the Dish here yet? Is she happy? Let's make sure she's happy, Bob, okay? Whatever that takes. Good. One second." Margo dropped her coat, briefcase and handbag on the guest chair and sat at her desk, pushed the buttons required to access her voicemail and listened to all the things she was very likely not going to take care of this, or any day in the near future. She made one phone call and headed to the ladies', then down the hall to the meeting.

The conference room was full of the weekly meeting crowd, and Margo almost laughed out loud as she morphed them all into dogs at the dog park. Bob was being his chocolate Labrador, overweight, supervisory self, trying to get Marion to stop rolling up spam faxes and shooting them at Kevin like a quarterback. One landed in Julie's latte and she retrieved it like a good little Dalmatian, threw it back trailing mahogany spit across the black lacquer table. At the dog park, Kevin the Golden Retriever would be trying to hump Cheryl the Viszla, who would probably bite him as a dog or the redheaded spitfire she was as a human.

"Where's Dish? Somebody go get her. All right! Let's get started. It's going to be a short day for me, so a long for you and I want both to start now." Groans all around. "Hey, Trish. Welcome. Sit here, okay?" A month ago Trish the Dish had gone ziggity boom, and it had taken the whole office two entire days to settle down.

"All right all right all right. Where are we? Start with you, Bob."

One last fax hit him in the side of the head. He grinned at Marion, threw the balled fax back. "As of yesterday we're sitting at $75,000 for the dinner dance in November, which means we're short by a bunch of thousand dollars." More groans. "No. Really. We have guaranteed 20 tables of ten and we've got 9 tables committed."

Margo raised her hand, "Bob, I'm sorry to interrupt, but yesterday I met with the two point people at GCD and, although they weren't up to speed, I'm sure Walter will be in for 2 tables, so that leaves 9 tables to get butts in seats. Julie? Can you follow up with Walter this afternoon and get a check on its way here? Thanks. Please continue, Bob."

"The silent auction has way too many low-end items and could use some higher value stuff. If you would all work your donors, I'd like to see some jewelry, a couple weekend hotel packages, a full day spa…"

Bob's voice droned into the background, and Margo's brain floated in the silence of contentment that stilled her neural network. Out the window, the two maples that had shared the same twenty feet of soil for decades, wore giant clown shoes of leaves. The foliage still on the tree was a gradient of colors from brilliant yellow to pink-red. The glory of their attire squeezed Margo's heart once sweetly, sending warm blood rushing to her extremities. She hadn't felt so glad to be alive in years. Vibrating the warmth was a small wand of fear, but she could feel it as the sort that means you're on your way to an adventure and can't wait to set your feet on that yellow brick road.

"Margo?" Bob's voice floated back into range like a scanned radio station on a country highway. "Yes?" Margo asked, blinking to clear the yellow brick road off Bob's face.

"Was there something you wanted to add?" Margo looked at the faces around the table, quiet and attentive for a change. Trish the Dish looked wise. What did she suspect?

"Yes, actually, there is." Margo stood up, smoothed her skirt with both palms, tugged on her jacket lapels and started a circuit of the conference table. She glanced down at her second favorite pair of shoes. Emerald and copper snakeskin slingbacks. Margo smiled. The girl at breakfast yesterday would have to wait for years until these shoes represented one week's pay. Ah, well. Maybe she'd apply for this job.

"I want you all to be the first to know that I'm going to be leaving…ah, now, wait. It's time for me to go. I called Lynn just before this meeting and gave her 3 weeks' notice. This will take us through to the dinner dance, and the first quarter events are all well in hand - thank you, thank you all for that. I'm going to be taking some time over the holidays to see my family, and then I'm going to figure out what I might do with my life after that." She stopped behind the Dish and put her hand on her shoulder.

"I congratulate all of you on the team you've put together here. You all care deeply about the mission, but you also care about each other, and that is the difference that makes or breaks a nonprofit. I'll be making my recommendations to Lynn in the next few weeks, and I hope you'll give the new director the same quality of performance, the same level of commitment that you've shown to me since I've been here. Thank you sincerely."

She stepped toward the door, turning before she exited. "Bob, if you'd like to continue with the rest of the meeting? Fine. I hope to see each of you individually before I go. Cheers!" And she was gone.

Dish knocked on Margo's office doorjamb three minutes later, just as Margo expected she would. "Have you lost your freaking mind?" Trish the Dish, the former Patricia Worthington, slid into the room and slouched in the visitor chair farthest from the door. She kicked off her shoes, and stretched her legs straight out, giving the impression of a middle school student, called into the principal's office for not wearing shoes.

Trish the Dish had been diagnosed with non-Hodgkin Lymphoma two years ago, and had been duking it out with the disease in private and without comment for most of that time. She spent her week's pay on gorgeous, undetectable human hair wigs, and achieved the hair height she wanted with a cloth breast form stuffed under the crown, sewn by the groups who met to sew whatever they could to help the cause, and stolen out of the size bins by Ms. Worthington. Patricia took herself to chemotherapy, threw up on her own when necessary in private and, except for the times she was on prednisone, could pass for any of the well people working at the society. When she was on the prednisone, she vibrated visibly, and constantly pulled her cheek curls into curlier half-circles at a dizzying rate of speed.

And then one Monday morning she came in at 8 a.m. with a platinum blonde buzz. Jaws dropped, papers floated to the floor. Gone was the tidy airline stewardess suit in navy with the blouse with matching pinstripes. Same with the sensible pumps and the flight attendant wig. What walked into the office wrapped around Patricia was a beater t-shirt, blue jeans that had been run over repeatedly by several large and dirty trucks: an unwrapped morsel of left buttock and right thigh exposed. She towered on platform shoes that an office pool would definitely *not* have bet she would be able to wear, let alone walk in; and a diamond nose stud.

She announced at the Monday meeting what was happening to her and her body, and assured everyone that while she was indeed still the same person, she was renouncing acceptable behavior in whatever form she found herself disapproving of, and began her pinkly fresh interpretation of work/life balance by sitting in Frank Maccarosca's lap and tongue-kissing him into senselessness. Frank quit the next day ("*Chicken! Buk buk BUK!*" the formerly sedate Patricia Worthington hollered after his fleeing form.)

Bye bye Ms. American Pi: hello Trish the Dish.

Margo smiled at Trish, comfortable in the chair and her life. "No. I'm not out of my mind. I just moved back into it actually." Margo put her elbows on her desk, settled her chin in her palms like a kid watching TV stomach down on the floor. "Trish. What was the moment - the precise moment - when you realized what you were about to do? I mean there's all that Hegel speculative reason and the difference between theory and practice: when was the sparkling second when you moved from thinking to doing?"

Trish frowned. "I don't know that I thought about what I was going to do. It just showed up. I was tired, Margo. Bone sick, bone tired. I changed. One nanosecond I was Patricia Worthington, Cancer Patient. The next nanosecond I was in the car on my way to the drugstore to buy hair dye. It rolled forward from there. Like the old home movies? When we were kids, the reel might get stuck in the projector, start to burn right before our eyes. You'd watch those brown-edged blooms, and then everyone would run to shut the thing down, and rethread the movie. That's sort of what happened. But not exactly." Trish frowned again, composed her face slit-eyed at Margo, a 1920s Best Friend in a film noir B movie, letting the star know the gig was up. "You having some of this? Is that why you're leaving?"

"I'm not leaving. I'm starting." Margo cryptically countered, sitting back in her desk chair, spinning it around once.

"For Christ's sake, Margo, what's Frasier going to say?" Trish pleaded for reason, tried to reel Margo back from the brink.

"I'm leaving Frasier, too, Trish." Margo sobered. "Or maybe Frasier has already left me and I just found out. Either way, I don't see us together on the yellow brick road."

Trish stood up, fumbled feet into shoes. "Look, Dorothy, we need to talk before you head for the Emerald City. Are you free for lunch today? I've got stuff I need to take care of still this morning."

"Lunch definitely. Sushi okay?"

"Fine. I'll be out front at 11:30." Trish bestowed one more worried look on Margo and disappeared into the traffic of the office.

Margo met Trish at the elevator promptly at 11:30. Trish was shrugging into a black velvet swing coat with big puffy sleeves studded with gold beads. "Channeling Shakespeare, are we?" Margo mocked and Trish closed her eyes once in regal ascent.

"At least *I'm* not channeling the Taz," Trish swished her swing coat into the elevator as it dinged its arrival. Trish twirled back to the front of the elevator, pushed "L" for Lobby and settled in to watching the numbers descend. Trish arranged herself in a grand theatrical interpretation of Shakespearean royal disdain, hands on hips, legs rigid. She looked like the carving on the prow of Henry VIII's favorite battleship.

Margo smiled fondly, "Sushi Iwa? If it's not too crowded?"

Trish said, "Yeah. I invited Claire to join us."

"Terrific! Are we picking her up or meeting her there? You drive then." Margo suggested when Trish acknowledged they'd have to pick Claire up at her gallery. Margo's little red sports car wouldn't seat more than one and a half. They took their building shortcut, past the mini-post office, through the janitorial supply closet, out the Emergency Exit Only back door to the parking garage.

Claire was standing on the curb when the women pulled up. "Is that thing made out of gum wrappers?" Margo asked, pointing to the life-sized figure of a woman with a winged helmet, posed like a speed skater in the window of the gallery.

Claire looked back where Margo was pointing. "Hell if I know. New girl brought that in. I haven't looked at it yet."

Trish glanced at the woman in the passenger seat. "You have an employee named New Girl? You don't know her name? And you let her bring in an artist? Little detached, are we?"

Claire attached herself to the seat with her seatbelt. "Bite me, Dish, I just can't remember her name this second. Is this important? You writing a review on deadline?"

Margo laughed in the back. Claire let out an exaggerated sigh. "I can't tell you how glad I am you called. The new kids are making me nuts. The gallery has turned into some dumb coming of age movie I am not writing, but got stuck starring in anyway." She turned her head sideways. "You two doing all right? Margo? I know Dish is never all right any more." Claire reached over, slapped Trish on the thigh. "Sushi Iwa, I hope, I hope? Let's go there even if it's busy." She took in Trish's velvet cloak. "Headed to Stratford this weekend?" Margo laughed again.

They were finally seated at a table, surveying the menu, when Claire said abruptly, "Kennedy."

"What? Where do you see that?" Dish said, turning the menu over.

"The new girl's name. Kennedy. I just thought of it." Claire revealed.

Trish resumed her study of the lunch choices. "That's a relief."

"Dammit, Trish! Can you take some of the edge off your little bon mots? You're ticking me off."

Trish was confused, then mad. "What's wrong, Claire? I'm not doing anything I haven't been. What's up with you?"

Claire tossed her menu on the tablecloth, took a breath for her salvo, then released it unfired. "I don't know. Thought maybe it was the time of year, all those soggy leaves, but it's not. It's something else, deeper; not dark, but definitely gray." She glanced at Margo, who was watching her with concern. "I feel soggy. Lumpy. I don't know how to explain it but it's as though all along I was headed somewhere, and now I've just stopped on the path. Less color in the world to follow." she finished weakly, smoothing the edge of the linen that extended beyond the edge of the table. "Weary."

The three women were silent.

"Sorry," Claire said, rousing and picking her menu back up. "I'm going tempura today. Dish, you want to share some edamame?"

"My teeth are breaking," Dish said, apropos of nothing. "That's what finally made me cry. My teeth are cracking off." Tears pooled rapidly in her eyes, spilled out on her cheekbone. "I was talking to a friend the other day, working my upbeat, positive language bullshit, and I was waxing enthusiastic on the medical advances made in my lifetime and the person I was talking to, said, 'that's not such a short time.' And it hit me that, even if I wasn't sick, I've been around longer than people had been just 100 years ago. I'm 57. If I was living in Shakespeare's time, I'd have been dead for a long time."

"Thanks, Patricia, that's cheered me the fuck up," Claire said, and Trish, drinking from her ice water, sprayed it back into the glass, laughing.

"It's the chemo, Patricia. It makes the body frailer." Margo soothed.

"I know. On a cellular level, I'm disintegrating. It's a damn good thing I look good, cause I've got nothing else going for me," Trish finished triumphantly, just as the waiter came by to cheerfully take their food order.

The three friends ate and talked companionably, the everyday conversation lightened by long years of shared experiences and warmth. Each woman felt her spirit saturated with color, hue restored to psyches that were grayscaled by the abrasion of being in the world.

"Margo resigned today," Trish confessed on behalf of her boss and friend.

"What?" Claire, astonished, dropped her chopsticks. "You love that job!"

"No, I don't. I love what the work does, but I don't love the job."

"And she's leaving Frasier," Trish also confessed, hunched over like a second grader who'd just ratted out the class bully to the teacher.

"Margo. What's happening?" Claire asked softly.

Her tall friend straightened, sat contemplatively. Claire glanced at Dish and Dish shrugged *don't ask me*, and both women waited for an answer. Margo didn't stir, examining her plate as though it were a rare manuscript.

She roused herself, rearranged her skirt on the chair. "One: I'm not leaving Frasier. He walked out of the house this morning and I don't think he'll be back. Not to the marriage anyway.

"I had a meeting yesterday with the new people from GCD," Margo waved her hand dismissively at Claire who was about to get some clarification. "It doesn't matter who they are, just another couple of talking checkbooks. Frasier came with me - I have no idea how that happened - but we parked, were walking toward the restaurant, and I turned into the wrong doorway. It was a door farther to the restaurant, but I turned into this doorway and I opened the door, and it wasn't the restaurant. It was the strangest little shop…"

Here Claire did interrupt. "Where were you?"

"You know that little breakfast place by Kerrytown? Near the Farmer's Market? We've gone there for breakfast before." Claire nodded and Margo continued.

"We finished the meeting, I sent Frasier home with the car, and I went back to that strange little shop. I opened the door and there wasn't anyone at the counter or in the shop. There had been a small older woman sitting at the counter when we bungled in before, but there wasn't anyone this time. It wasn't much of a shop; it was dark and had a few furniture pieces, a couple of items on display, but not what I'd call a going concern.

"I walked to the back of the building where a curtain hung in a doorway, and yelled 'hello' but no one answered, so I opened the curtain just as the small woman did the same from the back room." She stopped, looked puzzled.

"There was a charming room back there, with a fire in the fireplace; beautiful, antique furniture. An old man had fainted in his chair, a younger man was trying to attend to him. The woman was unconcerned, oddly calm and I, for some reason, moved to take the old man's pulse. Make sure he was alive. He'd dropped his cup."

Margo stopped the story once more, still with the same puzzled look. "The cup was in a pattern that I found on some dessert plates when my mother died and we were sorting her precious things. It's a golden pheasant pattern, a Czechoslovakian mark." She looked at one friend, then the other.

"I just found the same pattern on more plates in my great-grandmother's cabin this summer. I'd never seen them before, not even after Grandma died.

Turns out the younger man and the old man both have family in Czechoslovakia.

When I got home last night, Frasier was gone. I made a martini."

"Blue cheese olives?" Dish sighed dreamily.

"Of course. Try to focus, Trish. And I put Mozart on, wasn't thinking about much, relaxing, and something made me look at the CD cover. It was the Prague Chamber Orchestra."

Dish and Claire looked at each other, cast their eyes down, glanced furtively at the other diners.

Margo caught the drift. "You can stick this in the file marked 'Bonkers' if you'd like, ladies - I couldn't begin to explain what any of this means, except when I woke up this morning, I felt really good, and I saw the yellow brick road of a plan in my mind's eye, golden pheasants and all."

Margo widened her own blue eyes comically. "I am taking some time off. If I wait until I'm old enough to retire, Frasier will have spent my retirement anyway, so I might as well start spending some of it now. I feel excited, adventurous, reckless even. I'm going to visit the sibs, see the nieces and nephews, relax, take long baths, and deep draughts of freedom, and then I'm going to find an adventure. Would you like to come?"

Her best friends were mute until Claire disagreed, "Margo, coincidences are happening all the time. Serendipity is real. Synchronicity. All that. People don't leave their jobs and take off into the wilderness because of it. Hardly ever, in fact."

"Have you ever known me to be spontaneous, Claire? I once confided to you that I was a rebel wannabe, and you laughed. Said 'yeah, right, a rebel who obeys each and every rule.' Well, maybe I'm done with rules.

"Lynn is a tyrant - she's wrecked the game for me." Margo turned to Trish. "I'd recommend you in a heartbeat for my job, and fight to make sure you got it, but I'm not sure that would be a task you'd appreciate, Trish. Is that true?"

Trish nodded immediately. "No. I don't want the job."

"Trish!" Claire was astonished.

"No, I don't want it. I don't know what I want, but that's not it." Trish leaned forward, folded her hands on the table, cradled her teacup, peering into it, maybe hoping to divine something there. "I'm thinking like Margo. This rotten disease is probably going to get me, no matter what brew I pour into my veins. Do I really want to keep doing that? Do I want to feel weak and semi-upright for the rest of my life?

I'm struggling to pay my bills." Margo and Claire looked at one another, alarmed. "My money is all in the equity in the house, but I can't get to it. That's stressful, and the cancer is stressful. Everything's stress. I'm tired. I need some joy to balance me. I'm pissed off all the time and that takes too much energy."

The clatter of forks on plates, hurried lunchtime conversation, bustle and flow around the restaurant continued on as the women sat silently.

"My therapist gave me a card," Margo started. "There is a store owned by two women and they've started a writers' group. I was thinking of taking a ride out there, to see the store and find out what the group is about." Margo laughed shortly. "You know how I feel about joining anything that requires me to actually participate. I'm good at getting things organized, and then disappearing on to the next task, so this would be different." She paused, raised her napkin to her lips unnecessarily, subconsciously wiping the words away even as she spoke them. "Would you like to come with me?"

Claire and Trish looked at one another, agreed silently that Margo having a therapist was a subject for another time, and Trish said, "Sure. Why not? When?"

"Davisburg! That's to hell and gone," Claire observed loudly, clicking her seatbelt home in the front seat of Trish's car on the following Saturday morning. Claire turned all the way around to fix an eye on Margo in the back. "There is nothing out there. Nothing. Less than nothing. Cows and a 4H camp. That's it. What sort of writers are we going to find out there in Cowland?" She bounced back to the front, crossed her arms like a Roman senator finished verbally annihilating an opposing viewpoint.

"Now, now, Claire. Cowland? It's a beautiful day, let's enjoy the country." Trish glanced right and left, commencing the appreciation of the landscape. "Come on, Claire, you're going to have fun. Think of the bumpkin stories you can tell the new girl at the gallery on Tuesday."

The day had opened its eyes this morning, blinking away the overcast of the last several days, rain glinted on the remaining leaves. Red and yellow stained the ground in brilliant patches, and the browns and coppers of the oak leaves were burnished with sunlight. November was thumbing its painterly nose at October, proud of the blueness of its sky and the fragrance of its earthy perfume.

In the city the color was raked up, blown into bags, put on the curb. Grass was still being cut in cross-hatched shades of green in town, and the trees planted on the streets were bare, long naked limbs exposed to the sky, obscured by the bricks at their backs until the filigree of top branches stretched above the roofline.

The women talked of their city lives. Claire wondered if the new girls would be able to handle Saturday holiday traffic without her supervision. Trish talked about the interesting people she'd met at chemotherapy. Margo offered candidates for her job for review, and her friends diagnosed some candidates as problematic, shuffled others forward in the line, sentenced others to remain with their current employment.

"Is that a black swan?" Margo pointing out the window, hit her finger on the glass, and hurried to depress the button that would lower the glass. "On the pond there. It's a black swan. I didn't think they existed outside of fairy tales."

"Is that a unicorn?" Trish asked shocked.

"It's a statue, Dish," said Claire, abandoning her usual disdain, caught up in the magic kingdom of imaginary animals, turning to watch the pond and its inhabitants disappear in the distance behind the car. "So that's Colasanti's. People from town drive out here for their produce.

It's supposed to be organic and reasonable, which we're not going to find by us. Organic, yes; reasonable, no."

From the pond on, the color balance in the world around the car was saturated with the intensity contributed by mythical beings. Claire gave memorized directions from the mapquest paper she no longer glanced at, and commented on the girth of trees, the height of sumac. Trish was quiet and relaxed. Margo kept her window open two inches, her nose lifted to the air rushing by like a puppy on its first car ride.

"I don't remember township signs."

"We don't care about townships in town. We never drive far enough to get out of one and into another."

"Indian Springs Metro Park. Never heard of it. We should go one time, huh?"

"We should go to the parks we can walk to at home and save the gas. Turn right here, then you need to turn left not too far up the road."

"You know, there aren't as many squished animals on the side of the road."

"They're either smarter out here, or there are fewer cars."

"Is that a skunk? Yuck."

"I like skunks."

"Is that an eagle?"

"Turkey buzzard."

"Oh."

"You know: I don't know much about trees. We live in a tree town, don't we? I wouldn't be able to point out an ash or a cherry. I think I can spot an oak by its leaves, but aren't there varieties of oak?" Margo wondered.

"You might not have any ash to identify soon," Claire observed. "Emerald ash borer. We lost over a thousand trees in Ann Arbor alone and several more thousand in the parks. I read the bug came into the country not too far from us in a wooden pallet delivered to a greenhouse. Can you imagine? A hitchhiker pestilence. I guess that's how most natural devastations happen though. Brought in on the back of something else."

"I just read that Congress has tabled legislation to stop foreign ships from dumping their bilges into the Great Lakes," Trish reported. "Tabled for years maybe. That's how we got zebra mussels, and white perch and tamarisk: on the hulls and in the bilge water of oceangoing vessels."

"And garlic mustard." Margo added. "Some of the women at work were at the parks in September, pulling the stuff out."

"George Carlin wondered if maybe six-pack rings weren't supposed to inherit the earth," Trish concluded. "Six-pack rings are smarter than both my exes."

They rode through the country, admiring the sunlit tall grasses in the ditches alongside the road, waving as they passed, happy as the women to be out enjoying the respite from clouds and rain.

Each woman ruminated on the good fortune to have friends to go out in the world with, and each subconsciously congratulated herself on the good taste to have chosen each other.

Margo's heart cracked a little as they passed a man in a lawn chair, obviously not active, who hung his head turned to the side to watch the traffic go by.

Claire wondered how to incorporate this renewed appreciation of the rustic into a gallery show. Her mind morphed the holiday displays featuring glitz-riddled drama into a brown gold display of pine cones, earthtones and hominess.

Trish felt her blood, generally sizzling with the chemicals battling with the invaders, wave a white flag of truce and settle down for a snack and a gab with the enemy cells. She stuck a note to the bulletin board of her memory to practice the visualization she was supposed to be doing using this Saturday car ride.

The giant thighs of oaks on either side of the road stepped aside as they descended a steep winding hill, at the apogee again revealing a panorama of muted color. In the distance the tops of orange trees looked like clown wigs lined up on a circus shelf. A farm field, turned to rich brown for the season, exposed itself to hawks circling for evicted mice, as a tractor churned a swath of deeper chestnut hue farther down the road. Trish almost missed the stop sign at the bottom of the hill, as the road ended at the crossroad of trees.

"Right," directed Claire, and into the town of Davisburg the women moved at 25 mph. Old houses, some restored to their original grandeur, aged gracefully along with the enormous trees on their well-groomed lawns, keeping a respectful distance from each other on either side of the road, their exteriors the color of their country enterprise. Butter cream, soybean green, corn, the brown of the tilled soil. The town buildings were a dilapidated hotel, a liquor/convenience store, a fire station, a saddler (not open), an abandoned, for sale gas station, a candle factory, and Sweetgrass, their destination.

"That's it. There on the left. Are we on time?" Margo asked, turning to examine the front of the tiny store. "Park there on the left – just make a U."

The friends got out, stretched, walked the half block back to the store, commented on the garden, and the fire circle in the back, the seats hewn logs uprighted for stools.

Margo led to the door, and turned the knob, opening the door into a miasma of sandalwood, cedar and palo santo wood and the sound of Ecuadorian wooden flutes.

The bell over the door tinkled.

Chapter 3

Room was small with a doorbell, No windows. Man who would stretch like Draggable Dan. I was cutting him up with scissors which was the only way to destroy him. Marian wouldn't help. No one would help. It had to be done a particular way. The pieces had invaded others and they were devil's spawn too.

Then a window. Out the window, a river. Coming down the river was an army moving like a circus. Lots of fanfare and dancing women and color. Place I was in turned into a hotel. Old. 20s. Fake Star Trek stuff. I'm looking for my doctor buddy. Told a red-uniformed soldier an army was coming. He said "who?" I said either the French or the Devil. Looked again out long wall of fancy gathered curtains.

Chantepleure

Devil's army was camped right outside the hotel on a shallow lake. Music playing. White-clothed tables set up. Waitresses dressed like French maids. Kept looking. Now I'm in a long gown with pantyhose that are bagged at the knees. Raspberry copper color. Both swirly and beaded. Hat too. 1800s shoes. Look out window again. Everyone is walking on water. It is the Devil's army. Devil himself is sitting at table. A waitress drops something on round table top. Devil smites the waitress and the two guests on that side. They drop into the water — waves start just where they land and fire consumes them.

Devil glances up, spots me in the window.

I take off fast.

Walking down hotel street. Hotels of different decades, different centuries. A themed hotel street. To my right is a river: looks like it would flow under the street I'm walking on. I try to find a hiding place. Old 40s limos keep pulling up and doors open and I won't get in. Revolving doors. Brass and bronze tones on the street. The burnt yellow light of gaslights gleaming reflected in the dark windows. The doors spin, but no people go in or out.

I'm trying to believe I have some power so the Devil can't find me. At some point earlier I found the rival for the Devil's affections laying on a table - depressed? I think - and her copper gown laid out to put on. I wanted to wear it.

I pick an Old West hotel with a saloon and out the window is a lone kayaker paddling toward the hotel. I go in the bathroom. All the toilets are running. I pull up pantyhose in a bunch around my waist. I wake up.

Trish woke up. Soaked, breathing heavily, she threw the damp sheets aside, flung her legs over the side of the bed and sat, head down, gathering her dream-addled wits. French maids? What silliness was that? She recognized the pantyhose scene as having to pee.

It was dark, Trish had to squint to make out the red numbers on the clock. 3:11. Yikes. She rubbed the platinum burr of her head, bringing her hand away wet. Even though spots danced in her eyes, she stood; dizzy, sat back down hard on the bed, making the antique boards squawk. She was wrung. Trish scooted her butt across the bed, swung her legs to the other side, struggled to get the simple door in the chifforobe open, and hauled out a new pair of pajamas, dumping what was around them on the floor. She pulled the top of her pjs over her head without unbuttoning them, and wriggled one cheek and then the other to kick the bottoms to the floor.

Naked, drenched, she stood again and holding onto the walls and the furniture made it to the toilet in time. She sat there for a long while after she had finished, head in hands. Dripping on her knees, sweat and tears.

After a shower, taken sitting on the molded bench in the stall because she was too weak to stand, Trish shuffled hand over hand on the peninsula counter to the coffee pot, pushed the brewer on, and sat at the dining nook table with the lights off, looking out the window at the gray, leaf blown day. Superimposed over the predawn was herself, white hair the same color as her robe, the whitest objects in the double exposure. Not enough light in the sky yet for more than the muted grayscale Trish viewed, her ghost image superimposed in the foreground.

Chantepleure

I'd like to see an infrared image, Trish mused. See if my innards are really percolating in the colors I think they are. She knew she wasn't the only person in the world going through chemotherapy and chemical menopause at the same time, but she didn't want to know the other women. Shared misery wasn't appealing. Trish had seen the faces of her friends when she whinged about what was happening to her body, and she didn't want to know the same look was on her own face. Complaining didn't change the facts. Crying didn't make her feel any better. And the doctors had their jobs to do. She couldn't afford a therapist. She remembered one of the counselors she had seen who took money to tell her "it feels like shit because it's shitty." Yeah, right.

Drained. That's what this is. In a vampire movie, I'd be the dead woman, whitened by the blood-sucker that went too far. No eternal life of damnation for me, no creature of the night endless future. Just grayscale. The sickly white skin of the woman who appears in the credits as "First Female Victim."

Maybe she'd call in sick today. Sick days - how many did she have. Six? A joke unless all she had was a cold. She wanted to take a few months off. A few years. Every job she'd had in her ersatz career she'd signed up for short-term disability and never used it. Now she couldn't afford to use it. The benefit had lessened every year, and the cost had risen. She'd have to wait a month without pay for it to kick it. Nice disincentive.

But Margo's suggestion of an adventure was appealing. In the nuclear stew of her body, Trish felt a tiny bubble of excitement. The possibilities were vast, the choices juicy, the barometer range of adrenalin colossal. Imagine a morning walk in an old growth forest, a raft trip on the Columbia River. Hiking the Smokies. Jet skiing in Maine. Bicycling Virginia. Paddling Idaho.

Trish got up, rinsed her coffee cup, headed slowly for the closet to get dressed. She wondered what time Margo would be in today. They needed to talk.

"Do you have a driver's license, Edgar?" asked Saima over the top of Lavoisiere's head. She gently held one of Antoine's arms and Edgar, bent at a 45 degree angle to hold the other, nodded twice. "Yes, of course."

"Good," Saima smiled and guided her portion of the senior's body sideways, as Edgar held the curtain out of the way. He would borrow Saima's old Volvo to tote Monsieur Lavoisiere home.

"I'm sorry to be this much trouble, Saima. It's inexplicable what happened just now, but I certainly appreciate your good attendance." Antoine Lavoisiere stopped completely to turn his head and smile at Saima. "You've been a blessing since I walked into this shop. You're an angel." Saima demurely said nothing, but nodded, eyes soft, and she tenderly urged Monsieur Lavoisiere's captive arm forward once more.

Edgar left, keys in hand, to locate the car, as the taller woman helped the diminutive man on with his coat and hat. One arm through the coat, the other reaching behind him for the held sleeve, his face crinkled; he was going to sneeze. Saima quickly grabbled her handkerchief out of her sleeve, got it positioned directly over his nose, and Lavoisiere sneezed twice in rapid succession. "Oh, my, sorry. Thank you! Handy place to keep a handkerchief." Saima said, "You're welcome," just as Edgar dashed into the shop, accompanied by a wave of wet leaves and rain.

"Well, the rain's arrived, as we thought it would. Monsieur Lavoisiere, you should turn up your collar. I left the car running, but it's not right in front of the store. You're going to get wet, I'm afraid."

He reached for the older man's coated arm, and Antoine started forward, turned and thanked Saima gallantly once more for her help, and was ushered out the door.

The leaves that had escorted Antoine to the shop earlier this morning were now plastered in forlorn groups in puddles on the sidewalk and, in a covey, were being ferried down the narrow river that had formed in the gutter. M Lavoisiere's socks were wet by the time they had slowly traversed the distance to the car. Edgar opened the door to the old Volvo, settled Antoine in, belted his seatbelt, and dashed around the rear to his own door. "Well then," Edgar assessed, as he wiped his eyes with the forearm of his coat. He found the wipers on the stick on the steering wheel, rolled the windows down to clear the water, quickly rolled them back up, fumbled for, then found the headlights, and set the car in reverse first, angling his way out of the parking space. He made sure he was in first gear three times before he made the final forward move into the street.

"You walk to the shop every day, Monsieur Lavoisiere?" inquired Edgar, peering straight ahead as far as his neck would allow his head to be extended. He looked like a hood ornament on a very strange car.

"Please call me Antoine. Yes, I walk every day during the week early in the morning, before the shop's open. The shop isn't open on the weekends."

"Odd for a shop not to be open on weekends, isn't it?" Edgar commented. He frowned briefly in concentration. "Were there hours posted on the door somewhere? I don't seem to remember…you know I came into the store this morning because the drugstore wasn't open yet. I'd gone to the drugstore for a newspaper, but the sign on the window, um, well, it was too early; the door was locked. Next door, yes, um, I went next door. I don't know why I tried the handle next door, but I just turned the knob and the door opened. But it must have been 7 o'clock." He glanced at Antoine, who benignly looked through the windshield, not contributing to Edgar's stumbling analysis of shops and doorknobs turning. "Monsieur Lavoisiere, why was the shop open so early?"

"Saima probably forgot to lock the door again after I arrived."

"Oh, well, then. That explains it."

"If you turn left at the light, and go up the hill, then turn right at the first opportunity, I live just around that corner. You'll want to go up in second gear; it's a fairly steep hill." Antoine pointed straight ahead while he spoke, and Edgar glanced at the hand guiding him forward. He hadn't noticed how large his hands were, and now that Edgar focused on the one issuing directions, he could see scars, whitened with age on the fingers and thumb. One long mark was on the side of his index finger, the finger pointing the way home. Lavoisiere turned to smile at Edgar, saw his regard, and brought his hand closer to his face.

"Not a handsome fist certainly, but these hands have served me well in my lifetime. They bear the marks of inattention and the badges of service. Mistakes left an impression and I learned how to avoid getting another reminder." Lavoisiere laughed abruptly. "Doesn't look like I was a fast learner, does it?" He rotated the hand for Edgar, then dropped it in his lap, cradling it with the other, equally scarred hand. "They're old marks, Edgar. Diplomas of my apprenticeship." Lavoisiere turned his head to look out the side window, though the rain coursing sideways across the glass obscured any view.

Edgar turned at the light, and started up the hill in second gear. "You walk this every day?" the surprise in Edgar's voice raising it. "This is challenging."

"I take my time." Antoine gestured with his chin at the window. "There are beautiful gardens along the way. Many of them are on the summer tour. The trees survived the elm disease, and now the ash borer. Hopefully they will survive the next invader, too, but I will be in the ultimate garden by then, I hope."

Edgar could see his cheek raise. Lavoisiere was smiling. The ultimate garden didn't disturb him, Edgar thought. I wonder if it will me when my days grow short. He sighed, put on the blinker, and negotiated the turn to the right that would take him to Lavoisiere's house. The houses on the street were an assortment of styles, typical of a university town grown up in the early 1900s, close together a hodgepodge of Arts & Crafts, Italianate mansions, and tiny bungalows.

"See the black car, on the right? Just in front of the FedEx truck? The driveway is in front of the black car, it's narrow but if you pull up to the back door, I can get out there and you needn't get out of the car."

"No, I'll help you get inside. Do you have your key handy? I'll open the door first." Edgar said this as he turned into the driveway. He sat a moment, turned the wipers on to full, peered at the house that presented itself sporadically: swish, house, swish, house. It was a lovely Arts & Craft house, deep porch columned at the front. Wicker furniture tops peeked over the edge from Edgar's vantage point, and the porch light, which had been left on, spotlighted the chairs arranged in a cozy conversation group, The porch wound to the left side that Edgar couldn't see, and a matching portico sheltered the back door Edgar assumed Antoine wanted to enter.

"Wow," breathed an appreciative Edgar.

"I've felt that way many times myself," said the owner of this beauty. "I've been fortunate to live here, and there are wonderful memories behind those bricks."

Edgar moved slowly forward, peering through the deluge on the windshield. There were spent flowers and red bushes to the right, growing in the 5 foot space before his neighbor's house rose two stories. On the left, the garden wound around the front, and back of the house. Stone pavers marked the way from the driveway to the back door, and rolling under the portico, Edgar could see the beveled glass of the heavy old door. He got out and helped Antoine do the same, taking the key from him as they walked to the door.

Stairs led down to a basement, and up to a room leftward that, when Antoine pushed open the door was clearly a pantry for the kitchen beyond. The pantry shelves were light on food, and heavy on books stacked cover to cover. A valet was hidden when the door was open, now Antoine took his hat off, set it on one of the valet's pegs, and put his coat on the chair seat. "Please," he gestured, inviting Edgar to do the same. "I'll make some tea, if you have time?" Antoine was already shuffling into the kitchen. "Saima won't need her car back until she leaves the shop and even then, perhaps not."

Edgar followed into the small charming kitchen. The gloom outside was kept at bay with a cheerful windowsill garden above the sink, beautiful tiles on the backsplash and countertop. The walls were a yellow that allowed pink some elbow room, all spotlessly clean and bouncing a muted glow around the room. Antoine double-handed an enormous kettle back on the stove from filling it at the sink, opened a beveled glass cupboard to retrieve two china teacups and saucers, and rubbing his hands together, invited Edgar to follow him into the living room.

The dining room was separated from the living room by an open archway, to the left was the large mullioned window Edgar had seen from the car, and next to the window, a corner fireplace. Two doors to the right probably opened onto bedrooms, and a narrow recessed door facing Edgar perhaps gave way to the upstairs. The floors were large planks of red oak, beautifully maintained, but still bearing the staple marks of old carpeting. The floor had been restored to reflect its valued life through the decades, without having the spirit ground out of it by the buffers of nonprofessionals. Through the tall narrow front windows, the wicker chairs still chatted quietly with each other.

The dining table was Stickley, the seat cushions replaced in a period chrysanthemum fabric with a black background. On the mantel of the fireplace were implements Edgar would like to have a closer look at later. Propped against the age-darkened mirror were small pictures Edgar assumed would be family. The tables in the living room were Mission style: once more Edgar saw in his mind the purpose-driven cabinet in Saima's shop that he'd meant to ask about.

Framed on the walls were what Edgar thought of as font proofs. Some were clearly ancient, the edges frayed and the page yellowed.

These were framed in shadowboxes, some with thick carved wooden frames. Others were newer, simply framed in narrow black metal. On the buffet in the dining room, Edgar stopped to peer at a tray of metal type, edges dulled by use. "Is this printing press type?" Edgar asked, touching the crossbar of a capital A.

"Yes, they are. Made in what was called hot metal, a blend of tin, lead and antimony. These are letterpress forms," he said, brushing his hand lightly over the tops of the small shapes with their knuckled curves and lines. This type is what was used for decades to print before the lithography of your former employer. This font is Bernhard Gothic, designed by Lucian Bernhard in 1930."

Edgar pointed to the framed set above the tray. "This is the same font on paper?"

Antoine moved closer, tipping his head back to look at the wall through his bifocals. "No, that one was designed by Adolphe Mouron Cassandre. It is similar in that it's a sans serif form, but it was created earlier, at a different foundry." Antoine smiled, embarrassed. "Forgive me. I can go on and on about this art. It's what I did for a living." He held his hands briefly at waist height, and then used them palms-up to shrug. "I was a punch cutter when I was young, and then I taught the history of letterpress when my memories became sturdier and more productive than my hands. I taught at the university, until I retired many years ago. Now I dream about the old days more than anything else." He sighed, lost in history and memory.

The two men moved to the living room, Antoine gesturing to a wing chair for Edgar to claim. Lavoisiere talked as he walked to the chair's twin, settling himself comfortably. "The difference between a typeface and a font has smoothed since the advent of computers, but a font could be a particular potion of a typeface family (Roman, Italic, Bold) but a typeface would include all permutations of the type family." Antoine set his teacup down, warmed with his subject now in place of the brew.

Edgar spoke then, setting his own cup down, "The word font is derived from the French 'fonte' (a cognate of fondue) meaning 'something melted'. Fount was a multipart metal type. In the mid 1980s users all adopted 'font' which means primarily a computer file of scalable outline letterforms.

"I would love to hear more about your work, Monsieur Lavoisiere," Edgar's voice shined his enthusiasm at Antoine like a flashlight in the dark illuminating a desperately sought destination.

"Indeed. And so you shall," Antoine laughed, rising and clapping Edgar on the back with one big hand, as he moved back toward the kitchen and the whistling teakettle that beckoned again.

The rain had stopped when Edgar waved to the old man standing on the porch of his house and drove back down the hill toward the shop. Wet leaves shone like pieces of colored glass shattered in the streetlights. The young man who had been beside himself with worry this morning felt restored, enthused, calm. No promise of work, no end to the troubles looking for work would bring, but Edgar felt better about the world and his chances in it than he had for some time.

No lights shown into the street from the shop and once more Edgar had the feeling there wasn't something quite right about the address. The drugstore was lit, the home interiors store on the other side was closed, but the Christmas tree set back from the window glowed softly. Imitation gaslights lit the sidewalk like a 40s movie; the holiday wreath casting a shadow halo on the street.

The handle turned just as it had this morning, and the firelight from the backroom pulsed orange into the shop. The green shaded reading lamp was lit, and turning, Edgar could see the same shadow halo of the wreath on the street outside, the gaslight shining clearly, but he hadn't seen the reading lamp from the street when he'd parked the car.

"Antoine is home safely?" Saima smiled at Edgar. "I'm glad you were able to keep him out of the rain. It's too easy to get ill at his age." Edgar smiled back at the woman. She wasn't much younger than Monsieur Lavoisiere.

"He is home and dry," Edgar assured their benefactress. "I appreciate the loan of your car." He held the keys out to Saima and she shook her head once.

"Take the car, Edgar. You'll need it for a few days to look for work, I'm sure. Bring it back when you've got a job."

"I couldn't do that, really. Um, well, I had been planning on taking the bus downtown tomorrow, and the car would really help me. Well, yes, if you're sure you won't be needing it, I truly would welcome its use. May I drive you somewhere tonight?"

Saima shook her head again. "I won't need the car. I just keep it for times like these. Please take care of yourself, Edgar, drive safely home, and I'll see you again very soon." She moved around the counter as she spoke, and Saima held her hand on Edgar's back, opened the front door for him to exit, and perhaps Edgar only imagined she was pushing gently. "Good night."

As Edgar adjusted the seatbelt, checked his mirrors to exit the parking space, he glanced at the window in the front of the store. No lights. Well, perhaps, she'd turned off the reading lamp. But the fire should still show. There were no curtains on the picture window. Shrugging his shoulders, tired and ready to relax, Edgar checked his mirrors once more, and pulled out into the street, headed south toward home.

Someone had parked in his space again. Edgar felt the anger spike briefly in his chest, drove to the end where visitor parking waited, locked the car, and walked the extra distance to the apartment building. He didn't recognize the car. Maybe a visitor who hadn't been told where to park. The tall man stood looking at the squatter car, a fleeting idea to leave a note scuttling back out of his brain. He walked away, let himself in to the building and his apartment, sat on the couch in the dark without taking off his coat. Within minutes he was asleep.

I'm wading through letters like leaves, like confetti, as I shuffle my feet the letters rise up into the air and spell nonsense words. Gieusn. henaoeiv. The words float upward, out of sight, and then drift down again like ribbons dropped by an unwrapping god. I turn my face to the ribbons and they fall gently on my eyes, drift down my outstretched arms. I turn slowly around and the ribbons wrap tighter. ereis. cndeicnchg. I can't stop spinning, faster, faster and the ribbons get tighter, tighter. I can't breathe. I'm choking. I fall to the ground in slow motion, and the swirling letters fly up, settle on me, burying me.

Edgar sat up, breathing rapidly. He wiped his sweating forehead with the back of his hand, expecting to see inked letters scribbled there. He laid back against the arm of the couch, his heartbeat adjusting to its steady rhythm. It was dark out, snow floating down heavily and slowly like the words in his dream.

He contemplated rising, getting his pajamas on, going to bed. Instead he pulled off his coat, rolling to each side to get his arms out, covered his body with it to his chin, and closed his eyes again.

They had talked about letters - he and Lavoisiere - and Edgar must have seen the snow in its directionless descent before he fell asleep. That explained the dream. But why choking? Why would words choke?

Breath. The words had been taking his breath away. Like a treasured book, a favorite poem, a powerful speech, all could hold your breath for you, and only when the rapture ended could you breathe freely again.

Words had tripped over Edgar's tongue as long as he could remember. Mortified by reading his book report in 5th grade, he had run from the room and cowered in a stall in the boys' toilet, until another teacher found him in there weeping. She was kind, but the memory of that moment was not her kindness, it was the humiliation. Avoiding speaking to anyone he didn't absolutely have to, he chose a career that kept his tongue from betraying him, and words, arranged beautifully and articulated pristinely were the province of writers and speakers who were strangers, even though the words were warm friends. He loved words from afar, his heart aching at the beauty he could only glimpse.

He saw Lavoisiere's scarred hand, caressing the letterpress metal, fingertips brushing the embrasures and merlons lightly, his love and respect evident in the gentle touch. Hot metal that had burned his hands, files that cut creating the letters; all wounds for the love of the letters.

What have I suffered to learn? Edgar wondered fruitlessly. He hadn't suffered, he'd slid easily onto the path on which he tread his work life. All of his life. He stayed away from events where he'd have to talk to people and thus, didn't meet anyone from outside his cubicle. He'd sweated through interviews to get the jobs he'd had, but his resume spoke for his skills, and most people didn't expect glib prose from an IT expert.

No muscles stretched, no personal walls toppled, no demons vanquished. No risk, no gain, no triumphs or tragedies. Have I ever strived? Struggled? Scuffled?

Am I proud? of anything? wondered Edgar. Not really. I have excelled in not excellent. Exceeds expectations is a category of dust and spiderwebs; an artificial achievement coveted by ghosts and management.

What of my life would I fight to save?

Pull on that thread, you'll unravel the universe.

As long as he was going to gnaw on a bone of contention, he'd do it in the company of Lavoisiere.

Tomorrow he would return the car to the funny little shop lady, and he would seek Monsieur Lavoisiere's counsel.

The waiting area of the restaurant was crowded when Trish got there to meet her friends, seats filled, future diners milling about in small groups, watching the new arrivals, carrying flying saucer vibrators that would flash and buzz when their table was ready. Shopping bags were huddled at the feet of the sitters, quietly displaying the gift-buying success of their new owners. Bas relief Dionysian heads lined the walls, plastic grapes dangled from the ceiling. Italian lights were draped in the bar area, overhead lighting dim as befitted the serious business of soothing parched holiday throats.

Trish the Dish walked through the vestibule to the podium to ask if there was a Margo or Claire waiting inside. As she spoke, Margo said, "hey" behind her. "Claire here?" Margo peered over Dish's shoulder at the table assignment list, as though she could sort it out. "Just asking," said Trish as she questioned the girl behind the podium, "Is there a Claire waiting inside?"

Margo tapped Dish again as Claire appeared, beckoning through an arch to the right. "Thanks," Dish smiled at the young girl at the podium, still looking for the name, and walked away.

Claire sat on the end of the booth, so Trish and Margo slid in together opposite. "I invited Dr. Amy," Claire said, picking up her water glass and sipping while peering over the edge at the women on the other side of the table.

"You didn't," Margo denied. "Why would you do that?"

"Because she came into the gallery today and seemed confused and lonely, so I invited her." Claire said, chin raised in defiance. "She can sit next to me and I can smite her if she gets out of line. Think of it as a chance to practice your people skills, Margo."

"Whoops," Trish sidled away from Margo at the end of the booth, as Margo sighed. "Fine," and that was all Margo said until the waiter appeared.

"I'll have a Grey Goose martini, very dry and very dirty," Margo relayed to the young man who introduced himself 'I'm Sean. I'll be your waiter for the evening' to the three friends, as he displayed a bottle of house wine on the table.

Trish helped clarify. "She means fishbowl. Opaque. If she can see through it, she'll send it back. I'll have a glass of the pinot grigio, please." Claire shook her head at the offer of further refreshment, holding up her water in salute to sobriety and sense.

"So, Dr. Amy just wandered into the gallery today?"

"She did. Distracted, distraught and disarrayed."

"Nice alliteration, Claire."

"Thank you," Claire acknowledged, bowing her head humbly. "She looked - well - sloppy, which she never does, so I figured she has a story to tell, and that you all know how to listen, if you concentrate real hard, and what the hell? It's the holiday."

"Speaking of," Trish refocused, "who's cooking next week?"

"You looking for an invitation, Dish?" asked Margo.

"No, I'm going to my sister's; I wondered if you all were going to be fed or have to feed."

"I'm going to my daughter's this year, which I'm looking forward to, but I'm bringing the pies. Margo, do you have to cook?"

Margo shook her head, "No, I'm going to the girls. Caroline's, actually. She's having dinner so she doesn't have to pack up my grandson and then leave early to get him to bed."

"Frasier?"

"Haven't heard, but I know he'll call me before then. He'll need to prearrange his forgiveness before he shows up. I, naturally, will forgive him, enjoy the day, and sort out the rest later. Honestly, I'm not interested in what he might be up to, which feels weird but good." She paused to thank the waiter who set a frosty glass of green sludge on the table in front of her, "perfect. thanks," and leaned back as he set Trish' wine glass before her, waiting until he'd moved to the next table. "I'd rather leave all of this until after the first of the year, but I'm going to have to tell him I'm leaving the job." She sighed, picked up her glass, raised it to the friends, "Prosit." The other women clinked glasses with hers.

"Well, this is a cozy scene," a voice interrupted.

"Amy, hi," Claire said hurriedly, standing up to let Amy slide into the corner of the booth. "You know Margo and Trish, yes?"

Amy nodded, shrugging out of her coat. "Sorry I'm late. I had a taping to finish. We did the Thanksgiving Friday show today." Margo and Trish exchanged brief glances, and Claire frowned a short, intense warning. "Have you seen the show lately?" Dr. Amy asked brightly. "We're quite pleased with the changes, and the feedback from the audience is really positive."

Margo opened her mouth to respond, and Claire tongue-trod into the pause. "We're not home during the day, Amy. I don't have a recorder, so no, unfortunately, I miss the show. What changes?"

"Well..." and Dr. Amy, Culinary Counselor launched into the extensive and exciting things that were happening on *Cuisine*. Celebrity guests *(yes, really, once she lets her hair down, and really COOKS, you'd be surprised what a down-to-earth person she is. Honestly.)*, décor, backdrop, camera angles, lighting, yes indeed...a new *couch*... in the most delicious shade of salmon with pesto pillows, and Margo and Trish did their best to be enthused. They only smirked once, and Claire aimed a perfectly placed kick at Trish's shin. Margo picked up her glass to cover a grin.

Abruptly Dr. Amy stopped, collapsed, and cried. Big wet tears slopped out of the perfectly mascaraed eyes. "Wo!" said Claire, handing Amy her napkin. "I'm sorry," Amy apologized, mopping saltwater from her cheeks, carefully dabbing her lower lashes. "All this crap on the show wasn't my idea. Ratings are down. A lot. If the new shit doesn't work, I don't either." She blinked rapidly, looked at each woman in turn. "I'll have to get used to being like everyone else. No offense, but it sucks."

"None taken," Margo said through her teeth, checking all vitals for any sign of sympathetic response. "Speaking for the regular folks out here."

"Did they tell you that - all this stuff - if ratings don't go up, they'll replace you?" Trish asked, curious.

"No, that's not how it works. I've been around the station long enough to know that no woman lasts past 35. I thought I was more immune to the aging stuff because it's a cooking show. You've seen cooking shows, right? All shapes, ages, wardrobe choices. Add the psychology of food, I thought, and I should be okay. But there isn't any protection from time. The network executives are under 40. And they're men. And the advertising people are 13, or younger. What the hell do they know?" Amy stopped, simmering in a soup of self-pity. "Demographics. Nielsen and the like. Shit. You said it, Claire, my audience isn't home during the day. Nielsen, my ass. The folks watching are so doddering they can't answer the phone when the survey people call."

Margo said quietly, "Amy, if I was home, I wouldn't watch a cooking show."

Amy froze, eyeing Margo like a rival buck in a clearing. "What's your point, Margo?"

"You're a psychiatrist. Why are you messing about with food?"

"Margo! Come on," Claire started, and Margo finished "No. I'm not being mean, I want to know. Amy, did you ever practice?"

"No."

Margo gestured, hand motion of confusion, "I'm sorry, I didn't mean to offend you. Perhaps I'm struggling with my own situation. My degree's in literature, and I've never done anything with it.

Circumstances, money, all of that alter our path. I wonder why cooking? How did you get there?"

Dr. Amy's shoulders relaxed a notch, but the hair on her neck was still bristling. "What difference does that make? What's your interest in this, Margo? An opportunity to belittle what I do for a living again?"

"I deserved that, but that's not my point. "We… " she gestured to Claire and Trish…"have been feeling well, astray lately. Perhaps it's a function of age, I don't know, but I've been thinking about how I got where I am, and where I might have gone otherwise. So, your story seems to fit here. Did you intend to have a cooking show on television, or how did you get one if that's not what you intended?"

Amy sat back, turned her water glass around with both hands, concentrating. "I took a part-time job in graduate school, working at a radio station in town, crunching ratings and other data. When one of the on-air people quit, I asked for the job. It was 2 hours prep a day for a twenty-minute show; a schedule I could handle along with school and studying, and it paid more than being a teaching assistant. Later I had a half hour call-in show; one of the early talk experiments. That's it. One thing led to the next, and here I am, 25 years later, about to be out of work."

"I'm sorry," Margo said again.

"Thanks," Amy said and sniffed. "I keep thinking about what my therapist said 'it feels shitty because it is shitty'" Margo hooted. "Mine said the same thing." and held up her hand, "No, don't tell me your therapist's name. I don't want to find out I've been paying for recycled homilies."

Everyone laughed.

"Previously-owned platitudes."

"Antique admonitions."

"Hurry! hurry! get your words of wisdom. Only spoken on Sundays by a little old lady in Burbank." Trish said, in a carnival barker drawl.

And so it was that the ice was broken, the floe that floated the women at the table, wobbling and chilly, melted, and the friends waded ashore. Claire talked of her creative wall: the new girls had the gallery handled. Her children were grown. There was a misty, treed path ahead that Claire couldn't peer beyond.

Trish talked about the short, treacherous path she found herself stepping.

Margo wondered if this was the time and these were the people that were supposed to accompany her through the woods, off the path so well-trod and familiar.

Dr. Amy analyzed. "This is normal. It's time to stir the pot." She smiled at the tsk tsk of the pun. "Age. It's about how long we've lived. We want new challenges, a deeper connection to spiritual things, we begin to let go of material stuff, and seek a closer connection to what we might believe really matters. Perfectly normal. Standard really."

"That may be the first time anyone has accused me of being normal," Margo chided. "And never standard. Never. Right, Claire? Unstandard. Abnormal, sure."

Margo raised her murky glass. "Here's to unstandard."

"Here, here."

"Amy," Trish began, serious. "How much clout do you have? I mean, I know host of the cooking thing is in jeopardy, but have you got any connection to the powers that be? Any pull?"

"I don't know. What do you have in mind?" Amy asked.

"A proposal. We're all intelligent, accomplished women (nods around, all eyes on Trish). "Of a certain age." More nods. There are lots of us out there. If we're not the biggest demographic group, we're close. There are plenty of marketing studies that put our influence in buying decisions in the high percentiles."

"We don't see our faces out there." Trish sat back, triumphant.

"What do you mean, Trish?"

"I've been noticing - standing in the grocery checkout line, looking at the magazines on the racks, seeing commercials on TV. Brittany Spears. Jennifer Aniston. Yeah, I know these are the celebrity rags, but look at the other, more prestigious sisters - *Cosmopolitan*, *Good Housekeeping*. Young faces. No one over 25. Even *More* magazine shows women just a touch over 40. Not many 50s. If we see them, they're nonstandard," nodding at Margo.

"Rarely 60s," Trish continued, warming her groove. "Never 70s or 80s. We're not represented anywhere. Even commercials for anti-aging goo have a woman 30 years old erasing her wrinkles with a stroke of her ring finger."

Grumble, grumble, nod, nod, all around the table.

Trish leaned forward again, elbows on the table, intent. "I was browsing the AARP site a few months ago. There was a call for volunteers in a little box on the home page. One of the task forces to be formed asked for media professionals to focus on getting age-appropriate images out there. I got excited briefly, but I'm not a member, so forgot about it for a couple weeks. When I remembered it again, I went to the site, and signed up, paid my $12.99 or whatever, and then went back to look for the task force. Nothing. No mention, nothing even close. There had been three or four bulleted committees with very specific goals listed when I'd last looked.

"I just figured I was missing it, called on my cellphone and got shuffled around to a few people, including a supervisor who couldn't identify - didn't know - what the hell I was talking about. Couldn't find the reference in any database he looked at. I thought I was going nuts. Still do. I didn't make it up. Regardless, I still like the idea."

"So: long story short..." Claire prompted.

"Oh, right. So I was wondering about changing the whole show, Amy. Mix it up. Cause trouble, be innovative. Have guests nobody else is clamoring to get. Be risqué, controversial, unique. Show us ourselves, at the age we are."

When no one joined in, Trish continued, waving her hands. "I don't know - have bull-riding grannies. What do insomniacs eat? Round up older folks who aren't working regularly, and talk about what they eat. Get the Peace Corps in there with how to barbeque beetles. What do you eat on a 600 mile kayak trip across Africa? Have celebrities show up looking like they look in the morning after a rough night. Have an organic cooking episode with unshaven hippies."

"Yuck!"

"Nobody wants to look at that."

"My sister said at the exact time you become comfortable with your naked body, nobody wants to look at it."

"I need to get that image out of my mind. Thanks."

Dr. Amy sat quietly, squinting at Trish. Trish squinted back. The waiter asked if anyone wanted anything, slipped the bill on the table, left. Still Amy and Trish squinted.

"Maybe," Dr. Amy said. "Maybe." Trish smiled widely.

"Cooking Up Trouble. With Dr. Amy." Claire mused.

Margo picked up the check. "Amen," she summed up.

Margo was early for her lunch date with Claire the following Wednesday. As she pulled open the gallery door, she saw the new girl, whose name Claire couldn't remember, standing in the center of the circular granite countertop.

The bell over the door tinkled.

"Hello," said New Girl, unrolling another length of gossamer ribbon and cutting it on a severe angle to match its opposite end.

"Hello," Margo countered cheerily. "I'm here to see Claire?"

"Claire!" new girl said, louder, not moving her head from her task, and then hauling another length of ribbon off the spool.

Margo smiled, breathed in the scent of holiday candles, fire making liquid wax in glass globes on the counter. She walked to the window to examine the Winged Wrapper. Gum wrappers. Honestly. Margo picked up the tag. $8,000 worth of gum wrappers. She congratulated herself for having made the wise decision years ago never to buy what she could make herself. Given enough time, and gum, she could make this statue, no sweat.

She turned, walked along the wall, the white oak planks of the floor hollering about her high heels on its head with each step. Some familiar items were missing from the shelves, probably moved to make way for holiday stuff. Glass bulbs hung from ribbons near the shelves, the end result of the ribbon trimming going on behind Margo's back. Stars, dreidels, glittery spirals sparkled season's greetings from the ceiling.

Claire's footsteps sounded on the boards. "Hey," Margo said.

"Hey, yourself," Claire responded, throwing her scarf around her neck. "Margo, this is...ah, Kennedy."

"Salinger actually. My name is Salinger. I'm glad to meet you."

"Really. Well, hello Salinger. Nice to meet you."

Margo spun, scrutinizing The Wrapper, lips clenched to keep from laughing. Claire glared at her side. "You're going to have to work on your word association skills," Margo whispered.

"Screw you, you harridan," Claire whispered back.

Margo spun 180 degrees. "What an interesting name you have, Salinger. Are you named for someone in the family? Pierre? Whom?"

"My parents are literature people. I'm named for J.D."

"Ah. Nice. Claire tells me you chose this piece for the window. Can you tell me, this...figure: am I understanding this work correctly as allegorical whimsy?"

"Actually the artist is a very committed environmental activist. It represents a warning about pollution. Very serious. Quite an impressive statement, isn't it?" Salinger paused a moment from ribbon cutting to be environmentally concerned, frowning greenly, lips pursed in disapproval at what the helmeted, striding sculpture portrayed.

"Indeed," Margo said. "Thank you. I see. Well, Claire shall we be going?"

Margo walked quickly toward the front door, pulled it open, sending the bell tinkling, as Claire brushed past onto the sidewalk. "Nice to meet you, Salinger. I hope to see you again."

Claire was two doorways down the block before Margo caught up to her.

Margo, amused, asked the stomping shorter woman "Since when does the gallery issue dire warnings about the environment via gum wrappers in the front window? Hey, Claire! Slow down, will you? I'm not wearing hiking boots here."

"It's sold, Margo."

"What? What's sold?"

"That beast you call The Wrapper. It sold."

"For eight bloody thousand dollars?"

"Yes, Margo, for eight bloody thousand dollars. It sold in five days." Claire started walking fast again. Margo stood stunned, then hurried to catch her friend. She kept pace, her long legs matching one for two the steps of her friend. Claire hunched, hands in her coat pockets, said nothing for a block.

"I'm superfluous." Claire mumbled, turning the corner at the light. Margo, three steps into the street straight ahead, glanced back, dashed out of the road, down the side street, and grabbed Claire's arm.

"What do you mean superfluous? What's going on?" Margo confronted Claire as she glared back up at her.

"She - the new girl - chose the art, signed the artist exclusively. It sold in five fucking days. Which part is confusing to you?"

"Claire, you need to explain what's in your head. I can't read your mind. Are you mad because you didn't make the decision? I thought that's why you hired Kennedy. Shit. Salinger. Didn't you? Doesn't she have an art background? Gallery experience? Which decisions are you unhappy about here? How far back are we going with this?"

Claire turned to walk away, and Margo grabbed her arm again. Claire yanked it away, stepped closer to Margo, tipped her head up to graze Margo's chin with her dark blowing hair. "She's better than me."

"That's not true," Margo started and Claire interrupted. "She is. She knows the market, she has the sense. Like a wine taster has the nose. I did once upon a time. I don't any more. I'm superfluous. In my own gallery. I'm spent, blown, call it what you want. I've become an anachronism. And I'm pissed. Let's go." Claire resumed her march down the sidewalk. Margo followed slowly, disturbed. Claire stopped at the Indian buffet, was in the door and at a table when Margo caught her up.

"Claire, Claire, what's going on?" Margo pleaded.

"There are two new girls. Right?" Claire nodded as Margo agreed to the accuracy of the math. "Both are under 30, fine art educated, smart, erudite, happening, awake and aware." Claire pouted for a second or two. "I used to be all that. Things have changed."

"We've all changed, Claire. It's what happens to people if they live long enough."

"Not helpful, Margo. Please let me wallow for awhile."

"Okay. I'm sorry, my dear friend. I really am. It feels shitty, I know." Margo put her hand on Claire's clenched fist on the tablecloth. "It feels shitty....

"...because it is shitty." Claire finished. Both women smiled, sniffed back the tears that were elbowing each other to be the first to escape. "'Getting old is not for sissies.' My mother had that on a t-shirt. I think I still have it somewhere. Maybe I should haul it out and wear it. Except it has cute bears on it. I hate cute bears more than I hate getting older. Are you going to do the buffet?"

Both women made their choice known to the waiter, got up and picked up a warm plate, ladled hot comfort food on its surface as they sidestepped the length of the glass-hooded food array. "We're all in the same shape," Claire observed suddenly. "You know what Trish was talking about the other night about what my cousins in England call 'being made redundant.' The night with Dr. Amy? Maybe there's an idea for all of us there. You're launching on an adventure. You're not going to wait to be made redundant. Maybe we should talk about sharing that adventure."

Margo smiled as she spooned spiced rice in an extra bowl, balancing it precariously on the edge of her full plate. "That's why I mentioned it, Claire. We all can use a change, something exciting, inspirational."

"But not expensive. Dish can't afford it, and I've got new employees to pay. I'm still getting used to having people besides me in the gallery. You know? I hired two girls because I needed one. I couldn't figure out why two, when it would be dicey financially." She looked at Margo. "It's because my subconscious knew I'd be needing to be away. Not just me, but the gallery needs me to step back. Weird, huh? Something I gave birth to telling me it doesn't need me any more. It's like the kids now. It's painful."

"It's a growth opportunity, Claire." Margo pronounced.

"Well, dandy. Let's hope this growth is not just my waistline. You think you have enough food there? Geez, Margo. Let's eat."

Chapter 4

The phone rang, waking Margo in the early dark the next day. Margo mumbled, telling Frasier to pick it up, and then, realizing Frasier wasn't there, answered the phone herself. "Hello?" she spoke with a dash of confusion, a hint of anger.

"Margo. It's Claire. I'm at Trish's. Get over here right now."

"What's happened?" Margo yelled into the phone, but Claire had hung up. Margo looked at the call-ended message on the phone screen for a few seconds, hit the end button, and ran around like a goon until she said "enough!" and got her body organized sufficiently to get it dressed, grab her handbag and car keys and move out the door.

The red sportster skidded on the slick street as Margo corralled it to the curb in front of Trish's house. An ambulance, lights pulsing red, pulled away and lit the siren. Margo put the car in first gear to follow the receding taillights just as Claire came running out of the house. Claire didn't stop running until she was sitting in the passenger seat, buckling the seatbelt. "Go!" Claire yelled, as the belt clicked home.

"Where dammit?" Margo yelled, too, frantic and frightened.

"Follow that ambulance," Claire quietly said, shaking her head and putting her face in her hands. "They're taking her to St. Joseph. We don't have to rush, the roads are slick and she's in good hands now. Just hurry, Margo, get going."

Margo was silent until she had negotiated her way through the subdivision, onto the major thoroughfare, and had a straight route to the hospital.

"Tell me what happened," Margo insisted, shifting into fourth gear.

Claire shuddered and took a gulp of air. "She called me, but didn't say anything. I think she was passing out and hit speed dial, and the number she got was mine. I answered the phone when I saw who it was, but nobody said anything. Oh, Margo, I was freaked out! I hung up on Dish, Margo. I had to. She didn't speak and I was terrified. I called 911, and then got in the car to come here, too." Claire was in her pajamas and boots with her scarf wrapped around her neck. "I don't even have my purse. I just grabbed my keys and left." She turned her frightened round eyes to Margo.

"She wasn't conscious. She was barely breathing. They wouldn't let me near her. When I got here, they were waiting outside - the freaking door was locked. I had to hand my key to the paramedic because I couldn't stop shaking enough to get it in the freaking lock. Oh, Margo," and Claire commenced crying miserably.

"Okay, Claire," Margo said, reaching to pat her thigh. "She's in good hands, she'll get the best of care and attention. Easy, girl. I'm sure she's just weak. Her body has been through hell and she's kept the same pace going. It was bound to catch up with her. Is she still running?"

"I don't know," sniffed Claire. "We haven't talked much about anything to do with her. I'm so wrapped up in my own shit, I've forgotten to make sure my friends are all right. Especially Dish. Poor sick Patricia."

"That's not going to do anybody any good," Margo cautioned. "No guilt trips here. I'm going to the drive-through for coffee. Hang on, sharp turn." Margo put her hand out like she was restraining a toddler in the days before seatbelts.

"Two large coffees, please, no cream, no sugar. Thanks."

Margo handed a steaming cup to Claire, pulled back into the street and, ignoring the beverage in the cup holder, drove both hands on the wheel, staring straight ahead the rest of the distance to the hospital, Claire sipping and sniffing at her side.

Even this early, the parking lot was full, and the two women clung to each other's arm as they tip-toed through the ridged slush toward the neon emergency sign.

"You'll have to go around to the other entrance," a burly orderly in greens sternly shepherded the two women out the emergency entrance sliding doors. "This is for ambulances only. Around there. To your right."

Margo and Claire huddled together, angled their way past the smoking people on the sidewalk, batting eyes against the densely falling snow. Margo left Claire standing at the door and walked rapidly to the desk. "My friend was just brought in by ambulance." Margo informed the disinterested woman behind the desk. "Where do we wait?" The woman pointed further into the building, where a sign overhead declared "Emergency Room Waiting." Margo turned back to the woman, "Who do we inform that we're here, that we need to be kept informed on Patricia Worthington's condition?"

The woman spoke to the papers she was flipping in front of her, pointed with one hand without looking up. "You'll be found in that room when there's anything to be told."

Margo retrieved Claire who was still standing in the doorway, guided her by the elbow to the waiting room, parked her on a couch in the corner. Margo took off her coat and draped it around Claire's shoulders. Claire was still shaking. She held her coffee tightly in front of her, a paper life-saving device, useless and necessary. The coffee cup was vibrating like a demented wind-up toy. Margo pried her friend's fingers from the cup, set it down on the table, and sat next to Claire with her arm around the back of the couch, hand touching the shuddering woman's shoulder.

Margo was halfway through an article she remembered nothing about, when Claire said, "None of the junk that's been on my mind matters, you know? You said it the other day. Stuff happens to all of us. What matters is Trish being well, and you being okay with your life. You know?" she turned, pleading to Margo. "Not many people have friends as precious as you and Dish. That's what counts. Friends and family. My grandchildren." Claire murmured into silence.

"I know, Claire," Margo hugged her friend's shoulder. "Tell your grandchildren next time you see them. Dish and I already know."

"Anybody here for Worthington?" a white coat man asked the room. Margo and Claire looked around for who might answer this question, and then Claire realized who Worthington was. "Here!" she said, standing.

"Are you family?" the man asked.

"Yes," said the two women together. The doctor frowned once, decided not to pursue the relationship angle, and looked at his chart. "She's a lymphoma patient, yes? She's got some white cell count issues that we need to address, and she's running a slight fever which we want to watch. She's being transferred to a room. Someone will be out to tell you what the room number is when she's relocated. Please keep the visit short. Rest is going to do her the most good right now. Do you know who her oncologist is?"

Margo gave him the doctor's name, looked up his phone number in her PDA, delivered that, and sat back down, expelling the breath she had been holding.

Claire and Margo held hands, waiting like lost children for their parents to show up to claim them, until a nurse beckoned them a couple hours later, pointed to the elevator they'd need to take, and the two ascended to the new white realm inhabited by their friend Trish the Dish.

Dish was laying with her hands folded on her chest, an IV stand tethered to her arm, bags of clear liquid dripping down the tube into the needle in the back of her hand. She turned her head and smiled at Margo and Claire.

"If you think you're getting out of work that easily, you'd better think again," Margo joked lamely. She moved to brush the stiff bristle of Trish' head tenderly. "How you feeling, Dish?"

"Well. It feels shitty..." Trish smiled. No one finished the thought this time. "They're going to keep me at least overnight. Since it's almost breakfast time, we're talking three lousy meals only maybe. I'll be needing an infusion of Thai food the second they spring me." Dish tenderly moved her IV'ed hand flat on the bed. "I feel fine except for this. My veins aren't in the best shape: it took a while to get this thing in. It hurts." she closed her eyes.

"You two should take off - you're late for work. Margo, I've been thinking about what you said. About an adventure? When I'm out of here, after I get the Thai food, I'm going to want to talk about that some more. I might need some help figuring out how to do it, but I'm in. Bye, you wonderful women. Thank you." Claire kissed her on the forehead, Margo ruffled her scalp again, and they quietly left Dish to rest.

"Mrs. Worthington? Mrs. Worthington, are you awake?"

Trish opened her eyes slightly and looked at the person standing at her feet through gates of eyelashes. Muzzy short person with an eye-liquid aura of light. White coat. Trish opened one eye a little more and saw the clipboard, the intent look of a newbie doctor, come to learn more of his trade and keep her from getting the rest she was sure the clipboard insisted she get.

"Not Mrs.," Trish unhelpfully answered.

"Yes, well," the newbie continued. "We need to check your vitals and also get another blood sample."

"What time is it?" asked Trish.

"About 2, I think, yes," he acknowledged, looking at his watch.

"When is lunch served around here?" Trish struggled to sit up, pushing the up angle button on the bed. Newbie didn't volunteer to help.

"I don't know. You haven't had lunch yet?"

"No, I haven't, and I'm hungry. Can you get someone who knows about these things please?"

"Well, I need to check your vitals."

"You need to get me someone about lunch," reinforced Trish. "First. No vitals until I have vittles. Okay?"

"There's a nurse call button."

"I've been pushing the call button while you're not getting me someone about lunch. I was pushing the call button when I fell asleep. Please help me here."

The newbie left the room, and Trish picked up the hospital phone, dialed. "Could I speak to Claire please? Yes, I'll wait." Trish watched the snow falling, drifting quietly, covering the cars who got here too late to get a spot inside the parking structure. They'd have to scrape when they left today. "Claire. Would you please do me a favor? I need some clothes. No, I haven't heard anything or seen anyone, but I'd rather be at home than in here. Yes. I'll get my doctor to sign off, but I need clothes. On the chaise in my bedroom is my fuzzy turtleneck and jeans. Top drawer of the dresser has socks and please bring the boots at the front of the closet. The brown ones. No hurry, Claire, no, don't rush out now. I've got to deal with several levels of white coats before I get sprung. But I want out before I don't get fed dinner, if it's possible. Okay. I'll see you around 4-4:30. Thanks, Claire."

Trish hung up the phone as the young doctor came in alone. "Someone is getting you a tray that should be here shortly. Meanwhile, if we can proceed?" He set down his clipboard and grabbed Trish's wrist, checked his watch, stuck a thermometer in her mouth and prepared a syringe for a blood sample, stuck it in the port.

Trish waited quietly until he was done with his assignments. "Would you please find my doctor? Dr. Webster? He's probably doing rounds in the hospital right now. I need to speak to him soon."

The resident was writing on Trish's chart, didn't answer, set the chart back on the clip at the foot rail. "I'm sure the nurse can help you with that. The call button?" he pointed again as though she may have forgotten its place, and had never mentioned its effectiveness. Trish smiled.

"You're a resident, yes?" The doctor nodded. "Are you an oncology resident?" He nodded once more. "So, you report to Dr. Webster while you're on your rounds. At least this afternoon, yes?" The doctor didn't nod.

"My guess is you know precisely where he is this minute, because that's where you're headed to report about me. Please tell him I want to see him. Quite soon."

The doctor turned and left the room without another word.

Trish sighed, returned to watching the falling snow, mesmerized by its lazy drift, she closed her eyes again, drifted down into sleep.

"Pssstt. Psssttt."

Trish turned her head toward the sound before she opened her eyes. Through the eyelash gate, she saw a ski mask. Her eyes flew open.

"Come on," the words muffled by wool revealed the masked Claire. "We're busting outta here. Let's go." Trish grinned.

"My ski mask?"

"Of course," admitted Claire, dragging it off her head, her hair crackling with static. "I found it on the floor of your closet and couldn't resist. I didn't know you skied."

"I don't," said Trish, torso rising up with the bed. "I use it for winter paddling."

"Two words that should never be in the same sentence," Claire said as she unloaded her grocery bag of clothes. "I brought your puffy coat, too. Did you find Dr. Webster? Has he given his seal of approval?"

Trish held up her unstuck hand. "They took the shunt out." She shrugged. "He said he didn't approve, but I was a grown woman and it couldn't hurt me to be in my own bed. But I need to take a few days off to rest and chug chicken soup by the cauldron."

"Well, then, my friend and yours, the inestimable Margo Sawyer, is even more gifted by foresight than we thought. She dropped a pot of soup off at the gallery. We can swing by there and pick it up on the way to your house. Here. I brought you a couple pounds of the ton of make-up you had on your bureau. You can spackle some on that wan face of yours, if you like."

Claire helped Trish get into the layers of clothes, and they both sat on the bed talking quietly, Trish fiddling with mascara lamely while they waited for the mandatory wheelchair chariot to cart The Dish out of the hospital. When one didn't arrive, Claire walked down to the nurse's desk, inquired and got permission to cut out on their own, as long as she promised not to jog. Arm in arm, the friends walked to the elevator, pushed the button, crossed the lobby. Claire said, "wait right here. I'll get the car."

Claire's toy car was puffing warm clouds of heated air when Dish got into the passenger door, and the mini-wipers were swinging mightily to clear the windshield of the big flakes of snow. "We'll take our time, not to worry," Claire nodded at Trish, who didn't like to drive in snow.

"I don't worry if someone else is driving," Trish clicked the seatbelt home.

Claire maneuvered into the roundabout that took them toward town. "For a person who goes paddling in February, you'd think driving in snow wouldn't be a big deal."

"I know my skill level on the water. There aren't dozens of idiots going too fast to cause trouble. It's their skill level that scares me."

"Ah," said Claire. "You know you can count on yourself."

"Without question or pause."

"Thanks, Claire, for coming for me."

"Any time Patricia. Any time at all."

Claire dropped Trish at the sidewalk in front of the shop, and Trish stomped her way into the store, nodded to the new girl behind the counter, and turned to look out the window at a car with a canoe strapped to its roof, was about to ask Salinger if she knew whose car it was, when Claire stomped in behind her.

"Salinger, you remember Trish." Claire said, pulling her glasses off and wiping them on a handkerchief she'd scrounged from the depth of her jacket pocket.

"Hi," both women said at the same time. Salinger turned to speak to a man that had just walked up to the counter. Claire nodded at the man as he looked up and smiled. Salinger walked around the counter, took the man's elbow and brought him before the two friends. "Claire, Trish, this is my dad. Caldwell. Dad, this is the gallery owner, Claire Chernikova," and Claire hauled off her mitten to take the man's hand, extended. "How are you?"

"And this is her friend, Trish," Trish took the hand pointed in her direction, smiled back at the smile glinting at her. "Hello, glad to meet you." said Salinger's dad.

"Caldwell, did you say? I sense a trend here."

The man laughed. "Yes, we literary types are literal as well. I'm named for Taylor Caldwell."

"Wasn't Taylor Caldwell a woman?" asked Trish.

"Yes, she was. You're correct. We were light on gender, but religious on naming. Salinger's mother came from a family as devoted to the written word, so her fate was sealed at birth, too." He shrugged, finished, ended on another white-toothed smile.

"What's your last name?"

"Spooner." both Salinger and Caldwell answered together.

"My friends generally call me Spoon," he smiled, shrugged.

Claire and Trish stared open-mouthed and Claire took to laughing until she was hiccuping into her handkerchief.

Trish smiled at the befuddled father and daughter. She grinned as Claire mumbled apologies. "Seems we've fallen into a nursery rhyme, " Trish started to explain. "It's a long story about how I got the nickname, but my good friends call me Trish the Dish. And now we have the Spoon. Claire (Trish punched her affectionately in the arm) here is thinking that a cow, the moon and a little laughing dog are about to show up."

"Serendipity," said Caldwell the Spoon quietly, admiring Trish's ice blue eyes.

"Indeed," agreed Trish the Dish, noting the liquid gold speckling the brown of his sparkling eyes.

Claire watched them for a moment, and clapped her hands together. "Well, I've got work to do, and Dish needs to get home with chicken soup in hand. I'll go get the soup out of the back room." She lightly hip-checked Trish on the way past.

"Did you need a ride home?" asked Spoon, "My car's right out front. I'd be glad to drive you."

"Well, thank you very much. Is that all right with you, Claire?" she yelled at her friend's retreating back. Claire waved her hand in the air, continuing on her way.

Salinger frowned slightly, eyes moving from her father to Trish. "Dad, we're still going to dinner, right?"

The eye spell, blue to brown to blue, snapped like a taut ribbon, and both Trish and the man turned to look at the young girl. "Of course, sweetheart. I'll be back directly."

All eyes watched Claire returning, toting a big Dutch oven toward the front. "Let me," said Caldwell, hurrying to take the pot from Claire. Trish stuffed the mittens she had taken off back on each hand, threw both arms around Claire. "Thank you for rescuing me, you wonderful woman."

"My pleasure. Eat soup, get rest." Claire hugged her back.

"I'll be back shortly," Caldwell said to the women remaining, and "Shall we?" to the designated rider. Trish smiled, opened the door for the brew-bearing man, waved good-bye to the two others, and walked out of the gallery.

"My car's got the canoe on top," he nodded toward the car Trish had spotted in front.

"You're kidding," Trish said, regretting immediately the teenaged sound of it. "I noticed it when we came in. That's an Old Town, isn't it?"

"It is," he stopped to look at Trish, surprised. "You're a paddler?"

"Yes. Some. I have a Dagger. Sojourn."

"Well! An experienced paddler."

"No, not really. It's more canoe than I can handle on some days. I paddle solo in it when the water's warm. But I find a doubles ride when it's cold." They continued the short walk to the car, he set the pot on the sidewalk, unlocked the door and opened it for Trish, ushering her into the passenger seat.

"Where do you paddle?" Trish asked while he buckled up, started the car.

"Wherever I can. Huron is my home river, of course, but I get to the Pere Marquette and the Pine as often as I can. Au Sable occasionally. And farther away when time and work allow. I've raced open boats for quite awhile."

"Well," Trish said, lost for words.

"So which way are we going?" he asked. Trish gave him directions, sat quietly contemplating how tired she was, and how curious, the pot of soup warm and comforting on her lap.

He gestured with his chin toward the soup pot, "So why are people making you soup?"

"Oh," Trish dipped her eyes and head. "I just got out of the hospital. Claire picked me up, we stopped at the gallery to pick up the soup another friend made." She turned her head to smile at the driver. "And then we met you."

"Chicken soup for the paddler, huh? I hope it wasn't something serious that had you in the hospital?" He modulated his voice into a question, but not enough to disguise concern behind it. Trish smiled at the generosity of spirit the voice quality revealed. She turned to beam the smile fully on this kind man. "I'm a cancer patient. I hit a rough patch, but I'm headed home, bearing soup, talking paddling. It's good right now."

They talked about rivers and paddles and boats for the short duration of the ride, and pulling up in front of Trish's house, he got out, opened her door for her and took the pot. Trish led the way to the front door, unlocked it, trying to remember what state the living room was in, and was happy to find it neat. She held the door for Caldwell, gestured toward the kitchen and led the way.

"Well then," he smacked his gloved hands together. "This is nice. Cozy. I like the lay-out."

"It's a kit house. I think rooms were added on as needed, but I like the open center. It's great for entertaining."

"I'll bet it is," he acknowledged walking to the back doorwall to look out on the snow-covered trees. "Nice view. No curtains. You're not worried about voyeurs?"

"I'd rather have the view. I don't like curtains."

"Me either. Well, I'd better get back to Salinger. She's about to be finished for the day. We're going out for sushi." He walked to the front door, put his hand on the knob.

Trish was quiet behind him. He turned to look at her, and Trish, meeting his eyes felt a spark she hadn't felt in a lot of years. "Trish - what's your given name," asked Caldwell.

"Patricia."

"Patricia. That's nice. If you're feeling up to it, would you like to paddle with me some day? The Old Town's rigged for solo, but I have a couple other canoes set up for doubles." He unzipped his jacket, reached into an inner pocket on whatever garment was layered underneath and pulled a bent card out. "Here's my card. When you'd like to paddle, just call the number there." He pointed with a gloved hand. "The cellphone."

Trish looked up from the card, and smiled again. "I'd like that. Have fun at dinner with your daughter. And thank you for the ride home."

Trish stood at the window, waved back as he waved, and watched the car with the canoe hat disappear into the distance. She looked at the card in her hand. Professor of Paleography. Wow. So, ancient manuscripts? But he'd said to call the cellphone, not work phone, not home phone. She sighed, took off her jacket and hat, set a match to the wood in the fireplace, and lit the stove under the soup.

The Tuesday before Thanksgiving rose mystically in a foggy world of 51 degrees. Antoine Lavoisiere stood at his kitchen window, watching the trees come into view, the lace of bare branches obscured in the rising mist. A patch of grass showed at the bottom, the twigs of variegated dogwood, lilac and forsythia bushes in clumps on the ground, decapitated by the thick haze. Curlicues danced at the base of the vapor, looping into fairy calligraphy before disappearing into the brume above, as though the mist was writing the story of the branches to be.

Evidence of global warming each year eclipsed by the denial of its existence.

Lavoisiere sighed, shuffled in his slippers to the kettle that was singing steamily, poured hot water over his teabag, and carried the cup to his desk. He was up before his usual early awakening, and he smiled to himself, recognizing the reason as excitement to meet Edgar Pavelka again today.

He blew into, then sipped his tea, remembering the phone ringing last night. "Hello?" Antoine had answered, curious about the sound that seldom signaled a caller he knew these days. "Yes?" when the caller didn't speak right away.

"Monsieur Lavoisiere?" the tentative voice asked. "Um, well, this is Edgar. Edgar Pavelka. I drove you home?"

Antoine Lavoisiere crinkled his eyes in a smile. "Yes, of course, Edgar. How are you? Good of you to call."

"Yes, well, thank you, um, I was wondering if it is your plan to go to the shop tomorrow morning. If you wouldn't mind, I'd like very much to hear more about your work and its history, and well, um, if you wouldn't mind - oh I said that already - might I join you there in the morning?"

"Yes, certainly! Delighted. I'll be there at 7 a.m., but take your time. I won't be leaving until eleven or noon, depending, so no hurry. I'll be glad to see you again, Edgar. Yes. Look forward to it. Good-bye now. Until then."

He had gently replaced the old bakelite receiver in its cradle, smiling at the rotary dial. He guessed how difficult it may have been for the boy - oh no, young man - to make the telephone call, and Antoine was appreciative of his courage.

This early morning, as Antoine swung his crossed slippered feet in his desk chair, sipped his tea, he thought that Edgar at his age wasn't much different than young Antoine had been at 14, when he was taken to the print shop by his father. His older brothers were already at their jobs by his age, but Antoine, shy and stuttering, lingered longer at his schoolwork than his father would have liked. It was a stern and resolute man who introduced his fourth son to the printmaker.

He thought about what he would like to tell Edgar Pavelka. About his own work and about the work of his own apprentice, Jan Pavelka. About his country and their shared heritage, his family, his passion.

In 1501 the Czech Brethren had printed the first Protestant hymnbook.

He would remind his young new friend that grimoires - textbooks about magic - were being widely printed and successfully published at the same time all the Bibles were coming out. Luther's Bible. The Polyglot Bible. The Kralice Bible.

Antoine Lavoisiere remembered with loving detail the first time he visited the permanent exhibition "Work of the Czech Brethren Printers." He wandered for an entire day among the iconographic materials and photographs, postcards and graphic art; the collection of mostly Czech orders and decorations.

The history of letter-print.

Czechoslovakia's art history is about applied arts, Antoine would tell Edgar. Applied arts being the application of design and aesthetics to functional objects for everyday use. Whereas fine arts serve as intellectual stimulation to the viewer of academic sensibilities, the applied arts incorporate design and creative ideals to useful objects, such as a cup, magazine, book or park bench.

Then, he proposed happily to himself, he would talk a little about cutting tools normally associated with metal engraving such as burins or gravers and a steel needle embedded in a wooden grip.

Goodness, thought Lavoisiere. What would a Polyglot Bible look like today?

He rose, rinsed his teacup in the sink, walked to the vestibule, wrapped his muffler around his neck, pulled his coat slowly onto one arm, then the other, sat on the valet to pull on his good walking shoes;

stood, settled his hat firmly on his head, and walked out the door, locking it behind him. Out into the fog of an early warm pre-Thanksgiving Tuesday morning, Antoine Lavoisiere was on his way to meet a new friend.

When Antoine arrived, having said "good morning" to the baker on his way (the difference being this morning, Lavoisiere had opened the bakery door, shouted "good morning" into the fragrant, floured air, and left before Joseph the Baker could come to the front, frowning at the old man's retreating back) Saima was decorating a small tree. Two large boxes were opened, many smaller boxes were on the floor around the two.

The bell over the door tinkled.

"Ah, Antoine, good morning. Happy Tuesday before Thanksgiving Day. I'm decorating a tree this year. Haven't done it in years, but I felt like decorating a tree."

Monsieur Lavoisiere set his hat on the coat tree, and walked over to where Saima stood holding a metal angel, unbuttoning his coat as he walked. "A real tree, too. How festive. I love the smell of evergreens. Reminds me of my youth and summers in the mountains."

"My youth was scented with pine, too. And my old age."

"Bah. You're not old yet. But when you do age, I hope there are pines to smell. May I help?"

"If you'd like, Antoine. Everything in the boxes goes on the tree. I've strung the lights already, but just got these downstairs," she gestured to the big boxes.

Antoine bent and picked up a small gold box. He pulled the cover, gently parted the tissue, and found a golden spider nestled there; a scroll rolled in one of its beaded legs. He lifted it by its gold thread. Saima smiled, "You, of course, know the folk wisdom of a spider in a Christmas tree."

"It's good luck for the new year, isn't it? If I remember correctly, to find a spider in the tree is good. German, yes?"

"Yes, it is. Put it anywhere, Antoine," and Lavoisiere walked around the tree to find the perfect nest for the spider. "I loved the markets at Christmas in Prague. Wenceslas Square would be full of stalls with trees, and food and holiday decorations. Our tradition is to eat carp for Christmas dinner, so in the market there would be bathtubs full of live carp. The fishmonger would prepare your choice for you, right out of the bathtub. At midnight mass, we would hear Jan Jakub Ryba's Czech Christmas Mass."

"Our fish was a salmon," Saima offered. "Fruit soup. Pülla. Before Christianity it was our custom to celebrate the return of the light at the solstice, much the way that time in December is celebrated now: honoring our gods, feasting, distributing presents. The Finnish word for Christmas *joulu* has its origin in the old Viking word *jhul* meaning 'sun disk'." Saima patted Antoine on the shoulder as she passed him, moving toward the boxes and another ornament. "Much has changed; much remains the same. Once I moved to America, I stopped eating fish. Don't miss it much at all."

Antoine picked up a tin bell, intricately wrapped with a small nut as the bell clapper. "South America?"

"Guatemala."

"I sense a trend."

"Most of these are handmade from all over the world. A few are family heirlooms, many are gifts. The glass bulbs in this box here still are hung by the butcher's string my mother tied to them. We reused everything we could. I suppose that's how recycling used to work."

Lavoisiere picked up a glass painted bird, a pheasant with a brush tail. "Well, my, here's a familiar chick." He flicked its tail on its new perch, center front on the tree. He watched Saima hang a woven reed angel next to the bird. "You know the story of each ornament, don't you, Saima?" The old woman smiled. "Yes, I do. If I did not make or buy the ornament, if I wasn't in the story, I was told it by my mother, my grandmother. We have a long history of storytelling in my tribe. I imagine your family too, Antoine."

"There aren't many of us left. In the old days, if you were running out of family, you told the stories to your apprentice, or your entire village as an honored elder, or your parish youth. There are stories that end every day in America, I think.

"It's a lonelier life here, perhaps."

"How so, Antoine?"

"It may well be the times, more than the place. I've been gone from Europe for a long time - you, too, I believe. But I imagine it's modern there too. Computers instead of communing, internet rather than libraries or cafes. Results expected for our work that we may not understand. We don't create the tools we use to work now. It has been decades since we knew how to make the tools we use or, if we didn't make the tools, we knew well the person who did.

"We do not see the results of our labor. We don't know how it contributes to the overall good. We cannot chart the course taken to deliver our goods to market. There is no good measure of the impact we make, for good or ill.

"We do not watch our hands work, with pride and purpose. We do not derive direct benefit from a job well done. And our neighbors do not either. Our food travels thousands of miles to reach our mouths. We're divided from our work. And now in this new century, we are divided from each other by our words.

"We do not honor our tribe's storytellers. The telling is mutated, the words misused and spun out recklessly, perhaps by laziness, maybe by ideology, witnesses not consulted. And that story is then copied, wrong word for wrong word, repeated until the tale is unrecognizable by the people who are living the story as it is told.

"I saw on the television this young man who wants to be president of America speak," Antoine shook his head in surprised wonder. "I believe it was he who said that the future is in the hands of those who go back to their roots and do one thing well. These people who do one thing well will replace what he called the heroic multitasker.

"I'm hoping that he may have true insight, but I think he may be young and therefore optimistically enthusiastic.

"Saima, I talk too much," Antoine clapped his hands together and rubbed them briskly. "Let's decorate the tree. If we see any young people today, you will fill their eager ears with the stories of the ornaments. That's a good day's work."

The bell over the door tinkled.

Edgar Pavelka and a squadron of wet leaves flew in the door.

Margo was dumping her reheated coffee into a lidded travel cup when Frasier let himself in the garage door on Tuesday morning. "I hope you didn't park me in, Frasier," Margo called toward the doorway, around the kitchen counter.

"I didn't, Margo. You're leaving for work?"

"As I have for the last eight years at exactly the same time during the week, yes. You were expecting something different, or is this small talk meant to charm me before the more serious matter you want to discuss?" Margo plopped, then secured the top on the traveler mug with a palm tap, and turned to face Frasier, standing wearing his falsely accused face in the kitchen. Margo crossed her arms and smiled.

"I don't have anything to discuss, Margo. I believe I said that the other morning when you launched your unprovoked attack. I thought I'd give you a couple days to calm down, so that we could talk about your issues rationally."

"My issues? I'm not sure I want to talk about *my* issues *rationally* just now, if that's your agenda, Frasier. Not when you come back after being gone for three days with no note, no phone call, leaving me to explain to our daughters that I have no way to reach you. Which I didn't do, by the way. I'll leave that little task for you to do yourself. That's if you're having Thanksgiving dinner with your family. Are you?"

Frasier hung his head in dramatic and entirely unbelievable remorse. Margo rolled her eyes over the perfectly coiffed dome displayed for her view. "Call Caroline. Or Morgan. Get the details, if you're interested. I'd have given you more attention if you had come home at a more convenient time. I have to go."

She pulled her driving gloves on, picked up her handbag from the back of the kitchen chair, slung it over her shoulder, picked up the travel mug, and marched past the still head-hung Frasier. What the hell did he want? Applause? Ah. The magic wand. The absolution that only Margo could bestow.

"I forgive you, Frasier. Once more. If the president gets to pardon a turkey today, then I guess I can do that little thing, too. Call Caroline this morning. No later than."

She didn't slam the door on the way out.

Margo backed the red roadster carefully out of the garage, creeping past Frasier's SUV, wishing she'd thought to take his car and leave hers for him. The fog was frozen in patches on the grass and bare trees, and shining leaves stuck to the ground would be slippery. Maybe not. It felt warmer than normal.

She relaxed into her morning routine, catching up on the news on the public radio station, sipping coffee, testing the brakes on the road that turned out to be not frozen, contemplating what she'd get done that day. Lynn wanted a talk at 10:00 a.m., had faxed an agenda. Margo's cellphone rang.

"Hello, sweetheart," she greeted her daughter's voice. "Well, of course your father is coming. Haven't you talked to him? Oh, Caroline, he's just busy. How's my grandson? Is he looking forward to tomorrow?" She listened to the happy baby boy news, smiling. "Yes, I'll bring the pies. I'll be over at noon. Will your sister be there in the morning? What do you mean? You haven't talked with Morgan? I'll call her; not to worry. No, I'll watch the parades at home making the pies. If you want me earlier, call me in the morning. Love you, too, honey. Bye." Margo left the phone open, pushed the voice button, spoke "Morgan" into the phone, waited for the inevitable dump to voicemail message. "Morgan

Valentina. This is your mother. Your sister and I are wondering if we're going to see you for Thanksgiving dinner at Caroline's. Call one of us, please, honey. Dinner's at 3. Love you. Bye."

Trish wasn't in, naturally, when Margo checked at the reception desk, and Margo reminded herself to call the hospital to check on her condition before the 10 o'clock call.

Bob wanted to discuss his telephone interview with Lynn, and Margo led him into the kitchen for coffee, and back to her office, while he talked the entire route. She assured him he hadn't screwed it up, shooed him away, and called St. Joseph Hospital. She was still on hold when it dawned on her to call Claire. "She was sprung yesterday, Margo. She talked her doctor into letting her convalesce at home, which was easy and smart. I gave her the soup you made. How are the roads? Good? Swell. I figured there wouldn't be ice. It's over 50 degrees. Gotta go. We'll talk more later."

At precisely 10, Margo's phone rang, Lynn's number appearing LED. Margo stuck her tongue out at the square digits, picked up the receiver, took a breath and answered cheerfully, "Good morning, Lynn."

"Is it, Margo? I'm wondering when my next good morning might be. You picked one hell of a time to abandon us, Margo. I wish you had given your decision more thought and our position more consideration." Lynn sighed audibly. Margo stuck her tongue out again. "Julie told me that Patricia isn't in today yet. Is she expected any time soon? I was hoping to talk with her about your position today."

And with that Margo knew who the mole in the office was. It had given her only a few minutes' discomfiture over the past several months, but now it all fit. Margo had brought Julie in from their former agency; she was excellent at committee-wrangling and a heck of a fundraiser. After a few incidences of information being revealed as already known by Lynn, Margo figured someone was informing. Ambition could be a terrible burden, if the person you were angling to replace found out too soon. Well, well, this was going to be more fun than she'd thought. Lessons could be learned.

"Trish isn't interested, Lynn. I asked her already. There's no need to talk with her about this process."

"But is she coming in today?"

"Lynn, call her phone after we're done here, if you have something to discuss with her. Can we start on your list that involves me?"

"Really, Margo, I wish you had a better handle on your staff. You still have two and a half weeks in that position. Let's not let the office get out of control."

"Lynn. The list?"

The two women wound their way through the five bullet points on Lynn's list. Margo motioning and seconding any movement forward that occurred. Lynn cajoled, bullied, whined in her well-known management style that Margo figured she'd honed as the oldest of three weaker sisters with absentee parents, and as the second banana in a small nonprofit where she'd elbowed her way in by the sharpness of her creases and her nose, and her knowledge of all the skeletons in all the closets.

"Margo, one more item not on the list: I'd like you to prepare a document with four or five external candidates you'd recommend, and the analysis why you believe I should consider them for the director's chair. I know this is a holiday week, but I can give you until oh, say, Tuesday? Email me the document by Tuesday. That would be fine."

"No, Lynn."

"Margo? I'm sorry, I thought you said no."

"I said no, Lynn."

"I don't understand."

"No, I won't make five external recommendations. No, I won't be evaluating any of my choices submitted to you before I make those choices. I'll make my recommendations to you in the next couple of weeks. That, I believe, ends any obligation for recommending. There's more important work to be finished before I go."

"Margo, honestly, you're not transitioning very well. Really."

"Lynn, I'm not transitioning: I quit. And Lynn? I forgive you for telling Harvey I wasn't transitioning very well. Yes, he told me you told him. Because we're *friends*, Lynn. Maybe next time you'll check first. Good-bye, Lynn." Margo gently placed the still connected line into its cradle.

Margo sat back in her desk chair, hands clasped behind her head, and spun around once. She stopped, facing her desk again, picked up the phone receiver, smiling and dialed a four-digit internal number. "Julie? Good morning. Would you come in for a minute please? Thanks." She spun around once more, just for fun.

"Just look at that moonrise," Margo observed much later that day, her chair swiveled to face the dark glass of the conference room window. "Makes you understand why the ancients would have feared and revered it."

Margo and Trish were in the office, shoeless, tired and determined to finish selecting candidates for director, crunching cheese puffs and drinking bottled iced tea. Trish had come in her Tasmanian slipper socks after 5:00 to keep her friend company. Papers were strewn on the conference table. Empty coffee cups stood sentinel among file folders and crinkled paper debris. Giant sticky notes were affixed to the wall and red, green and black marker notes were bulleted, crossed off and circled, like modern petroglyphs on the stippled wallpaper.

Trish had her bare feet on the marbled surface, legs stretched out from her tipped-back chair. "Claire would have a snit if she knew we were eating this junk," Trish commented, licking yellowed fingers happily.

"We won't ask her over to join us then," Margo said, sipping tea loudly. "This is work therapy. Back in the day, we'd have gone to the bar. So. Where are we exactly with this succession business?"

Trish dropped her legs from the table to the floor, tilting her two-legged chair stance down to four legs on the ground. "We've got three. One internal, two external. By the way, you're not dazzled by any of them," Trish gave a swift glance up at Margo.

"I'm not?" Margo asked, in mock surprise.

"No," Trish concluded.

"Hmm."

"Let's review the three again. We've got Marion," Trish floated the paper with Marion's stats into the air.

"She's suitable, Trish. Only one tiny detail that bothers me. She works with the fierce urgency of maybe next week. I prefer the urgency of a week ago Thursday. Maybe I'm being picky."

"Picky's fine, as long as you actually end up recommending someone, Margo. What about Bob?"

Margo frowned. "He's not on our list of finalists."

Trish tipped her chair precariously back again. "Why not?" she asked, putting one bare foot back on the conference table, using it to swish other papers out of the way.

"He's boring," Margo said.

"Yes."

"Undynamic. Not exciting."

"Yes."

"Reticent. It takes him a long time to make a decision. He's slow to act. Thoughtful." Margo put her hands flat on the table, picked her

121

head straight up from her shoulders, awake again. "Oh ho! You wily wench! He's just the nonconfrontational, steady, reliable, contemplative person we need! Lynn would have her hands full trying to pull his strings. She won't find the ends! Bingo, Trish. You're a genius."

"As I have said," Trish saluted with a puffy cheese curl, and triumphant, chomped it into smithereens.

Dish was still wriggling her toes in her Tasmanian Devil sleeping socks, enjoying a second cup of coffee at the dining room table in front of the big picture window, feeling like a kid cutting third grade when the phone rang.

Trish frowned. Did collectors call the Wednesday before Thanksgiving? Sure they did. Hoping to catch their degenerate, irresponsible targets home from work, recovering from a stay in the hospital, shopping on eBay, spending their money.

She shuffled her feet into the office to listen to the message, screening the call.

"Trish, this is Caldwell Spooner. We met yesterday at your friend's gallery? I know it's a little soon, but I wondered if you had plans for lunch today. I know you have a lot of soup, but…."

Trish picked up the receiver, said "Hello, Caldwell" into the middle of his sentence. "I have soup indeed."

"Oh, yeah, that was a big pot of chicken soup. If you'd prefer another choice, I'd be willing to share my limited knowledge of other varieties of soup. Or if you'd rather go nonliquid, well, I'm flexible about solid foods."

Trish smiled into the phone. "Sounds nice. Solid foods. Yes, that would be just fine. Shall I meet you?"

"Not necessary. I'll pick you up. 11:45? You have my cell number if anything changes, but discounting that, I'll be in your driveway at 11:45, looking forward to talking with you again."

"Okay. Thanks. I'll see you then."

How about that? A trip to the hospital in an ambulance = date. Go figure. Dish did a little jig in her souvenir Tazmanian sleeping socks, set her cup on the counter, turned on the shower, ditched her Buzz Lightyear pjs on the carpeted floor and submitted her body to a massage pounding shower, singing.

She wrapped in her robe she'd made for herself back in the marriage days, this one thicker than the one she made for the ex, longer, too. His was the prototype, hers the perfect production model. She retrieved her cup with fresh hot coffee poured, set it down and looked in the triple mirror. It would be easier if I saw more images of women my age, Trish thought again. This is hard because we're not used to seeing women age.

Ten years ago, Trish discovered she looked like her worst hangover morning all the time. Now she looked like her mother, with promises of grandma to come in the not-too-distant future. She was reasonably athletic, and up until the cancer thing had worked to maintain her shape and her stamina. Not as much in the last two years, but Patricia Worthington was not disappointed in Trish the Dish who stood tall, gazing back at her. Chicken skin, fat pads and sagging breasts weren't a bad price to pay for continued existence. She'd look older yet if she lived. To Trish, it was just as simple as that. She picked up her Maybelline to put into practice her motto "When you are young you should wear lots of mascara. When you are old, you should wear much, much more."

Trish got to work.

She finished dressing before 11 o'clock, so she used the time to tidy the house, thinking about her plan as she moved from small room to small room.

She'd owned five houses in her life; two she walked away from; left to the exes, Trish stuffing the paperwork representing her share in her purse. One other house she sold at a nice profit, another a loss, and this one she'd been in for the longest period of her life. Ten years. It was a lovely little house in butter cream vinyl, with a fireplace and a mud room, red oak floors that Trish had restored. In this smallest house she'd owned, the bathroom was the biggest, with a shower stall and a garden tub with a skylight. The main house was open from the front door to the back door wall, with a partial windowed wall separating the living room from the kitchen. A counter peninsula separated the dining space from the rest of the kitchen.

There were big windows all along the south wall of the house, opposite the two bedrooms, bath and laundry room. The small dining area windows she'd had cut out and replaced with one 96 inch span of glass. The house stood at the side of a double lot, so the southern exposure wasn't close enough to another house to worry about whether the curtains were closed or not. In the corner of the kitchen, a pink chromed refrigerator from the 50s chugged coolly.

What was special about this house was the quality of light. Aunt Suoma had traveled the world, but remembered Venice most tenderly because of the light. It was like nowhere else in the world, Aunt Suoma had mused, her voice soft and far away.

Like nowhere else, Trish mused to herself, enjoying the quiet light.

If she had to sell the house, the memory of the light would be with her always, and she knew where to find other special light, in secret places that she and a big blue heron knew. In the other locales she was the two-legged who walks where blue heron flies. She remembered a sign she saw more than once in England "Priorities Change Ahead." Yes, indeed. She glanced one more time out the big window, just as a car with a canoe strapped on top pulled into view.

Trish watched him sit in his car. She assumed he was shutting off his phone, leaving it in the console, organizing his approach. He got out and stretched, looking up at the two 30 foot cottonwoods, their leaves still strewn in piles at the corners of the yard. He was over six feet, not much taller than Trish, and he moved confidently, maybe favoring one knee. His hair was on his head, and that's as much attention as he'd paid it. It was clean. His clothes were sensible, not stylish; useful, not showy. He wore jeans and worn hiking boots and a Henley shirt in forest green with the sleeves pushed up. His arms were well-muscled paddler's arms, with a light coat of the same ash brown hair that was on his head. He looked in the kitchen window, didn't acknowledge seeing Trish, and came up on the porch, and rang the doorbell.

Trish opened the wooden door to his ready smile. Caldwell opened the screen door himself and stepped into the house again at Trish's invitation. "It's a nice house, Trish. How long have you lived here?"

"Ten years," Trish answered over her shoulder, going to the dining room for her wrap and handbag. "It's been host to a lot of good times."

"And more to come. Definitely. You're ready to go, that's nice: shall we then?" He held the door for her, Trish turned the tumbler and yanked it shut locked. Trish led down the stairs and stopped at the bottom, glancing first at the car and back at the man behind her, still holding onto the railing, one foot on the steps.

"You changed boats."

He laughed. "I did. I put a doubles up. It was warm this morning and when I thought of calling you for lunch, I thought maybe, if you weren't busy afterward, and of course, if you were feeling up to it..."

Trish grinned, reached into her bag for her keys. "If you want to come back in and wait for a second, I'll change clothes."

Caldwell waited on the couch, his arms stretched across the back of... what is this? Patio furniture? admiring the vaulted ceiling in the living room, the tall bay window, the art on the limited wall space. "That's an unusual sculpture over the fireplace." he said loudly into the bedroom doorway.

"My sisters got that for me. It's from Peru, I think."

Trish appeared wearing blue jeans, gortex ankle boots, a wicking undershirt, a zippered pocket vest, and a hat that read "Dances with Rocks."

"I'll get my life vest and paddles out of my car, and then we're ready to go."

Caldwell stood up, slapped both hands on his thighs. "Good with me. Wow. A woman who changes clothes in less than 10 minutes. Rare."

Trish laughed. "I'll let you out the front, and then get my stuff out of the car and come out through the garage. Meet you on the driveway."

"All right."

They saddled up after tossing Trish's gear in the back of the Jeep. Trish patted the skirt of the Mad River Malecite KX shining upside down on the roof. Oh boy, you're a beauty, thought Trish.

"How much does it weigh?" asked Trish before her belt was clicked.

He shook his head and frowned slightly and then it dawned "Ah, the boat? Yes, of course, the boat. 51 pounds."

"It's Kevlar, isn't it? What? 16 feet? 16 and a half?" Trish asked, finishing engaging her seatbelt, turning fully to face Caldwell, who was eyeing her suspiciously. Trish gave him her best puzzled alien expression, as Claire described it *"Who me? I'm just a visitor here."*

"I have a rival and we haven't left your driveway." He put the car in reverse, and turned to watch their exit. "Tsk. I understand your instant admiration. But." He treated Trish to another of his special golden light smiles. All right, Dish, she warned herself. Head over heels is not a good look for you. Easy does it, old girl.

They talked about what food to have for lunch. Caldwell had sushi yesterday, so they decided on Thai. Trish had promised herself an infusion in the hospital, and Caldwell agreed she should have it. "What do you like?" asked Trish as they sat reading the menu in the restaurant.

"Anything without coconut milk," answered Caldwell. "I'm not a milk fan, even if it's out of a shell." Trish smiled, made no comment. She hadn't had milk in her refrigerator for decades. Her friend Joel tried to call her lactose intolerant, and Trish insisted she was more lactose *un*tolerant, and they agreed to disagree. Joel drank soy milk. Soy schmoy. None of it was in Dish's fridge. Shell, plant or udder-wise.

They talked of the small things that make up a life. Trish discovered he didn't teach at the University of Michigan, he taught at Sienna Heights. "Oh, Catholic," said Trish. "Well, yes, the college is," and they moved on to other topics. "Married twice?" he asked, confirming, and Trish admitted that it used to be true. He was separated, his wife had lived and worked in another state for fifteen years. This logjam rested half-submerged as a subject for later.

They talked of rivers, and boats and adventures taken, adventures wished for; conveyances, companions and charts. Each portaged the rough spots, set the conversation back in the flow when ready, and soon both Dish and Spoon were glad to have run away.

Over tea, Trish asked about college once more, gently. "How did you get to Siena Heights?"

He pushed his cup to the edge of the table, leaned back and crossed his arms. "My area is ancient texts, which academically amounts to religious materials. It was the college with the most active research program that I could find, without leaving Michigan. You wouldn't be surprised to discover that this area of study is more popular these days. It isn't the reason I stay though. Marygrove College has a new PhD program in sacred music, there's a stirring of activity at all levels of academia."

"You don't sound pleased," Trish pushed.

"There are many reasons one chooses an advanced degree in a subject, beyond talent and personal affinity. Perhaps there were as many reasons people produced the texts that survive. There are certainly few reasons that any survive at all: the Church protected those it wanted protected. Any other survivors are accidental." He leaned forward and rested his elbows on the table. Trish was drawn into the triangle of his intensity. She leaned her elbows and her body forward too.

"You're familiar with the finding of an important religious tract in a bog in Ireland? A bulldozer driver had the wit to pick it up out of the mud, and give it to a person who understood it may have value. Under the gilt of the sacred art was discovered formulae that may have been written by Archimedes."

No, Trish shook her head. Caldwell continued, "It's known as the Archimedes Palimpsest. a tenth century manuscript. Imagine. It languished in a private collection for most of the twentieth century, and was sold at auction in 1998. The new owner, bless him, delivered the Palimpsest to The Walters Art Museum in Baltimore. It is a unique source for *The Method and Stomachion*, and a unique Greek text of *On Floating Bodies*.

"It survived in a monastery for most of the time between the tenth and twentieth centuries. If it had not been scraped and overwritten - perpendicular to Archimedes writing by the way - and gilded with religious icons, it would have been lost to history. We have the Church to thank for its preservation."

"Scraped?" Trish queried.

Caldwell nodded. "Scraped. It's animal skin, goat or sheep. That's how papyrus was first made. Monks and scribes would conserve a bound book by scraping the iron gall ink off the pages, and overwriting. Recycling, 10th century style."

"Fascinating," Trish commented.

"Really. It is to me and a handful of other scholars. So…" He stretched his arms over his head and groaned happily. "The guy who got to take the pictures of the pages was a PhD researcher studying spinach."

"Spinach."

"Yup. Spinach. His mom saw an article on the Palimpsest and sent a clipping to him in a letter. 'Thought you'd be interested in the enclosed; love, Mom.' And the rest, as they say, is history. History in the making while we sit here. Enough of this. We've got a 55 degree afternoon, no rain, light breeze. What does that suggest to you?"

Trish grinned a happy reply, sighed in anticipation of submerging in a beautiful day, grabbed her hat and slid out of the booth, headed for the door.

They wound their way to Gallup Park, each coaxing the use of a favorite shortcut. Each teased the other about distances and routes, and circuitously, the two arrived at the park by the canoe livery, scattering the geese gathering there. "Don't those birds ever go home? Even at Thanksgiving? It's called home-made pumpkin pie! Go get some!" Trish hollered, looking over her shoulder at the geese on the slope down to the river, as she untied the stern line. "We'll carry the boat down, okay?"

Caldwell, untying the front, laughed out loud. "You'll walk in goose poop, but you don't want the boat dragged through it. I like the way you think." He pulled the untied boat off over his head, flipped it on his thighs, and set it gently on the grass in the cleanest spot. They busied themselves with water and dry clothes in the dry bag, set paddles in the canoe. Caldwell stuffed a banana and two apples in the bag, cinched it closed, tethered it to the center thwart. "We're ready. You prefer bow or stern?"

"Bow, please." answered Trish, picking up her front end, looking back to wait for Caldwell to get his. "Ready? All right."

It was a beautiful boat for touring. Trish smiled at the water she could see through the Kevlar flowing behind and into the grip of Caldwell's paddle. "I'm not going to work up a sweat," he mentioned. "We'll just take it easy. Relax. Lay back if you like. Let me know when you're ready to turn around."

"We could get out at the gardens and kick the kinks out of our legs, if that's okay with you," Trish called over her shoulder.

"Fine, fine." Caldwell answered.

The sun stayed out of sight behind the mackerel sky. Oak leaves, giving up their grip that should have taken them to spring, floated zigzag into the river. Trish smiled at how many landed on their toes, rather than their backs. Tenacious. Survivors. Holding on right to the end. She saluted one with her paddle as they moved past. A woodchuck crossed the river just ahead, taking its time, used to canoes on the water. A big turtle that ordinarily would have been buried in mud, sunned itself on a log, long neck stretched to catch the dim rays.

Thank you, mother, Trish closed her eyes in appreciation. Thank you for this day.

"Sorry?" Caldwell spoke. "Did you say something?" Trish just shook her head. Just before the Arb she pulled her paddle up, stuck it behind her head, and leaned back first, then forward.

"We're almost there. We'll get out and stretch, get a drink soon."

He got out first when they eddied out river left, and held the boat with his paddle while she stretched her legs before she stood up and slowly stepped out. She'd been having trouble with egress lately. It took more time than she wanted, as though her blood was slow to get back down into the straightened legs, but she'd have to learn to adjust. Life was all about change these days.

A big chocolate Lab came galumphing up, barking, bashed into Caldwell to be petted so that he almost upended into the river. Both humans laughed. "Hey, big boy!" Caldwell patted the huge head, picked up a stick and threw it and the big Lab lumbered away in search of a new playmate. The unseen owner whistled and the dog picked up speed, recognizing the call.

Trish automatically reached for the gunwale to drag the boat onto the bank just as Caldwell's hand arrived under hers at the same time. Her blue eyes met his brown eyes. Both people smiled. "My lady," Caldwell bowed, and removed his hand, letting Trish pull the beauty out of harm's way.

Patricia Worthington took two lungs full of autumn air deep into her body, the smell of wet earth, damp tree trunks, and burning leaves sending healing endorphins rollicking into her bloodstream. She started to walk up the hill beside Caldwell's long stride. "I love the fall. Reminds me of college, all new and shiny. Excitement. If you could bottle the smell of excitement, this would be it."

"Did you go to school here?"

Trish shook her head. "No. Wayne State."

"Aha. You were political."

Trish laughed, "My friends would crack up to hear me called that. No, I was a good girl, quiet and studious. Big glasses, good grades, the works. I had friends here at school, and spent a lot of time in town. Then my brothers came here, and I lived in Dexter for a while. Feels very comfortable."

Caldwell braced himself on a steep section of hill, and reached down to grab Trish's hand. His grip hit her hand the wrong way, and she gasped, pulling her hand flat to her chest, wincing. "I'm so sorry!" Caldwell cried. He two-stepped down to look at the red bruise already forming on the back of her hand. "Gosh, I'm sorry, Trish."

"No need to feel badly. It's one of the side effects of the chemo. The structure is weak. I hurt myself on the dumbest things that wouldn't have made a mark five years ago. Adjustments." she mumbled lamely, tears forming in her eyes.

Caldwell moved closer to put an arm around her. This tenderness pushed the tears over the edge and a tiny waterfall splattered on her cheeks. She brushed them away with the injured hand.

"Does it hurt, Trish, or just look horrendous?"

Trish smiled into his face. "It doesn't hurt now. It's not my power hand," she joked. "I could still beat you in a sprint."

"One day soon we'll see. Just not today. Do you want to continue on, or just sit, share an apple?"

"Sitting sounds good. And why is that? You sit for hours in a canoe, and you get out and want to sit. Strange."

"Life is strange. There's nothing strange about paddling," he observed as he pulled out his knife, expertly cut the apple in half, and helped Trish sit against a maple tree that had been waiting quietly for them to show up and share its footing.

Chapter 5

"Welcome, Edgar. You're early this morning." Saima turned back to place the glass icicle she was holding on a bough. "We're decorating a tree. The kettle is warm in the back, if you'd like some tea, or you can join us here. Hang up your coat and lend a hand. The ornaments are in those boxes there. Help yourself."

Edgar returned to the duo after hanging up his coat, and bent over to begin pulling boxes out of a bigger box. "Shall I pay attention to the order I pull these out?" he asked over his shoulder.

"There was order in there once, but not now. Don't worry about it, Edgar, just enjoy." said Saima.

"Entropy," stated Edgar flatly, emerging with arms loaded with small gilt boxes.

"Sorry?" said Saima, turning to Antoine and raising an eyebrow.

"Oh, no, I'm sorry. Well, um it's the second law of thermodynamics. Entropy is a measure of disorder, and nature moves from order to disorder, therefore disorder is more probable than order in any isolated system." He tried to gesture toward the box he was emptying, nearly dumping his armful to the ground. "And, of course, there are Maxwell's Demons." He smiled at the two old people who stood, dangling ornaments from their still fingers, watching Edgar fumble his packages to the glass countertop. "Statistical mechanics and so on. Really fascinating subjects; I always thought when I was more settled I'd study those areas that most interested me." He stopped, smiled hesitantly at his cohorts in ornamenting who had quit decorating and were staring. "Did I say something?"

"You're a different speaker when you're passionate, Edgar," observed Antoine.

Edgar smiled broadly, almost wiggling, like a puppy pleased on his first day in obedience class, anticipating his treat. "There are what I call sidebar studies that I bumped into getting my IT certification. Algorithms, light refraction, closed systems, so on.

"Maxwell's Demon is a thought experiment described by JC Maxwell in which a microscopic demon guards a gate between two halves of a room. He keeps slow molecules in one half the room." Edgar walked past the tree, turned around with his arms spread. "The demon opens the gate to let fast molecules go into the other" he explained, as he walked with arms outstretched back to the counter, turning around.

"By eventually making one side of the room cooler than before and the other hotter, it appears to reduce the entropy of the room, and reverse the arrow of time. Many analyses have been made of this; revealing that when the entropy of room and demon are taken together, this total entropy does increase. Modern reviews take into account Shannon's relation between entropy and information. In my field which is modern computing, some resulting data are closely related to this problem — reversible computing, quantum computing and physical limits to computing, for example."

Edgar dropped his arms to his side with an audible impact, raised his eyebrows, grinned. "So what may appear to be the stuff of metaphysics is slowly being converted to the stuff of the physical sciences."

"Naturally this only works if you believe the initial state of our universe holds, so if we find out the Big Bang didn't blow, all bets are off," Edgar finished, placing his moon and stars dainty on the tree, and setting it to spinning with his finger.

"Edgar, you're a scholar," praised Antoine, "and a wit as well."

"Monsieur Lavoisiere, I don't know how much of a scholar I am, but that's why I came here today. I feel as though you have something to teach me, and I must know what that knowledge might be. There is a Buddhist saying that when the student is ready, the teacher will appear. I've given this some thought, and that is the only explanation - beyond the tendency to disorder of the universe - that I opened the wrong door the other day. The only explanation I can find." He cast his eyes down, folded his hands, as though in prayer. "I feel a sense of urgency, Monsieur. I sincerely hope your schedule permits some time for us to talk. I would be most appreciative."

Lavoisiere's eyes shown at the taller man. "Well, it has been said that a gifted teacher is made great by the eagerness of his pupils. I'd be delighted, Edgar. If you would please call me Antoine, I'd be even more grateful." Lavoisiere busied himself opening a red and green box, which contained more moons and stars. He began to hang them on the branches. Saima hummed "O Tannenbaum."

"Tell me, Edgar, if you will, how you came to America. When we talked last you said you had been born in Prague, a city I love very much." He gestured to Edgar as a conductor might, ready for the orchestra to play.

"My father always told the story that I was born in chaos. I was born January 19, 1969."

"My! What a legacy!" Antoine remarked sharply. "I remember that day. Jan Palach set himself on fire in Wenceslas Square in protest of the Soviet invasion. Such a day to be born." Lavoisiere shook his head sadly. "I'm sorry. The memories of that Prague Spring. Please continue."

Edgar shrugged, continued. "I don't have any memory of Prague as a child. We moved when I was four - something to do with my father's job situation - and lived in the country on a collective farm.

"As for Czechoslovakia herself, we know the turmoil from 1969 onward. When I was old enough to read, and understand, I read the writings of Karel Capek, and tried to grasp his understanding that philosophy itself is a place 'in between' much as Maxwell's Demon sits 'in between.'

"He believed we face a world in which values are losing their firm contours and decisions in life, their static divisions. To adapt, we must deal with the problem of how to rethink the relationships between chaos and order, continuity and discontinuity, unity and multiplicity, the relationship between concept and image.

"But I no longer speak Czech fluently," Edgar sighed. "Linguistics define a worldview. In order to change the way one thinks about himself, his place in society, and in the world, he would have to change the language he speaks. A map that shows linguistics in the world would correspond nicely with a map that overlays the music of the world, for music represents the Weltanschauung - what? the world view of its peoples."

"Find the countries with similar epic folktales, and you will find language shared. If the language is singular, as it is in Saima's homeland, the subject and characters of its heroic folk stories will be singular as well." Antoine agreed.

"Yes, just as you say, Monsieur Lavoisiere. I'm sorry, I drifted from our discussion," Edgar apologized. He walked the few steps to the box, chose another crystal treasure, and returned to the Christmas tree. "My mother never really adjusted to country life after we moved from Prague. She was sad as I remember her, little though that is. Seldom smiling, always distracted. She died in childbirth after my sister Halina was born. I can sometimes see her beautiful face, picking vegetables, hanging frozen laundry." Edgar glanced at the crystal angel in his hand, and impulsively kissed its forehead before placing it on a branch.

Antoine smiled gently at the young man, reached up to put his hand on his shoulder. "What was your mother's name, Edgar?"

"Irina," Edgar smiled down at Antoine and caught him as he stumbled. "Monsieur, are you all right?" Saima ran to get the stool from behind the counter. Antoine waved the stool away, "I'm fine. Just a little overwhelmed." He stood straight and grasped Edgar's shoulders with both strong hands. Edgar touched the big scarred hands, enthralled with Lavoisiere. "What is it, Antoine?" Edgar asked gently.

"I knew your parents in Prague, Edgar. I knew them both, may God forgive me."

Edgar grasped the older man as he slouched toward the floor. Saima moved to hold an arm, and the two guided Lavoisiere through the curtains to the firelit room where the chair received Antoine into its stiff arms.

Antoine hung his head, moved it slowly side to side once. He began to speak again, the syrup of time and memory slowing his tongue. "I wasn't born in Prague, even though Prague became the city where my heart was born. My family came from Paris, although my father was Bohemian, my mother was French, and Paris was our home when I was a young boy.

"My father was a letterform foundryman, and worked for the Deberney et Peignot typefoundry on Rue de Marais-Saint-Germain in Paris, a position he had secured as my mother was distantly related to Louise Antoinette Laure De Berny, and after a trial period, he was secure in his chosen profession, and had been employed there for the entirety of his working life.

"As I mentioned before, I had four older brothers, all of whom had been apprenticed by the age of 12, as was common in the late 1800s, early 1900s. I was late, and at 14, my father presented me to the head man at his place of business for training in letterform making, a position he had not asked for my elder siblings, but because I was old (almost too old) he was more assured of a positive response to his request for an apprenticeship at the place he had worked for 18 years.

"I was a shy boy, timid of strangers and given to slow responses when questioned by people I did not know, and I did not fare well for the first months of my apprenticeship. Grievously prone to nervous starts when addressed, I either dropped what I was working on, or drove a tool into my hand as my nerves took hold of my arms.

"My father was beside himself, afraid he would lose his job over my ineptitude, and my mother, wanting peace as well as prosperity, took me aside and addressed me as the man I was yet to become, asking for my assistance in securing the continuation of a prosperous future for my father, and a sublime and harmonious home life for all of us. She advised me to work harder at controlling my nerves than my tools, and the instruments would eventually work for me, as long as my demeanor achieved calm first.

"I did as she asked, and struggled to gain control of my nerves. Within another six months, I was so in love with my work, because of its utility in the world, and its contribution to literature and learning, but more so because it had given me the composure and attention to detail that would see me through to adulthood, and contribute to my quiet understanding of personal balance, that after the first year of my apprenticeship I was promoted within the company ahead of boys much older than I.

"My brothers did well in their professions, one a set builder in the booming Paris theater district, another a sous chef, one grocer, and another a haberdasher; the hatmaker and the grocer having been sponsored into the business by the men who would become their fathers-in-law. One by one, they married and moved into their own households."

Antoine set his head against the chair back, closed his eyes and sighed. The firelight danced on the veins of his eyelids, the delicate skin moving as his eyes wandered in the early century. His thin lips, drawn tighter by time, began to tremble before words emerged.

"We were just three at home, when my mother suddenly sickened and too quickly, was gone. My father, who I do not believe ever cared for Paris wrote to his family in Bohemia, received word of a position in a printmaking establishment there, and as I was still not of age, he and I packed up and shipped our belongings to Prague, and a few weeks later, followed our household goods to our new home.

"Art Noveau architecture, cubism alongside the old Renaissance and Italianate architecture from centuries gone coexisted below Vysehrad Park where we took up residence. We had only been relocated for a few months when the Emperor and the Empress Sofia were assassinated in Sarajevo in 1914 and the world was plunged into war.

"My father had always been a man who spoke few words, fewer still after my mother's death; after the war he barely spoke at all. In 1918, when the new democratic republic of Czechoslovakia was formed, he went with me to Vysehrad Park and waved the flag of his new country and listened, smiling, to the speeches by Tomas Masaryk and the other hopeful.

"But he, like his infant country, soon would remember old grievances and discords, and slowly my father faded, and at last, one day at work as always with his gravur and files, he slumped over his work table and passed away into a realm perhaps more suited to his being.

"Prague was a volatile place to be in those years. People moved to the city from the countryside, as the German speakers moved to Vienna and elsewhere. The country itched to establish its national identity, with a long and treasured history as backdrop.

"The census of 1922 had done little to help foment national pride, asking for 'language spoken in everyday intercourse' rather than nationality, and a schizophrenic straw man of a Czechoslovakian appeared, distorted by language spoken, land inherited and religion practiced, and identified inaccurately by flawed questions and intentionally or accidentally divisive questioners. Yiddish was defined as German language, and Jewish was identified as a nationality as well as a religion.

"But men including Franz Kafka wrote to his love and asked her to please write to him in Czech, rather than German, and national pride began slowly to rise."

Antoine once again found himself opening his eyes to anxious faces, murmuring kind words in soft susurrations. His vision was faint, his grasp of the world tenuous, and paying homage to his own long-winded spouting of the possibility of fractal time and space, he saw his mother's face, backlit by the fire in the hearth, rubbing his head, asking if he was feeling better now?

He was six or seven. He had taken the worst of a scuffle with one or more of his older brothers and hit his head on the corner of the table, upsetting the bowl of peas. Before he opened his eyes, he smelled the soap in his mother's apron and felt its stiff cloth against his cheek. Her hand was soft on his head and cheek, and the sound of her fingertips gently stroking his hair was woody and scratchy, but the feel of her comfort warmed his heart. He smiled, pushing his nose into her apron, feeling her stomach beneath, and he put both arms around her, and was completely cured when he heard her laugh out loud.

The woman rubbing his head when his eyes and mind returned to the present, made the same sound on his grayed head, but she smelled of pine and lavender. Antoine smiled at Saima, just the same.

Edgar got up from his knees, asked a quick question, and left the room by the back door returning in another mini-vortex of swirling leaves with an armload of small firewood, which he put carefully in the firebox, removed the screen from the hearth, and dropped two pieces into the coals there. The logs were covered in snow fritters, patchy blobs with ice rime edges, kept alive in the unusual Thanksgiving warmth by the shade of the building. The frost-crusted wood hissed at the room's occupants. as the fire bit the ice, and heads turned momentarily to the sound.

"Thank you all. Too kind." Antoine assured the careful attendees that he was recovered, and rubbed his own head until it tingled. "I seem to be making a habit of dropping out of your good company." He chuckled at his weak joke, then sobered and shook his head.

"Edgar, it is apparent to me once more that whom God wants to punish, He first makes remember." He touched his forehead with his first finger and his thumb, the gesture of someone plucking a memory from a brain that was reluctant to give it up. Antoine licked his lips and bit the lower, the words dammed behind his teeth, until with a whoosh of a sigh, he turned to smile at Edgar.

"I told you I knew your father and mother in Prague. Your father, Edgar, if I'm not mistaken was Janus Pavelka?" After receiving an astonished nod of assent, Antoine continued. "Your father was my apprentice in the shop at the foot of Vyreshad Park. I first met him when he was the same age I was apprenticed to the printer in Paris. Fourteen. He was tall and long-limbed like you, and shy the way I had been at that age. I remember the day he came into the shop as though it were this day."

The bell over the door tinkled on that long ago winter day.

Antoine listened for a moment to hear the bell's tiny peal again, indicating a person who had come in, found the wrong shop, and exited back to the street. But there were tentative footsteps on the wooden floor, and Antoine set his file down, checked his apron for metal flotsam, wiped his hands, and went through the curtain to the counter. He startled a young man into dropping his hat. As the boy bent to retrieve the hat, the snow that had doused his shoulders fell to the floor, melting into sparkles of water as quickly as they landed.

The boy stood again, looking at Antoine with determination, his lips clamped in a tight line, his eyes resolute. "I've come to ask about apprenticing." he said emphatically and then ran completely out of steam, so quickly it seemed to dissipate directly from his body into the air, like a deflating balloon.

Antoine watched him for a moment, evaluating his determination in spite of his obvious fear. He was tall, perhaps 16, which meant he might not be done growing. His back was straight, arms muscled as though used to upper body work. His hands were large, the fingers long and supple. The beautiful hands worked at dismantling the structure of his hat, turning it and combing its edge until Antoine guessed the wool would be shining and thin soon. The boy's feet were enormous. Antoine wondered where he would find boots to replace the worn ones he had on; there was no way his feet were dry after the deep snow outside. His green eyes were clear and looked straight at Antoine. His hair was the nondescript brown of his people, but his skin had the lucky coloration of his Czech heritage: a golden, creamy, ruddy-cheeked translucence that Antoine had missed from his Czech father, instead inheriting the pale alabaster of his French mother. "I see," said Antoine. "And who is your sponsor?"

Hesitation winked in his eyes, but his mouth won the battle against retreat. "I am sponsoring myself, as there's no one else to do it for me. I have no family. I can take care of myself. Have done so." He nodded abruptly as in punctuation.

"What work do you want?" Antoine questioned. "What skills do you have?"

"I want to make letters, like in books," the subject matter gave the boy strength. "I'm a fair drawer, but I need training and cannot go farther in school. I have to have a trade. Drawing isn't a trade, but letter-making is. I've made my decision, and offer myself for apprenticing."

Antoine melted the smile forming on his face, respecting the youth's solemnity, and asked the boy, "why this place?"

"Because I heard it is the best work to be done that comes from this shop. And I want to learn the best."

"Where is your father and mother? Where are you from?"

"My mother and father have gone on. I'm from here." He turned his upper body slightly and gestured outside to the street. "From Prague."

"Where do you live?"

"I live in the orphan house. Have done since I was eleven. I am fourteen now, and I need to find my own way. They will apprentice me or bond me to another place, and I..." here the boy hung his head, shuffled his big feet, realized he was knocking dirty snow on the floor by doing so, stopped and finished his sentence in a rush..."I left out the window today to come here to ask for apprenticing. This is the work I want to do, and I will have no other, even if I have to leave the city to find it. I will go away but I would, I would like, I came to ask here first."

"What is your name?"

"Janus. Jan Pavelka."

"How old are you?"

"Fourteen. Sir."

"What business was your father in, Janus Pavelka?"

"He was a woodcut maker, sir. The finest." Pride straightened young Pavelka's back even more. "He would have given me a trade, he would. Had he lived."

"What happened to your father?"

"He was killed in the war. My mother disappeared not long after he was killed." The young man who had escaped the orphanage to make his case to Antoine Lavoisiere struggled to maintain his grown-up demeanor. "The orphanage took me, and here I am today, asking for work and a trade, sir. I am asking, sir."

Arrangements were made. Antoine took Pavelka back to the orphanage, signed papers for the apprenticeship and custody of the young man, collected his meager belongings, which did not, unfortunately, include a better pair of boots or a spare hat, and Janus

Pavelka, fourteen-year-old fair drawer, came into the care and tutelage of Monsieur Antoine Lavoisiere.

As quickly as Antoine could teach Jan a chapter of the art of bookmaking, Pavelka could repeat the task with a skill and speed that Antoine himself would find difficult to duplicate. He started working the chemicals, the hot metal, and somewhat to Antoine's chagrin, did no harm to his long fingers and beautiful hands. He learned to mix the tin, antimony and copper with a precision and accuracy that astounded. He did not complain about any work given: he cleaned the hearth, shoveled the sidewalk, dumped garbage with as much speed and attention to detail as he devoted to practicing drawing the minimal woodcut work Antoine sprinkled his way in the beginning. He was eager, apt and a delight to watch at his work.

Perhaps some people are born to work who actually find the particular job that pleases them more than anything else would, Antoine thought. Many of us find our trade through assignment or necessity. Few are fortunate enough to find a craft that will not only keep food on their table and a roof over their heads, but a craft they will love as long as they have the wit and sinew to continue doing it.

Jan Pavelka was a lucky man. He loved his gift and a beneficent deity had brought him into Antoine's shop to be given the one trade he was born to perform with joy.

Within two years, Pavelka was handling the smaller runs himself. He took care of the invitations, the announcements, the one-offs that were single woodcuts for direct retail sale or for the street hawkers in larger volume.

When he wasn't making letterforms, or woodcuts or cleaning the shop and its tools, he studied his craft. He combed the library for references to typefaces and forms and he would regale Antoine at the work table with stories like the tale of Augustine of Canterbury and his delivery of uncial script to England.

He spent a day telling Antoine about Tironian Notes, shorthand developed by Cicero's scribe Marcus Tullius Tiro, who invented 4000 signs. "Monsieur Lavoisiere," Jan set down his file, set shining eyes on Antoine, "there are two Tironian Notes still used today. The ampersand, loosely translated as "et," and another I can't recall but is still used in Ireland. Imagine! The use of Notes was first reported by Plutarch in 63 BC. 63 BC!" and exhausted finally, he shook his head in wonder, sighed and bent back to his file work, the tool flashing in the firelight.

In his spare time, sometimes well into the night, so late that Antoine would have to come downstairs and insist he get some sleep, Jan designed typefaces.

He regaled his mentor with the history of Czechoslovakian printing, which Antoine listened to quietly, although it contained stories he knew, and some he had lived.

"The Bible was first translated into Czech in the 1370s, Monsieur," Jan revealed one morning, as though he had uncovered this truth himself. "Of 44 known books printed in Bohemia before 1500, 39 were in Czech. In the next hundred years 4,400 titles followed. The earliest Prague publishing house employed eleven people in 1577. In its 30th year, it published 223 books; 111 of them were in Czech, only 75 in Latin, and only three in German. Only three!" Jan set himself back on his work stool, having placed a steaming cup of hot tea he'd prepared in front of Lavoisiere.

"Did you know, Monsieur," Jan continued, "did you know the first modern newspaper in Czech started publication in Prague in 1789? And its editor Vaclav Matej Kramerius opened the first modern Czech publishing house the next year?" Jan set his newly retrieved tool down again, his eyes shining with pride in his heritage.

By the time Jan Pavelka was 21, he was in every way a journeyman artisan. Antoine spent more of his time in meetings with colleagues, and accepted a part-time teaching position at the university, while Jan handled all the work and business of the shop. Lavoisiere had even stopped checking the accounting books at the end of each month: within two years Jan had taken on this duty as well, there had been no errors. Jan was not only a craftsman, he was well-liked in their little community and a credit to his master craftsman, and as Antoine privately considered himself, his surrogate father.

Both men were enjoying a cup of tea and a chat about the job log for the coming month one fine April day, when the bell over the shop door tinkled.

Robinson

"I'll go," said Jan, setting his cup down, pulling his apron over his head, and reshuffling his already shuffled hair, stretching his arms over his head which had finally reached its 6'5" view of the world when Jan was nineteen. "You sit." He put his hand on Antoine's back affectionately, and walked through the curtains to the counter in front.

Antoine could hear low voices, but could not discern who might be in the store. If it were a customer, Jan would have been talking in his business voice, steady and easily heard. Lavoisiere set his cup on the workbench, pulled his own apron over his head, parted the curtains and entered the store.

Jan turned to look at Antoine, but didn't move, so the person on the other side of the counter was obscured by his big frame. Lavoisiere moved slightly to the side, and sighting the woman who stood there, stopped in his tracks.

Lavoisiere could never remember if apple blossoms were really drifting to the ground behind the glass panes onto the sidewalk, but in his mind, she was framed by pink petals and a soft azure watercolor cloudless sky.

She was petite, her hands so delicate and pale, Antoine wanted to bring them to his face to feel if such porcelain fingers could really have warmth. Her face was gamin, a heart-shaped study in alabaster that was home to oval eyes the color of finest Dutch chocolate, framed by a charcoal mist of eyelashes. Her mouth was a roller coaster of rosy dips and bows, over a chin rounded enough for character to balance the piquant point of its adventurous apex. She smiled shyly and two dimples appeared of such exquisite secret depth, that Antoine thought Jan was probably as stricken with regard and tenderness as he felt himself.

One glance at Jan's face proved true. The boy was blushing from the top of his head into his gargantuan boots.

"Monsieur," Jan coughed and began again. "Monsieur Lavoisiere, please allow me to introduce Miss Irina Slobovoda. She has come about a position."

"How do you do, Monsieur Lavoisiere," the vision curtsied. "What Mister Pavelka said is true. I am looking to find a suitable position, just as soon as may be. I have brought references," she reached in her bag to hold out two envelopes. "I have been trained as a clerk assistant and have a diploma from the women's business school at Karlovy Vary. In one of the envelopes you will find a letter of introduction from my uncle at University, who is my guardian as well as my benefactor in terms of my education and training."

Lavoisiere reached slowly to relieve Miss Slobovoda of the envelopes. "And who would your uncle be, Miss?"

"Professor Franz Slobovoda."

"Ah, yes, I know the good Professor."

"Yes, he sends his compliments and hoped you would recall his acquaintance." Here she blushed a delicious shade of peach, lowered her lashes and added, "He would appreciate any consideration and courtesy he is confident you will extend, and is grateful for any opportunity you may devise to challenge me further."

"Please do return my compliments to Professor Slobovoda, and I will be glad to consider his niece for a position." Antoine smiled widely at the young woman, and cuffed Jan on the shoulder, realigning his eyes back in his head. Jan smiled sheepishly and scuffed his giant shoes a small dance on the wood floor, stuffed his hands in his pockets and looked entirely an enormous colt caught outside the fence on a fine spring day.

And the following week, after conversations with Jan and Professor Slobovoda, Miss Irina Slobovoda came to work for Lavoisiere. As she would be dividing her time between various small jobs of the print shop, and clerical duties attached to Lavoisiere's position at the university, in addition to her annual salary, she received a stipend for travel between the two concerns, as a young woman unescorted should most certainly travel by covered coach. Jan had howled at the notion of this back and forth, and Lavoisiere put it down to a case of overprotectiveness. Irina was hardly a shrinking violet, and even so, Lavoisiere himself was very often headed in one direction or the other, and could escort his clerk to and fro.

She was a conscientious worker and well-trained in the secretarial duties she engaged. Above that, she was charming and convivial, and Lavoisiere found his office at university the center of some attention, while Ms. Slobovoda was wooed, curried favor with, and taken into the confidence of, a salmagundi of staff and students.

As Lavoisiere's appreciation of her skill and charm grew like the heady, fragrant blooms that beautiful spring, so did Jan Pavelka's admiration grow. His early coltishness changed to a clumsy horse when she was in his presence. Antoine watched with alarm one late spring morning, when Jan, relaying a tale of a too well-fed customer and his almost permanent fixture in the doorframe of the front door, waddled around the work room with such a gait, holding his arms out like a circle of big pants, pretending to be wrestling his girth out the door, sidled too close to the workbench and almost overturned the table and its load.

Lavoisiere contrived to have Irina spend more time at the university, and less at the shop, only to discover that Jan had found his inner stallion and had asked her out to the theater. As the autumn bade farewell to the leaves and late blossoms, it was obvious Jan was in love.

But Irina was more quiet, less scintillating in conversation, the outer office of Lavoisiere's quarters not as crowded as it had been in early spring.

As the winds of winter swept through the cracks in the work room at the print shop, and caused Lavoisiere to stuff paper in the window seals in his office at the university, Irina was pale and agitated.

Concerned for her health and well-being, Lavoisiere asked her in to share tea one dark, snowy afternoon in December. The city was readying for Christmas, lights shining haloed in the frosted windowpanes. Irina sipped her tea, sighed, smiled at the lace on the window. "It looks like its own fairy kingdom under glass, doesn't it? I love winter. At no other season is there the majesty and strength of the weather, together with the delicacy and fragility." She stopped as though she was a wound-down ballerina, dancing confined in a music box. She looked up at Antoine, the liquid in her brown eyes reflecting the light from the desk lamp.

"Jan has asked me to marry him," she said simply.

Antoine's heart leapt once and was still. "And what did you answer him?" he whispered, needing to know, desperate not to hear.

"I told him I would need a little time to think," Irina said quietly and the tears that had been hovering on her eyelashes, dashed out onto her cheeks, coursing down her chin.

"Irina, Irina," Antoine cried, coming around his desk with his handkerchief out, wiping gently at the water on her face, taking her teacup from her, setting it on the desk. "It is a good match, is it not? You care for him, don't you? Jan has a future you can be a part of, and he loves you, I'm sure."

Irina took the handkerchief from Antoine and continued transferring her tears into its cloth. She sat quietly for a moment, her hands turning the handkerchief, lower lip quivering so that Antoine's own heart took up the motion. Without knowing what to do with his hands, he folded one over the other at the front like a preacher. Irina took a deep breath, stood and wrapped Antoine's eyes with her own chocolate orbs.

"It is a fine offer, yes," she said, quietly, her eyes fixed forever in Antoine's. "I had hoped for another."

The quiver that was Antoine's heart moved into his head and he started to shake it no, no; left right, left right, until he was sure he could not stop the motion and his body would fly off in pieces, in different directions, forcibly surrendering his soul to the winter wind's whim.

Irina moved toward him and cupped his face in her hands.

"No," whispered Antoine. "No, it cannot be. No, this will not be. No. No," until God save him, Irina touched her rose lips to his rigid white ones, and Antoine was lost, lost, his tranquility terminated, his dream deserting him to follow his soul into the wind.

Chapter 6

Tradition for the girlfriends' portion of the Thanksgiving holiday weekend meant Margo, Claire and Dish met for breakfast at The Broken Egg early Friday morning. The meal was followed by judiciously and self-righteously not shopping. No shopping allowed. The breakfast tradition gave each of them an opportunity to share stories of The Feast Day itself, and also any family plans that looked juicy, hair-raising or law-breaking, and that might bite into their own weekend plans, goddesses forbid. When Claire's children were young, and she and Vik took Jaqueline and Nikolas to Detroit for the Santa Claus parade, Claire used to call this Friday morning friends' breakfast Parade Rest.

For the rest of the year, there would be little time for the friends to get together at leisure, except for phone calls and email. Nostalgia was served with the toast and eggs on Thanksgiving Friday morning.

Margo was the first to arrive, as usual. She had her coffee already in front of her when Trish came in tandem with Dr. Amy. While Amy was hanging up her coat, Margo gestured *what's the deal?* and Trish slid into the booth, whispered, "she called me." Claire slid in next to Margo who hugged her around the shoulder, set her menu on the table in front, helped Claire bounce her arms out of her coat.

"Well, now that we're all here, you want to start with grandchildren pictures or didn't any of you lightweights pick up the new ones?"

Groans and hoots, as Margo passed around a couple of new shots of the bouncing baby grandboy. "What's the baby's name again, Margo?" Trish asked, studying the pink cherubic cheeks in the picture.

"Ezekiel. No idea why. His father is already calling him Eazy. I predict his real name only shows up again at his wedding to shock his new bride."

Claire showed a small new family shot, which included her and the Amazing Teknicolor Viktori as well. "Oh, Claire, that's nice! Vik has clothes on even."

"Isn't it though?" said Claire. "It was my granddaughter Annie's idea, and Jaqueline picked up the studio tab as my holiday gift. I get an

8x10 framed for the family room, and Vik didn't object to putting it on the wall."

"How is the fair Anastasia?"

"Wonderful as ever, thank you for asking. Her parents are looking for buyers, if you're interested. They've had as much teenager as they can tolerate already. I told them to wait until she's 17, that they'll get her back at that age, but if she hasn't returned to her senses, I'll buy her then."

"Trish, how about your family? Everyone misbehave?"

"Happily, yes," Trish sighed. "I'm glad I was feeling up to going. It's great to see all the family together. Twice a year. And then I'm just as happy to hug everyone good-bye until Memorial Day weekend."

"Amy?" Claire prompted.

"We had a quiet dinner, just the three of us, and it was pleasant, thanks for asking," Dr. Amy said formally and without further comment.

"Come on, Amy," Claire poked more. "That's it? How's your husband taking the news of the show's ratings?"

"What he said was 'I told you that was a dumb idea when you first came up with it.'" Amy replied primly. "I don't recall anything more."

Claire laughed, shook her head. "Amy, Amy. You didn't throw anything breakable, did you?"

The other two women looked wide-eyed at Claire, and as though pinioned in the center like bicycle handles, both turned to look wide-eyed at Dr. Amy, who was glaring at Claire. "I did not break a thing."

Claire guffawed, shook her finger at Amy and explained to the rest, "Amy has a temper. A famous one."

"I do not." Amy flatly denied. "My temper is not famous."

"Okay, not famous. Maybe notorious." Claire slapped the table in glee.

Dish quietly asked Margo, "Did Frasier show up?"

Margo smiled at Trish. "He did indeed. He was charming, Caroline and Morgan were happy, and then he didn't come home last night. I don't know where he went."

"What are you going to do, Margo?" Trish asked.

Margo shrugged. "I'm not going to do anything. I'm going to work next week, and if Lynn hasn't made a decision about my replacement by the third week, I'm thinking of forcing the issue and taking the rest of the year as vacation. I'll stay if she condescends to hire someone, but not if she doesn't." Margo bent her elbows, turned her palms face up at her ears. "After that, I'm free as a bird."

"Tall, skinny bird."

"Old bird. Stringy."

"Ar ar ar. Let's eat, huh?" Margo lassoed all the wits back on breakfast task.

They took turns delivering their orders to the waitress, extended their coffee cups for refills, and talked with light hearts of the celebrations yesterday and the plans for the holidays coming up.

The meals arrived as did conversations about the coming work weeks, the changes in Margo's life, and the possibilities for Trish. Claire had found a modicum of peace regarding the new girls at the gallery. Salinger had the holidays covered right through to the spring shows, and Claire, finding no fault with her itinerary and selections, had decided to relax and enjoy.

"Maybe I'll take the sculpture class I've been eyeing. Or tile making. I've sort of made up my mind that being mad about getting old is a damn waste of time. Not that I haven't heard this from Vik for a handful of months. Including in my ear at night. I remember telling my mother 'Mom, all my doctors are younger than me!' and my mother saying 'get used to it.'"

"Everyone goes through it. Some more gracefully than others."

"I remember standing in the building, talking to Marilyn," Trish began, "from the plastic surgeon's office down the hall? It was after business hours, we had bumped into one another in the hall and were catching up before going home. The elevator door opened and a small, tidy women came trotting up to Marilyn. 'Oh, hello, dear, I'll just go on in, then?'

"Marilyn said, 'Where is it you're going?'

'Why, to see, Dr. T.'

'Ma'am, Dr. T. is gone for the day. The office is closed. If you call in the morning, I'd be glad to make you an appointment.'

'But I need a little refreshing,' the woman refused to understand.

'That's fine. If you'll call in the morning, we'll make an appointment.'

'But I *need* it. A little *refreshing*,' the woman had her hand on Marilyn's arm.

'Ma'am,' Marilyn said, gently removing the woman's hand that was now pawing her arm like a cat after a nip. 'Call in the morning.'"

"Wow."

Trish nodded. "I'll never forget the look on that woman's face. She was so tight you could bounce a quarter off her upper lip already." Laughter floated around the table, until Dr. Amy stuck a pin in that balloon abruptly, "That's what I wanted to talk about."

Six eyes waited to hear.

"About aging." Dr. Amy said.

"You've found a way not to do it?" Claire asked.

"No, Claire, I haven't. And I'll get *refreshed* if I damn well please when the time comes. But meanwhile, Trish mentioned an idea the other night that I've been giving a lot of thought to, since I'm done thinking about the show I've got now."

"Not the naked aging unshaved hippie cooking show? Not that one."

"Not exactly, no."

"What is it then, Amy?" Margo frowned at the rest of them, taking lead on the courtesy wagon train, too.

"Trish told the story about the image task force, the amazing vanishing image task force…"

"Now you see it, now you don't," Trish quipped.

"Right," continued Amy. "She talked about some other ways to handle the cooking show, but that's if it remains a cooking show, which I'm not sure it should."

Dr. Amy gathered her thoughts and her breath and launched into her proposal. "An adventure show. With women of a certain age. Are you familiar with Title Nine?"

"Title IX basically stated that no person in the United States can be denied participation based on gender in any educational program that receives Federal assistance. 1972, I think. All the whiners had fits about collegiate athletics, but it applies to math, science club as well. Is that it?" Trish asked, excited.

"Yes, that one. But I'm talking about Title Nine - n-i-n-e - the women's clothing outfitter. Athletic and casual clothing. Google it. See what I'm talking about, but the point is that the women who model the clothes are real women. Athletes, successful business women who run, professors who jog, scientists who wear brassieres, engineers who race ice boats on hard water."

"I've seen that website!" said Trish. "I have one. Title Nine has one of the few no bounce, nonsquishing Double D running bras on the market."

"Trish, I don't think the cook heard you in the kitchen," Claire snorted.

"Double D," Margo pouted. "Sheesh."

Trish passed her a dirty look on the way to Amy. "What's your idea, Amy?"

"Well," she leaned in, hands flat on the table, and the other women leaned closer to hear the idea. "We have a show, a series - don't know the name - we'll leave that to the naming gurus. In each episode, or maybe over a couple of episodes, one of these women who model in the catalog take several other women; older, maybe only mildly familiar with the sport, on an adventure. So, an iceboat champion would take two or three women out for an afternoon on the ice. Or for an overnight trip."

"Iceboating?

"Hard water sailing. On steel runners. Pay attention, Margo."

"A whitewater rafting guide might guide a couple rafts of 50/60 year old women down the – what?" Dr. Amy shrugged, hands up.

"Salmon."

"Snake."

"Youghioheny."

"Overnight. Two episodes. Something happens. Cliffhanger first night."

"Wow."

"Wow."

"Yes, wow."

"Iceboating?"

"Oh for crying out loud, Margo! It started right here in Detroit. All iceboats are DN racers. DN for Detroit News. It's an international sport. The international championship was in Michigan a couple years ago. They have to go where the ice is. All over the world." Trish looked up when she was finished and all eyes were on her.

"I met a terrific woman who does this. She's an engineer, too. She's been written about as 'the fastest woman on the ice.'"

"Where'd you meet her?"

"At writers' group."

"Writers' group! Since when do you have a writers' group?"

"Since you numbskulls drove me to one a few weeks ago." Trish made a Popeye face back at Margo, who was eyeing Trish as an interesting, but hideous life form.

"You went back?" Claire asked, surprised. "I thought it was too far."

"Appears not," Trish said. "Look, I'm sorry I didn't announce I was going, but I wanted to test my own wings on this. It's new for me to try something new, and I wanted to fail on my own, if I was going to fail.

You're all so good about propping me up, I was trying to practice my own propping. Geez. I didn't mean to hurt anyone or keep secrets."

"Fair enough," Claire said. "Margo will get over being disappointed in just a second. One thousand one, one thousand two… you done, Margo?"

Margo smiled, licked her lips and winked at Trish. "Only if you are, Claire."

"Could we get back to me, please?" Dr. Amy insisted, her manicured hands resting on her chest.

Trish guffawed. "My sister yells 'One, two, three, all eyes on me.' She's such a trollop." and Trish laughed some more.

Claire laughed along. "How is the remarkable redhead?"

"She's dandy. Just dandy. She was at dinner yesterday."

"Ahem," Amy now folded her arms and tapped her foot on the floor for attention.

Margo waved her arms, hands flopping. "Go for it, Amy. It's a show I'd watch. We probably all agree on that, don't we?"

"Yes, definitely, I'd watch."

"Yeah, sure."

Dr. Amy closed her eyes, sighed, raised one eyebrow. "I can get focus groups about who's going to watch, for crying out loud. I don't need you to *watch*. There are thousands, maybe millions who will watch. What I want to know is if you'll be part of the first show. Be *on* the show."

The noise of clattering china, short orders being hollered and repeated, silverware striking plates, conversations rising and falling filled the silent space at the table.

"I need to make a presentation, a knockdown, take them out at the knees presentation, and I need real people to be a part of it. You're the women. Pick the sport."

Margo was making herself a tuna sandwich for a late dinner in the kitchen Saturday when she heard the garage door open. She felt a little nerve thrill, but she was calm overall. These mini-scenes had happened too many times in the last 25 years to be overly excited.

Frasier gently closed the back door. His demeanor, draped in the kitchen doorway, was quiet resignation, just enough of the wasabi touch of arrogance to ignite Margo's anger, but she stuffed it down. "I'm making a sandwich. Would you like one?" she asked. "No fat mayonnaise."

"I'd like to talk," Frasier said.

"Fine, I'll meet you in the dining room in a second."

Frasier turned slowly, moved mechanically like an automaton sent to take his part in this drama. Margo rolled her eyes, calmed herself again, wrapped her sandwich for later, and carried her tea into the dining room.

"What are we doing here, Margo?" Frasier asked.

"Explain," Margo said.

"How do you see us in the future?"

"Frasier, what is it you want to hear?"

"Margo, it's a simple question: where do you see us heading?"

Margo sighed, gathered her thoughts and her teabag, set one in the saucer, and the other muddle out on the conversation table. "I'm not going to get into this from the back door, Frasier. You've been gone from this house for a week. I'm glad you came for Thanksgiving dinner, but other than that, I don't know your whereabouts. I think the question is for you to answer and the question is this: do you still want to be married to me?" Margo was a little surprised at how difficult it was to ask that question.

"I don't think that's the issue here," Frasier said.

"And what is the issue as you understand it?"

"I'm just not happy."

"Oh for crying out loud, Frasier. Who is?"

Frasier stood up. "I'm not interested in anyone else. And it's clear from your answers that you're not interested in anyone but yourself."

Margo sighed. She looked at her husband, felt the frost forming in the room between them.

"What are your plans, Frasier?"

171

"I'm not sure. You don't seem willing to discuss the future."

"All right. Fine." Margo stood up, faced the cold stranger across the table. "You emptied the joint account, Frasier. I assume that means you are through with this marriage. I can't imagine what else it could mean, unless you're willing to explain? No? Fine. When you leave this house today, please take everything of yours. Unless I hear from you otherwise, I'll assume you're filing for divorce."

Frasier lifted his hands limply, shrugged his shoulders. "It didn't have to be this way, you know."

"Didn't it?" Rage flared briefly, choked itself to death. "I wonder," Margo said quietly, and carrying her teacup, walked away.

It was less than an hour later when Frasier stopped outside Margo's home office, set his bag down, said, "I'm off then." Margo watched him pull on his coat, wondering when this man that stood before her had changed from the man she married. Maybe he hadn't changed. Maybe she had.

She stood, walked around the desk, and straight to Frasier and put her arms around him. "Take care of you," she said over his shoulder. She wouldn't cry right now. Not right now. Maybe later.

He didn't hug her back. "You, too, Margo. I'll be in touch." With that, he picked up his bag and was gone. Just like that. Margo felt a chill, rubbed her arms, walked back to her desk. She stared at the picture of the two of them. Happier times? Perhaps. Margo felt the burn at the top of her nose, scrubbed it back and forth hard a couple times, sniffed and picked up the pen she'd dropped to say good-bye to Frasier.

She dropped it again quickly as she dashed to the powder room to throw up.

Trish picked up the phone at the sound of Margo's hello.

"Hey, Margo."

"Trish, are you busy tonight? I don't mean to bother you but would you be able to come over?"

"I've got my pajamas on, Margo. And a cup of tea."

"Have you got a travel mug?"

"Oh. Like that? Okay. Give me a half hour. I'll be over."

32 minutes later, Margo's front doorbell rang.

"Ah, Trish, thanks for coming." Margo hugged the taller woman and then helped her take her coat off. Margo laughed. "You left your pajamas on?"

"What, you're expecting somebody else? I was comfortable. Now I'm still comfortable." She held up her travel mug. "And I brought my tea."

Margo laughed again. "Come on in. I just had the kettle on myself."

"You should open the blinds, Margo. It's snowing beautifully out there. Soft fluffy stuff." Trish accomplished the blind opening herself. "Ah. Nice. I'm glad I can enjoy it now. I didn't used to, because I was scared to drive in it. But I sure do like to look at it. Imagine living somewhere that you don't get to see this."

Margo came to stand next to Trish. "We're lucky, aren't we?"

"Sure are. So, what's going on? Where's Mr. Happy?"

"He left."

"For tonight?" Trish stared at Margo who didn't answer.

"For good," Trish guessed.

"Yes, I think so."

"Oh, Margo, I'm sorry." Trish sat hard on the couch.

"It's not as though it's a total surprise." Margo said, joining Trish on the couch.

"I know. But it still must be hard."

"I don't know what I'm going to tell the girls." said Margo.

"They may know more about this than you may think, Margo. They're not girls. Caroline and Morgan are grown women," Trish observed.

"Why? What do you know?"

"Nothing," Trish said quickly. "But I find that children usually know more than their parents think they do. And parents more than their children. It's one of those immutable laws. This is wisdom from a person with only two parents and no children. Caroline is married and a mother herself now, Margo. Morgan is what? 31? They probably know, my friend."

"Oh, you're right, Trish. Morgan asked me how Dad and I were getting along yesterday. I just said 'as well as can be expected' and she seemed content with that."

The two women watched the snow fall lazily in flakes the size of silver dollars, a treasury of lace dropping from the sky. It was wet snow and when it hit the carriage lamp glass, the flakes disappeared in a pool that dripped down the light like a lava lamp.

"He closed the joint account."

"Ah, nuts," Trish sighed.

Margo watched the snow some more. "You know, I may not have told you about how we got together in the beginning." She looked at Trish questioningly.

"I don't think you did. Go ahead." Trish settled in with her feet on the couch, knees to her chin, travel mug on her knees.

"I bought him."

"I beg your pardon?"

"I bought him. He was living with a politician's daughter at the time, and he owed her a decent amount of money. I don't remember how he brought it up, but we were already thinking about a future, and there was this woman and she was pissed, and therefore adamant about the money. I wrote her a check." Margo laughed out loud. "I'll bet she was surprised. I think it was her way of holding on to him, his inability to pay her off. So along comes another woman and writes a check to free him."

"Holy shit." Trish watched Margo's face. "Did you love him?"

Margo settled in the couch, same way as Trish, opposite corner. "I honestly don't know, Patricia. I really don't. Infatuated, sure. Dazzled, absolutely. He's got appallingly effective charisma." Margo was silent for a spell. "I loved him later. For a time." Margo shook her head. "Then the extracurricular activity started back up, and the circular accusations, and the pain and then the numbness. I was happy when I knew nothing. Once you're awake, you can't be unawake."

"Do you remember the partners' Christmas party we all went to, must have been 1986 or '87?" Trish asked. "At the Athenaeum? I went with that doofus podiatrist client who annoyed the hell out of me, lecturing me how bad the shoes I had on were for my feet. Cripes! Ann Marino red suede? Bad?"

Margo giggled, "I do remember. You said the red was the exact color of an enemy's blood. Very old world diva. I wore that black sequined Joan Crawford thing. I still have it somewhere. And you wore the teardrop cutout turtleneck red knit dress. That was hot, Trish."

"Yeah, a preview of the Dish to come. Anyway, I was standing on the mezzanine lobby with two of the partners from Frasier's law firm when you and Frasier walked by down on the main floor. One pointed and said "Is that Sawyer?" and the other said, "Yeah, it is, but who's the new babe?" The first guy said, "I don't think that's a babe. I think that's his wife.""

Margo smiled weakly. "You never said."

"My sister tried to tell me how to tell you ways to find out if Frasier was cheating on you. Remember me fumbling around relaying the stuff she told me?" Margo nodded. Trish continued, "You stopped me, told me that if you were that interested in getting the goods on Frasier, you'd be able to figure out how all by yourself."

Margo nodded once more. "You weren't the only one, Trish. I appreciate your trying to help in hindsight, I really do. But I wouldn't have done anything if I'd had any proof. It didn't make sense to stir the pot that hard." Margo stood up, stretched, picked up her cup to refill it. "Better the devil you know, I guess. We were comfortable for a long time. Maybe we're just no longer comfortable."

The two women went together to the kitchen, Trish leaned against the counter and fiddled with a teabag while Margo poured hot water into her mug. "Are you still going ahead with your plans then?" Trish asked her friend.

"Yes, I am. Hey! What did you think about Dr. Amy's idea?"

Trish stood up straight, eyes smiling. "I like it a lot. I've been trying to get you birds out on an adventure for a while. It's perfect. I hope it works out."

"Me, too. Let's make a fire, shall we? And tell me honestly: how do you feel about hot chocolate and peanut butter cookies?"

The two women put the tea aside, made hot chocolate with real heated milk and fat marshmallows, lit the fireplace, put on some Christmas music and talked companionably, watching the snow pile up.

Trish asked to sleep in the guest room, and after another hour of laughing and reminiscing, the two hugged good night, drifted to their rooms and off to sleep.

Trish was up and in the shower when Margo banged on the bathroom door, stuck her head into the steamed room, yelled "There's coffee on the counter." Trish pulled the curtain back, winked at Margo, said "thank you!" and got back to showering.

"What's your plan for today?" Trish asked, dressed and coffee-ed and ready to knock the snow off her tires.

"Just relax, I guess." Margo was watching the birds at the feeder, yellow finches delicately taking a seed, flying away to eat it, and then flying back for one more. Tiny hearts and brains that knew the luxury of enough. "I'd really like to have a good look at the accidental shop, though."

"The accidental shop?"

"The place where the old man fainted, with the broken teacup? It was an intriguing place, and I wouldn't mind bumping into those people again. I'd like to hear more about that golden pheasant pattern."

"Show me these plates, Margo. I don't remember you using them."

"I haven't," Margo said, reaching into the small cupboards above the refrigerator, pulling down a box. "I don't remember how I even came across these dishes. They're not pieces I bought." Margo unwrapped one ziplocked dish and handed it to Trish.

"It's a lovely pattern," Trish said. "Do you have other pieces?"

"Uh huh. Just dessert plates. Four of them here, four of them in the cabin. Isn't that odd?"

"It's odd you don't remember buying them. If your mother bought them, that explains the cabin, but not here. Your grandmother maybe?"

"My grandmother would only have dishes like this if it was a gift. She wouldn't buy good china. My aunt would though. Aunt Suoma. These look like her taste. She enjoyed lovely things around her, and she shared. But I still don't understand how they got here. I have my aunt's monogrammed barware, and a teapot and a serving dish, but I have no memory of these plates at all."

Trish shrugged. "Have you asked your daughters?"

Margo barked a short laugh. "I didn't think of it. But, thanks, Trish, I sure will." She rewrapped the plate, put the box back in the cupboard. "So how's this? I'll drive us to the shop in your car, we can have tea and dessert later if you have time, and then I'll take you home. I can get a cab from your house?"

"What time you hoping to be home?"

"No later than four."

179

"All right then. It's a plan. But no later! I have a date tonight." Trish batted her eyes and did a Betty Boop pose.

"Trish! You track down Frank?"

"Gosh no. That coward! No, I met this man at Claire's gallery. She's the new girl's dad."

"Salinger's?"

"Yes, indeed."

"Oh good grief, let me guess. His name is Faulkner."

"Nope."

"Wordsworth."

"Wrong."

"Capote."

"No! Caldwell."

"Well, that's not too bad. Wait, wasn't that a woman?"

"Maybe. But he's not. Saddle up, Sawyer. Let's go! I'm not going anywhere with you in those pajamas."

The only snow moving that had been accomplished this early was done by the cars sending sloppy slush to the curb and back again, but the major roads had at least two tracks cleared by this activity when the women finally dressed, set out in Trish's Jeep for the accidental shop, as Margo called it.

"Kerrytown? I don't remember seeing a shop like you describe there." Trish said.

"Me either. It's off the beaten track. It was an accident I went in the door at all. Did you have anything you wanted from the Farmer's Market? Shoot. Is it even open this time of year? Any other errands you want done?" Margo asked. Trish shook her head no.

They talked about Trish's date tonight. Caldwell was driving them all the way to Detroit to see the renovation of the DIA which had opened on the 23rd. "70,000 square feet, Margo. I can't imagine. The review said the museum has 90 percent of their major pieces on display now. I'm looking forward to seeing what's been done."

"Claire went last Sunday during the Members' preview," Margo remarked. "She said she liked how the paintings were regrouped in a much more user-friendly way. Easier for folks who weren't art aficionados to appreciate."

"I forget which way to turn now. Is it Fourth or Fifth? Oh well, can't go too far wrong either way," Margo said, turning left onto Fourth.

"There's the restaurant," Trish pointed, and then "Is that it? The Artcraft Shop?"

"Where do you see that?" Margo asked, leaning over the steering wheel.

"Right there. Big sign, Margo. Hard to miss. It's beautiful, the sign."

Margo made a u-turn, pulled into a space half a block below the shop, put the car in park, cut the engine, and sat quietly, looking at the sign. "Funny. I don't remember a sign. I don't remember a sign at all."

Trish and Margo sat in the car looking at the sign extending from the side of the green brick building. It was about four feet long by three feet high. Not easy to miss. It was covered on its top edge with snow. It had substance, weight, mass.

"Why wouldn't I have noticed that sign?" Margo wondered under her breath.

"Ah, you were busy, distracted. Point is, we see it now. Let's go in, shall we?" Trish opened her door, stood on the curb looking up at the sign, pulling on her gloves.

Margo waited for traffic to clear on her side, opened the door, got out of the car. "Hey! HEY!" she yelled.

Trish spun her head to see what Margo was hollering about. Margo was waving her hand in the air at someone down the street. Trish focused on the sidewalk and spotted Claire and her granddaughter, waving back, standing in front of the steamed windows of the restaurant on the corner. "What are the chances," Trish muttered, and waved at the two herself, starting forward to meet their friend.

Margo joined Trish on the sidewalk and both walked toward the two approaching them. Trish glanced up at the garland on the light poles, surmounted by a French horn and holly banner in shades of gold and green. She could smell the pine, saw the big clear lights wound through the garland. It would be pretty to see this at night, she thought. The sidewalk was cleared except directly in front of the shop, where the two women slowed, Margo taking mincing high heel boot steps through the frozen footfalls.

"What are you two up to?" called Claire loudly before the pairs had joined up, dodging another pedestrian headed the other direction.

"Hi there. How are you Anastasia?" Margo asked, smiling at the young woman.

"Fine, thanks," Annie answered.

"We're coming from breakfast. What's up with you guys?" Claire asked.

"Margo talked me into coming to see this shop," Trish offered.

"The shop you stumbled into?" Claire asked, craning her neck around the two friends. "Is that it?" she asked pointing at the green brick exterior. "The Artcraft Shop? You didn't say it had a name, Margo."

"I didn't see the sign. Either time."

"Ooookay. Well, let's go see this place. Mind if we join you? All right with you Annie?" and at her granddaughter's nod, everyone turned around to walk back toward the green brick façade. "Weird color, isn't it?" Claire commented.

The double doors were recessed into a glassed alcove so that the two picture windows faced the street, and two narrower windows of the same height approached the door at a 45 degree angle. Margo was still looking up at the sign, when they all reached the first display window. "Oh, Grandma look," Anastasia exclaimed, pointing at something in the window the rest couldn't see yet, as she was the first to reach the glass.

The window was deep with white netting, strewn with glittery white plastic snowflakes. The netting was draped to the top of the window, tiny white lights strung in abundance along the edges, looped into the middle, trailed on the tiered structure beneath. Music boxes, musical instruments, snow globes, sheet music, antique toys were strewn on the steps. From the middle step, a white tree trunk rose, the top obscured by the window upper edge. Wooden dowels painted white poked upward like tree branches. From the branches hung dozens of crystal snowflakes, stars and icicles, twirling iridescently in the tiny white-lit universe of under the Christmas tree. "There's more over here!" Annie had walked to the window beyond the door alcove.

Claire didn't move from her examination of the window display. Margo tipped her head slightly to catch her eye. Claire glanced up. "It's just map pins. Map pins, sewing pins, thumb tacks. That's what's holding up the tree ornaments, probably the lights, too. Some white paint and a couple dozen yards of taffeta. This is so unstudied. Remarkable really. There isn't a formal arrangement, but it's mesmerizing and engaging. It draws you in, doesn't it?"

"Charming, completely." Margo smiled. "Are you questioning your gifts again, Claire?" Claire looked at Margo, surprised. "No. Just admiring. This is really good. Makes me feel...warm. Happy."

Claire and Margo walked to the next window to join Trish and Annie. "Grandma, don't you have a bird like that?" Annie asked. Claire came up to put her arm around the taller girl. "I sure do. From my mother. That's Oiva Toikka for iittala, I'd bet. Finnish art glass. Wow. "

"What is it, Trish?" Margo asked standing next to the silent woman with her hands shoved in her coat pockets. Trish gestured with her chin "There. The paper snowflake."

"That one?" Margo pointed. Trish nodded.

It was origami folded by an enthusiastic second grader - glue dollops visible under the smattering of glitter that adhered here and there like snow melting in the midday sun. It spun slowly, catching the light and refracting it in Rorschach glimmers that dripped over the dowel branches and nestled on the netting around it.

It was heartbreakingly tender. "What is it about it exactly?" Margo put her head on Trish's shoulder. Trish smiled. "We all made something like it. Long ago. Can't you feel the excitement? Folding as carefully as our clumsy little hands could contrive, sprinkling glitter we would never be allowed to use at home, waiting for the glue to dry, disappointed when the teacher said we couldn't take it home until tomorrow. Running, carrying it home from school the next day, triumphantly hanging it on the tree, right in front as high as we could reach."

"Every school kid's memory," Margo said.

"Yes," Trish sighed.

"Are you coming?" Anastasia called to the loitering women, her hand on the door latch, nodding her head to hurry the other women along, her teen-aged body bouncing.

"Let's go," Claire said, following Annie to the door, as she flipped the latch open.

The bell over the door tinkled.

Anastasia was jumping up and down in front of a rack next to the counter, "Grandma, Grandma, these are what I was looking for. Look! Glittens, The fingers fold over, see? Cool colors!" Claire walked over to see what she was so excited about, first casting a short frown at Margo.

Margo was frowning herself. This couldn't be the store she remembered. Not in less than a week. She recognized the music cabinet at the back of the room, but it was different, wood shinier, well polished. The chifforobes were open and scarves, hats, hand-beaded purses spilled from the shelves of one; ornaments, delicate gold filigree, bisque and woven rattan crowded the shelves of the other.

From behind the walls, the motets of Anonymous 4 played softly.

In the center of the room gleamed a real Douglas Fir, strands of lights sparkling from the trunk to the branch tips. Bulbs and ornaments danced in the breeze from the ceiling fan, shimmering on the polished wood of the furniture pieces standing nearby like rocks in a fast river on a bright sun day.

Annie had just wound up a music box on the counter, and mice danced on typewriter keys as a letter to Santa rolled off the platen, to the tune of "Santa Claus is Coming to Town."

Claire was staring at the corner of the ceiling near the front window. Margo walked over to where she stood. "Do you know what that fragrance is?" Claire asked, barely audible. Margo didn't answer. "That's frankincense, Margo. Real, crushed, essential oil, expensive beyond belief frankincense. And do you know what that is hanging up there? No. There." Claire pointed to an intricately carved stick figure suspended in the corner. "That's a Japanese shadow puppet."

Claire and Margo turned as the woman with the braid came through the curtains into the shop space. "And that, I'm going to guess, is the Puppet Master."

"Claire, you're spooking me," hissed Margo. She smiled, walked quickly to the woman, extending her hand. "Hello again."

Saima took the hand offered, smiled in return, put her other hand over the top of the joined ones. "Welcome back. I'm glad you've brought friends." She nodded smiling at Claire. Claire didn't quite smile back.

"It's remarkable what you've done here. I wouldn't have believed you could make this much progress." Margo gushed.

"I had good helpers," Saima demurred.

"I wondered if the old gentleman who had fainted, is he all right?"

"He's fine. Antoine is in the back, if you'd like to see for yourself. And young Edgar as well. Please." and she held the curtain aside as she gestured for Margo to enter.

Saima saw the blonde-buzzed Trish standing by the tree watching her. She walked slowly toward her, and as she was within a foot of her, Saima threw out her arms and hugged the tall woman tightly. The two stood, arms around each other, eyes shut. Claire and Annie had stopped what they were doing to watch this tender tableau, amazed.

Saima stepped back, still holding Trish's shoulders with her hands. Trish smiled. Shook her head. "Grandma."

Saima smiled wider. "Patricia."

"What?" Claire said. "What? Grandma?" She was holding a pair of glittens in her hands. She gestured to Trish, then Saima, then Trish again. "Grandma?"

Trish took hold of one of the hands on her shoulder, tucked it into the crook of her arm, and walked the smaller woman over to Claire. "Claire, this is my grandmother. Saima Aaltonen. Grandma, this is my friend Claire Chernikova." Trish continued the promenade to where Annie was trying on woolen caps. "Annie, my grandmother. This is Claire's granddaughter, Anastasia."

"Anastasia. A lovely name for a lovely girl. I'm delighted to meet you both."

"Grandma, may I have a word with you over here?" Trish put a hand on the old woman's back, leading her toward the counter. "Excuse us, please," she said to Claire and Annie. Claire leaned in as the two passed. "*Grandma?*" she hissed between her teeth. Trish gave her the Popeye look, swiped a flat hand across her throat.

Trish waited until Saima was seated comfortably on the stool behind the counter, then she bent closer, darted eyes to see if Claire was in hearing distance. She was not. Claire still stood, holding the glittens outstretched in her hand, eyeing her friend and her friend's grandmother, mouth open and unmoving. Trish searched the blue eyes of the smiling woman in front of her, who waited primly and quietly, hands in her lap.

"Grandma," Trish said. "You're dead."

"Oh Patricia. Such a final word." Saima shut her eyes, made a dismissive gesture with her hand. "So dreary."

"But you are. You passed away."

"And what's your point, dear?"

"My *point*. Passed. Away. You can't just show up, running a shop where I live." Trish was flipping her hands around like a young porpoise signaling friends.

"Patricia, calm down. I'm not going to be here for long. Just enough to get this shop established, tidy up a few loose ends, and then I'll be on my way again. Not to worry." Saima slid off the stool, patted Trish on the arm. "Let me see how our other guests are doing, dear. Look around, have fun." Saima kissed her on the cheek, said, "excuse

189

me for a minute" to the gaping Claire and disappeared behind the curtain.

Trish was watching the undulating curtain. Claire leaned in again. "Grandma?"

"I don't know what to say, Claire. Yes, she's my grandmother."

"Whose side?"

"My mother's mother."

"Why wasn't she at your mother's funeral?"

"She doesn't do funerals." Trish stared at the curtain for another second. Then she laughed loudly. "Really doesn't do funerals."

"What's going on, Trish?"

"Claire, I wish I knew. I'll go ask. Be right back." Trish headed for the curtained room.

"I apologize for intruding. Mr. Lavoisiere, are you all right?" Margo asked as she let the curtain fall behind her, hurrying to Antoine's side. "You seem ill again."

Antoine pushed himself upward from the wing chair, shuffled slowly to Margo, picked up her hand and holding it with both of his, kissed it gently. "I'm fine, thank you for asking."

Edgar tipped another log over the screen into the fire, sending a fireworks display of sparks fleeing up the flue. "We were just talking about redemption and forgiveness."

"Really? How interesting. I just looked 'redemption' up on google. I wanted a synonym that was more suitable to what I was writing. There were quite a few about how to redeem a mortgage, but a surprising few others. Not much on the etymology end either. Being saved from, or for something. Credited as late as 1255. I don't believe that's all there is to it." Margo looked up. The two men were listening intently.

"I'm sorry again. Blathering. Research fanatic. What were you two being redeemed from or for?"

Edgar sat on the little lip of the hearth, dangling his arms. "Antoine was sharing the story of his life in Prague. He knew my father and mother there."

"Really? What are the chances?" Margo asked, subdued.

"Edgar is being kind. I loved his mother and father. His father was like a son to me, and I was in love with his mother. She married Edgar's father, whom she loved."

"I see." The new log crackled and hissed. Margo could feel the warmth on her knees. She could feel the cold on her back.

"Were your parents content, Edgar?"

"As much as any of us are, I think," Edgar replied after some thought.

"I wonder. Do you think it's possible to actually make someone happy? Isn't it hubris to think we have that much impact on another's life?"

"It reminds me of a story my mother told me when I was a boy," Antoine said. "About a turtle. The turtle jumped into the air from a high cliff. It landed spinning on its shell at the bottom of the valley. His brother, looking down from the cliff, wept. 'I should have stopped him.' His friend, weeping also, lamented she had not encouraged him more, been kinder to him. His sister wiped her eyes, 'I repent not showing him the other way down the mountain.' The turtle on the ground, the spinning slowing and finally ending, said, 'I regret thinking I could fly.'"

"When did you understand what she meant, Antoine?" Margo asked.

"Just now." Lavoisiere replied.

Margo nodded. "My grandmother told me that regret and worry are wasted emotions. One mourns the past and the other anticipates more of the same for the future. Not a good way to live a life. But we all do it. Regret and worry. If we're lucky, in between there's work to be done, and skills to pass along. To keep our minds off the worry."

"Hope," Edgar said. "Hope is the counterweight."

"Can you teach hope?"

"I don't know. I think you can remove the distractions that discourage it. It's how I think about writing. Or sculpting, the way Antoine does it. Focus on the center and you'd be lucky in a thousand years to reveal what you're after. Remove the layers, the distractions, the loose metal or mud that does not get you to your goal, gently, with love, and what is revealed is what you seek." Edgar stood up, paced, his shadow trailing behind, animated by the firelight.

"Is this what I mean? It's just there, just beyond the words. If I stare at it, I can't see it. Like light refraction: Evanescent means 'tends to vanish', which is appropriate because the intensity of evanescent waves decays exponentially with the distance from the interface at which they are formed.

"Mirror matter. Shadow matter. Bosons and Maxwell's Demons. Experiments that attempt to disprove theories that are not experimentally proven. An historian named Henry Adams used Maxwell's Demon as a historical metaphor, attempting to analyze history as a move toward equilibrium. But this cannot be correct, as nature tends from order to chaos in closed systems.

"You're familiar with the glass of water and the glass of water with ice chips? The glass with ice chips appears more disordered, but the chips actually limit the ways in which the water molecules can be arranged. The water without ice has many more possibilities for order.

"But, given time, nature will return to disorder." Edgar squeezed his head with his hands. "What am I saying here? I thought I had it. I thought I did." He sat down on the hearth again, defeated.

"We were talking about hope, Edgar," Antoine said gently.

"Yes. But hope for what?" Edgar rejoined. "Hope for order when disorder is more natural? Isn't what might calm us acceptance?"

"That's rather defeatist, isn't it?" asked Margo.

"I don't think so," Edgar responded. "Maybe we should look at this out of the side of our eyes. Not directly at it. In the mirror, as it were. Do you know why diamonds sparkle? Diamonds sparkle because a diamond has a refraction index of 2.42. A light ray refracted in a diamond undergoes many internal reflections before it emerges to be seen by our eyes. In just this way is the word 'hope' refracted. The definition is to desire with expectation or belief the possibility of obtaining. But for what do we hope?"

"Happiness?" Margo asked.

"By what means? We've all been exposed to what our religions would have us believe is the ultimate attainment. What we hold hope to realize: salvation."

"What if we hoped for acceptance? The peace of knowing that divine chaos is the best we can expect? Give up reordering the universe to fit our beliefs, or the beliefs we have been taught are normal. Relax and allow. Let our lives unfold as the time is meant to be revealed. Accept that the universe is infinite and that is not a concept that has any meaning to the human mind."

"Accept that nothing we do has meaning?" asked Antoine.

"No. Accept that everything we do has meaning. It is the province of tyrants who are constantly afraid to believe that nothing they do has meaning. This is what allows them the totalitarian purity of their actions. There are no clarifying moments in those lives. Forgiveness, redemption: unnecessary because nothing has meaning."

Edgar stood again. As he talked he walked the room. "We're educated to be part of society. Society requires order. We are trained to remain orderly. When I was little, I could see colored lights around my parents. My mother's was pink with a yellow center. My father's, blue. I could see the glow surrounding them and today I know it was their auras shining. I cannot see auras now. It is not in order.

"I was driving through the park last winter. There was snow on the ground in the woods. Brown leaves strewn in the snow. The oaks still held their leaves in the canopy. The trees were dense, a thicket. I said out loud 'show me the deer.'"

Edgar stopped pacing in front of the fire, his figure backlight shadowed, grayscaled to black.

"Like blinds opening, the scene changed instantly. Five deer stood watching me pass. I had not seen them in the copse. Until I asked to see them. The trees disappeared like slats turned to their edges. As soon as I had seen the deer, the scene changed back. There were only the trees. The deer disappeared."

Margo was excited, "In cognitive science, confirmation bias is a tendency to search for or interpret new information in a way that confirms one's preconceptions and avoid data which contradict prior beliefs. It represents an error of inductive inference, or disconfirmation of an alternative hypothesis. It happens all the time. A study of confirmation bias on the subject of the death penalty delivered the exact same document to the pro and con teams of a debate society, each of whom then used identical arguments to prove their side."

"Therefore, if we're to be conscientious critical thinkers, equally rigorous scrutiny should be used to analyze evidence challenging, as well as evidence supporting, yes?" interjected Antoine.

"Of course," Edgar said. "But if I came to you today and told you I'd seen a leprechaun - green coat, vest, hat and all - what can you offer me to refute what I saw? That leprechauns don't exist? Can you prove a negative? That seeing one is an illusion, magical thinking?"

"And yet we believe - we hope to believe - that a deity we've never seen exists. And is the sole proprietor of redemption. Contradictory. An experiment, the results of which we are not allowed to study, to disprove an experiment that hasn't happened, as you say," Margo said.

"If I hoped to prove how I saw the deer, I may as well try to climb a spider web," Edgar observed. "If I ask myself why I saw the deer that way, well, that way lies madness. If I accept what I saw, and that there is meaning I do not - perhaps cannot - understand, then I'm fine. I can replay the transition from trees to deer in my head and be content. Maybe it will happen to me again, maybe not. And still I'm content. If there is any message here, the message is just 'allow.'"

Edgar gestured to Antoine, the hand motion elegantly encompassing the dignified plea for awareness that fired Edgar's heart. "My mother was unhappy, regardless of whether she suffered from your presence in her world at that time or not. There was nothing you could do. You did what you thought best for people you loved. You should be content." He finished on a plaintive note.

Antoine gazed at Edgar, stood, walked into the shadow and hugged the tall man tightly. Edgar hugged Antoine back.

"Well," said Margo, standing herself. "I wandered back here to find an answer to why you have the same dessert plates I have."

Antoine and Edgar glanced puzzled at each other. Margo pointed to the teacup. "That pattern, Czechoslovakia. Golden Pheasant. I have the same plates."

Laughter shook Antoine's shoulders. "It's a common pattern. Like, what? Like milk glass was. No mystery." He clapped Edgar on the shoulder. "None that we can prove. Not without unraveling the universe by climbing spider webs."

"Which universe is that?" asked Trish, holding the curtain between the rooms out of her way. Six eyes were fixed on Trish. She nodded. "Hello." Trish the Dish took a moment to admire the room. "Nice. Uh. Excuse me, please. Margo can I talk with you for just a second?"

Trish took the few steps to be in the old man's personal space. "Hello. I'm Trish. I'm sorry to intrude, but I need to talk to this woman for just a second."

"Antoine Lavoisiere. How do you do?"

"Hello, I'm Edgar Pavelka," Edgar enjoined, shaking the hand offered him.

"Margo, if you would, please?" Trish gestured once emphatically past the drape of the curtain she was holding, expecting Margo's rapid exit.

"Trish!" Claire exclaimed, as Trish and Margo returned to the shop. "I've been thinking. It's just not possible that woman is your grandmother. Not possible."

"Really?" Trish said weakly. "How interesting." She turned to Margo, escorted her into the space in front of the music cabinet. Annie gave them a curious glance, moved toward the front of the shop.

"Tell me again how you found this store," Trish insisted.

Margo looked confused. "I walked in the door accidentally on the way somewhere else. It didn't look like this. It was emptier, older, I don't remember there being a sign, the…"

"By accident," Trish said. "Of course."

Claire inserted herself between the two friends. "Trish. I think your grandmother's dead." Margo glared at Claire, shocked. "Well? Is she dead or isn't she?"

Trish bit her lip, played with her gloves. Spinning around, she said over her shoulder, "I'll check. Just a second."

"Margo? What's going on here?" Claire asked. "What's in that back room?" Margo stood, cemented to the spot like a flagpole. Claire took one giant step toward the curtain, then another, flung it open, disappeared into the back room. Margo, ungluing her feet from the floorboards, hastened after her.

Trish touched her grandmother's knee. Saima was still seated on the stool behind the counter, waiting for Trish to return to her. "The first time I saw a psychic," Trish began, "when my friend told me it was my turn, as I got close enough to the table to hear the psychic, she said, 'your maternal grandmother is with us.'"

"And what did you say?" Saima asked, placing her hand on Trish's hand resting on her knee.

"I said 'I know. She's always with me.' I didn't know she meant it literally."

The younger woman and the old woman were silent. The Chenille Sisters sang about waiting for the man with the bag. Annie hummed along with her iPod nubs stuck in her ears, oblivious to anything but her personal music. A burning candle on the counter flung fumes of caramel apples and cinnamon into the shop. The tree lights glistened in the glass of the countertop, multiplying the lights in the back panel. Trish could see the lights like a tiny galaxy in her grandmother's eyes.

The buzz-haired silent woman spoke finally. "You know about the new treatment. The mouse hormone. It's $32,000 a shot, Grandma. I'm waiting to hear if my insurance will approve it. It's experimental. No guarantees."

More silence.

"It won't matter, will it?" Trish asked, watching her grandmother's blue eyes that were so much like her own, including the orange spot in the left eye.

Saima gently picked up Trish's other hand, idling at her side. She touched it to her wrinkled cheek, moving her head to caress the skin on the back of her granddaughter's hand. Grandma's face did not change, but Trish felt the smile. Felt the warmth of her spirit through the cold skin. Felt the softness of her hands, like a favorite t-shirt, worn and warm from the dryer, the threads and the skin so thin, the blue mystery of the universe shown through. And all of it, every particle in that infinite galaxy, immanent and transcendent, wished Trish eternal blessings.

"Okay, Grandma," Trish sighed.

Trish nodded brusquely, sniffed back the tears, scrubbed her nose with the sleeve of her coat. "What's up with the shop?"

"Your friends, Patricia," and Saima nodded toward the back room. "Will need a place to find you when they need you. Just as you found me here."

"How long, Grandma?"

Saima did not answer. "Well, then. Better get moving." Trish breathed deeply through her nose, filling her lungs, and breathed out the air through the O of her mouth. "Will you come with me? Then?" Trish asked into her grandmother's ear. Saima nodded.

"And help me get reacquainted with Mom?" Trish socked her grandmother playfully in the shoulder, skipped over to see what Annie was oohing over, and then headed for the curtain between the rooms.

Claire flung the curtain with such vigor, it sparked the flames in the fireplace. Both men started as she apparated into the room like a Valkyrie, bent on cold revenge.

Edgar was about to introduce himself once again, when the woman's jaw dropped and she stared at Antoine Lavoisiere. "Uncle Antoine?" she said once feebly. Her eyes closed to slits, and her jaw snapped back up. "Uncle Antoine!" Claire shouted.

Margo stumbled into the room behind her. Claire put her hands vigorously on her hips. "What are you up to, Uncle?" Claire asked belligerently.

"Claire! Please. I think you're mistaken." Margo cautioned.

"No, I'm not. What are you doing here, Uncle?" Claire insisted.

Edgar hesitantly stepped around Antoine, knees raising high with each step in a comedic imitation of someone tiptoeing around a ghost in a Bob Hope movie. "How do you do," he breathed, as he reached Claire and put out his hand. "I'm Edgar Pavelka. And this gentleman," he said, gesturing at Antoine, "is Monsieur Antoine Lavoisiere."

"Is he?" Claire said. "Is he just." Antoine said nothing, looked apologetic.

"Is he who?" Trish asked, coming into the room, and directly to the fireplace, warming her hands, smiling.

"Uncle Antoine."

"Uncle Antoine. My mother's brother," said Claire, still frowning.

"How nice! I'm glad to meet you properly, sir," smiled Margo.

"My Uncle Antoine. Who joined his older brothers in the Great Beyond in 1999."

"There really isn't any 'Great Beyond' my dear Claire. If you're going to insist on a specific locale actually…"

"Uncle Antoine!" Claire interrupted in her best mom voice. "Fine. Dead. Uncle Antoine. You're dead. Very like your grandmother, Trish."

"It's all something more like another state of mind really," said Saima, coming into the small room to make a crowd. Margo and Edgar zipped eyes from Claire to Saima to Trish to Antoine and round again, until Edgar, dizzy, plopped onto the chair, long legs bouncing once on his heels.

"What is it you're angry about, Claire?" asked Uncle Antoine.

The fury flew out of Claire, up the fireplace and out to trouble the afternoon sky elsewhere. "I'm confused," said Claire, wiping her forehead to sort her thoughts, moving to rest her rear on the worktable opposite the fireplace. Claire dropped her hand, looked at Saima. "That's a Japanese shadow puppet in the front corner, isn't it?"

"Actually it's Balinese. But a shadow puppet nonetheless."

"I've been looking for one for a long time." She turned to Margo. "You know the spring show I told you the new girls are organizing? It's a puppet show. From around the world. I never said a word about puppets to them, that I recall. They just came up with it all on their own."

"There's a famous marionette theatre in Prague," Edgar volunteered, having decided to participate in this mad hatter's party until a real Maxwell's Demon came through the curtains, at which time he'd bolt.

"I know. Uncle Antoine loved the puppet theatre," Claire said quietly. "Uncle. Uncle, Why are you here?"

"I'm not altogether sure, my dear. Saima was coming and I tagged along." He touched Edgar's arm. "Perhaps there were some small ends to tidy up."

"We haven't sold your house yet, Uncle Antoine. It's been rented for all this time, but the market is terrible right now."

"I think I can help you with that, Claire." Antoine Lavoisiere came to his niece, looked up into her eyes, and laid his head on her shoulder. Claire stood looking over his head at Trish. Trish winked. Claire grinned, and hugged the small man until he grunted.

Margo went to sit on the edge of Edgar's chair. Edgar looked shell-shocked and Margo felt the same. "Will someone please tell us what the hell is going on here?"

At that moment, Annie materialized out of the curtain between the rooms. "Hey you guys! It's snowing. Come look, it's really pretty."

And that's just what everyone did.

Chapter 7

Three weeks before Christmas, on a Wednesday, Margo's phone rang early in the morning, as she sat at her desk, writing holiday letters. "Hello," Margo greeted the caller, wondering who had something to discuss at 7:45 a.m. She hoped it was one of her daughters with exciting news or a fun offer. She set her pen down in happy anticipation.

"Hi, Margo. This is Trish. I have a favor to ask."

"Good morning, Dish! Of course, what is it?" Margo smiled.

"You know the clinic where I get my blood drawn?"

Margo was alert now, sitting straight in her chair, fumbling for her pen. "Yes, I think I do. What's up?"

"Are you busy now? Can you meet me there?"

"Yes, certainly I'll meet you. What's the intersection? Right. Got it. I'll be there in about 15 minutes. Do you need anything else? No? I'm on my way, Trish."

When Margo got to the clinic parking lot, there was only one other car in addition to Trish's Jeep. Margo pulled quickly into the spot next to Trish. As she unbuckled her seatbelt, she expected to meet Trish's eye, and had a bright smile ready to greet her, but Trish sat, staring straight ahead through the windshield. She did not turn her head until Margo tapped on the driver's window glass.

Trish opened the door, not looking at Margo. Fear spit adrenaline into Margo's bloodstream. "Trish? Are you okay? What's happening?"

"I can't see, Margo." Trish said as she stood, closing the car door beside her.

"What do you mean you can't see?"

"I can't see. I'm blacked out and conscious. I need to get my blood drawn." Trish's face was wan and sweaty; her voice thready but stern. She took a tentative step forward.

Margo, confused and anxious, reached for Trish's elbow.

Trish snatched her arm away.

Margo's fear instantly shifted into anger. "Fine. I see what you need. You need me to shoo cars away so you're not squished in the parking lot when you fall down. Good. I can do that. The front door's right there. Do it yourself, like always."

Trish took a swift gulp of air and wobbled on her feet.

Margo's fear and anger spun dizzyingly into concern, spilling more adrenaline, prepared for swift action. "Trish, I know this is difficult for you. But you need help. You are still strong. You just need an extra hand, baby girl."

"There are wheelchairs in the lobby, Margo. I'll wait here."

"Do you need to sit back down in the car, Trish?"

"No. I'll just wait here."

"I'll be right back, Dish. Hang in there. Put your hand on the hood. There you are. Just a second. I'll be right back."

When Margo returned with the wheelchair, Trish's face was wet with tears. Silently, Margo gathered Trish into her arms, her own tears dripping onto Trish's Shakespearean coat, clutching her tightly, as though the power of this contact could restore vitality to her sick and troubled friend.

"Margo," Trish whispered. "I don't know what to do. I'm afraid."

"There, there," Margo whispered into Trish's neck, unconsciously rocking the sick woman. "So so, love. I'm here, Trish. I'm here, sweet friend. I won't leave you."

They were clutched together still, in the gray misty morning of a December day, as snow began to fall and melt on their entwined forms; rocking and crying, as two staff from the clinic hurried outside without their coats to let the women know that an ambulance had been called for, and that it was on its way.

The friends gathered around Trish's hospital bed through the waning weeks of December, bringing her ice cream, books, cards, good jokes from the internet and all the love they could squeeze into the room. One morning Claire came in to find Trish holding a badly-folded origami snowflake, slathered with glitter and gobs of glue.

Trish had just awakened from a dream.

I will hold his tah. Her friend looked like a Chinese dragon, but was really a dog. Little girl came running from far away calling "Mama."

She had hit the dog in the head and thought she knocked out his "hard palate." Green goo. Dying. The woman would not shoot the dog. Then I said I would hold his tah and she did.

She met me and still threatened me back with a weird comb like a rake, dipped in mustard.

Around a campfire in a steel drum she told a story of going to Poland to look at/buy from a steel train and the communist government didn't want them to even see it. She acted out standing at one train place while over there the train went by. 'They never intended to sell us any,' she said.

I stayed. We got to be friends. She told me the story of the steel business. Lived underground. Big train caverns. Slept on the ground. I had a companion. Male. I think Chinese.

There was a friend of hers - not Chinese, maybe not male. We slept on the ground at night and this friend kept chowlers off us. Leeches using live frayed electrical wire which we slept around. Red coal hot got chowlers off bodies. This friend did this. We ate white chicken breast-like meat cooked in water.

We made a friend ritual. I woke up when the dog was shot even though there was no noise.

"Claire," Trish said, softly happy to find her friend in view, exhausted from her journeys in the world of surreal and lucid dreams. "Claire. You must get The Artcraft Shop."

"What do you mean, Trish?" Claire asked, sitting on the edge of the bed, wiping sweat from Trish's face with a hospital cloth.

"It's a friend ritual," Trish whispered. "Keeping chowlers away. Friends do this."

Claire stroked Trish's cheek with the back of her fingers, scared. "I don't know what you mean, Trish. Were you dreaming?"

Trish reached slowly to hold Claire's hand still on her fevered cheek. "You and Margo. Buy The Artcraft Shop. Grandma said she came back because my friends would need a place to find me. The accidental shop must have a purpose. Grandma came back to find us somewhere to keep our friendship, Claire. Please try," her voice drifted off as her eyes closed in sleep once more. Claire cried quietly at her side, grief pumping her heart until Claire thought the swell of its pain would drown all the joy in the world.

"You're going to do Dr. Amy's show, aren't you, Margo, please?" Trish asked, when she woke, finding Claire gone and Margo in the chair next to the bed. "You're going to have an adventure just as we talked about. If you do it on the river, I'll go, too, Margo. You'll like it. You will. Do it." And Margo said she would.

Trish dreamed about Auntie Suoma. Auntie's advice to Patricia's preteen self.

This is what you do: you play. All the time. You learn how to play with others, that others are allowed to play; there may be time limits to play, but you play and play. You learn about yourself as you play. You learn what you like and what you love. That you have curly hair. Dark blonde curly hair. That your eyes are deep blue. And shiny. As blue and shiny as two stones in a shallow lake with the moon shining on them. That your smile makes everyone it beams on want to smile too. That you are tall. Right now people say 'tall for your age' but you will always be tall. That you are very beautiful. And smart. And funny. You like pizza, but not pineapple. You like to run, but not to wait. You like ladybugs, but not mosquitoes. You learn about you and more about what you love.

And then one day soon you think about what you might like to do when you're grown. You learn about you and what you love and you learn about what you'd like to do. And you play still more.

And you try to make play and who you are and what you do and what you love be all the same.

And you'll have a pretty happy life.

"Margo," Trish began, laying upright in the elevated hospital bed, pushing her tray away at lunch time on a frosty Tuesday morning. Margo wondered worriedly if Trish was eating at all, and if the medical staff would push the issue soon, as though forcing Trish to do anything she didn't want to do was a possibility that could actually happen.

"Margo," Trish began again, wiggling one cheek, then the other, smoothing the crisp cloth of hospital sheets over her thin body. "I've told Claire, I think, and now I'll tell you. You must buy The Artcraft Shop."

"What? Whatever for?" Margo asked, curious and amused.

"You're going to need it."

"A store? You're kidding."

"No, I'm not."

"Trish, darling friend, I have no intention of owning a store, and no means to buy one, if I did."

"Yes, you do, Margo. You will. Please think about it, at least. Talk with Claire. You won't do well with nothing to do but think, Margo. You're a world-class thinker, but you need to work on your feeling skills."

"Oh, I do, do I?" Margo bristled.

Trish smiled at her friend, placed her own IV'ed hand over top of Margo's on the bed sheet. "Yes, love, you do." Trish pronounced once more. Margo answered her smile. "You must go on Amy's adventure, too, Margo," Trish, pleased with her success at corralling Margo in any direction Margo wasn't interested in going toward, pushed on. "You'll need adventure as well. Go climb a spiderweb, my dignified, elegant friend."

Margo disengaged her hand, patted Trish's bruised one lightly, shocked once more at the bones evident through the blue skin. "Well, all this need identification reminds me. You need to drink something, Trish. Water for you, skinnydo," and Margo held up the paper cup with the bendy straw for Trish to have a sip.

Claire promised Trish she would go on a river adventure with Margo, when Claire came to visit next. "Claire, is this a dream?" Trish asked, closing her eyes weakly, in a voice fading as quickly as the flesh on her frame, one Thursday the third week of December. The weather had warmed, and green grass poked through the patches of snow struggling to stay in this world as quietly as Trish struggled to leave it.

This is what I want to tell you, Claire. Margo, all the children I did not have. 'If you want to build a ship,' counseled author Antoine de Saint-Exupéry, 'don't drum up the people to gather wood, divide the work, and give orders. Instead, teach them to yearn for the vast and endless sea.'

Trish opened her eyes. What was that? No light in the world yet, so she closed her eyes and fell into a dream again.

I wake again in the dream and my eyes are already open and I realize it's raining on my eyes. I can see straight ahead the drops hitting the water surface of my eyes; the concave edges swollen up like a thickly-glassed candy dish. It's a lot of rain.

A soaker. One after another drops hit my eyes and splash in the pool. No sound. I can see my sheet warped by the water, the closet door, the IV stand - all warped by water.

Am I a fish? Is the Great Beyond under the sea?

"Have you figured out what Uncle Antoine was doing?" Trish asked quietly. Claire was sitting on the bed the afternoon after the fish dream, sharing a hospital ice cream on a wooden spoon with Trish.

"I think he had wandered back into the world to make peace with his apprentice. And his apprentice's wife. Maybe he couldn't get their address in the Great Beyond, so he had to show up in Michigan," Claire licked her spoon, gazing at it as she rotated it in her hand. "Do you remember talking about sacred contracts? A long time ago, soon after we'd met. I commented that it was unusual to become so close after so short an acquaintance. Maybe it was Margo who thought that we agree to meet special people at an arranged time before we are born."

"I remember, " Trish eyes were gleaming, out of focus with warm memories of the world with her friends in it, and the world she was packing her thoughts to join.

"Anyway," continued Claire. "Uncle Antoine apparently was supposed to meet Edgar Pavelka. He just forgot before he died. So, he put himself back in his path, and I think it was supposed to work as a sacred contract, although Uncle Antoine was always a little befuddled.

"Edgar is buying Uncle Antoine's house. We gave him a very attractive price, and the house and its treasures will be well-loved. Honestly, Trish, it was stuffed to the rafters with old metal letterforms, some quite nice copies of old manuscripts. Salinger's dad Caldwell had a peek at some of them - turns out that's his specialty - and he's dazzled by what's there. Said it's almost a lifetime of research work. Books in Czechoslovakian, German, Austrian and who knows what all. Caldwell insists it all requires cataloguing.

"We think - Margo and I - that Uncle Antoine may have had a contract with Jan Pavelka to help his son, Edgar, find his way onto the path he is intended to walk. So, my wonderful friend, your 'need to know' way of living extends even into the next dimension. Janus and Irina Pavelka needed to know their son was guided gently into the future he is likely to have. And to enjoy.

"You know, Trish, Margo and I drove by the shop last week, on the way to see how Edgar was getting on with the house. I wouldn't attempt to explain this to anyone else, but there was no shop there. The sign was out front, just as clean and pretty as can be. But the façade is toast. The big picture window on the right is boarded up. Thready, nasty drapes are in the other windows. We peeked inside. There's a toilet sitting in the middle of the floor, the ceiling is dripping onto the stairs from the apartment above." Claire took another wooden spoon of ice cream.

"And?" Trish prompted.

"We checked with the restaurant, got the owner's name. He's an old coot, fighting with the city about the building - won't rent, won't sell. He pays the taxes, but won't pay the fines." She licked the spoon, smiled at Trish, rubbed her friend's bald head. "We'll get it, Trish. It's just what we all need. The new girls can run the gallery, and we'll turn the shop into what we already know it can be. Margo will find her entrepreneurial spirit soon enough." Claire barked a laugh. "She said it would take more than two spirits from the Great Beyond to get her into retailing."

Trish coughed, lay back on the pillow, the work to breathe getting harder to do. "Caldwell came to see me yesterday. I appreciated the visit a lot, Claire. He was excited about the history windfall at Edgar's new house, too. He's a good man. He said he'd like to go on the river adventure with you all. Please call him when you're going." She opened her eyes. "It doesn't have to be all old women, does it?"

Claire smiled at her fading friend. "No. It doesn't have to be all old women. I told my daughter Jaqueline about it, and she suggested I ask Anastasia if she was interested in going. If it doesn't take too much time away from school. Sort of an old women training expedition, according to my darling offspring. I don't know where she gets her attitude. Yes, Caldwell can go, too. Annie can discover there are more good men out there than her father and grandfather. Edgar has been hinting he'd be up for a little splashing about in rivers, too. He could use some wild and wordy women training."

"Claire," Trish began, and then rested for a moment. "Please find Dr. Webster. I want to go home."

Claire waited at the nurse's station after the nurse had paged Dr. Webster. She was drained, felt disembodied and distant, the noises in the background wafting through awareness like waking to a train whistle in the middle of the night. *I want my mommy,* Claire thought, shocked. Perhaps Trish was ready to move along, but Claire was not ready to have her depart.

"Mrs. Chernikova?" Dr. Webster held out his hand to Claire when he arrived. "What can I do for you?"

"Dr. Webster," Claire started, coughed, pushed the geyser of emotion back into the pit of her stomach, and started once more. "Trish wants to go home."

"Ah, yes, well," Dr. Webster pushed his glasses up on his nose, only to have the frame return to where it belonged, covering the red groove that was home. "Mrs. Chernikova, how much do you know about Patricia's present condition?" He glanced hesitantly at Claire's face, before dropping his gaze back to the floor.

Claire rallied her vocal cords back to the starting line, coaching her voice to return from the brink of a clean getaway. "I'm guessing she hasn't long here. With us. Is that close to the truth?"

Dr. Webster shuffled his feet and paperwork once. "We can release her right away, if that is what she wishes. I will suggest that you talk with her about hospice care at home while we get the paperwork organized. I'll call Ann Arbor Hospice, if Patricia agrees, and perhaps we can get someone here to talk with you all before she is discharged this afternoon."

Claire, shot through with adrenaline, was shocked at her voice jumping the starting gun on its own. "How much time have we got, Doctor?"

"I wouldn't delay the conversation, Mrs. Chernikova."

Claire was nakedly grateful to see Margo hurrying through the parking lot a surprisingly short time later, her sigh of relief mingling visibly with the cold air, until Margo was close enough for Claire to see the thunder in her face. "Shit," whispered Claire, sucking the cold air back into her lungs. Margo had barely come to a halt inches from Claire, the cold wind from her arrival shrouding Claire like a malevolent ghost.

"Hospice, Claire? What the hell have you talked her into?"

Raw emotion took both women into its clenched fists and shook them both mercilessly.

"What have *I* talked her into? Have you seen her? Do you know what she's going through?"

"Yes, I've seen her, Claire. She's been fighting hard. It's our job to help her keep doing just that." Margo's jaw was rigidly clenched. Claire thought she could see the veins in her temples pumping hot blood through her head. Tendrils of icy mist coiled around her neck.

"Margo, it's up to Trish to decide."

"It's not for you to claim what Trish should decide or not. Why are you doing this?"

Claire was confused and shocked and furious. "I'm not doing anything! Trish wants to go home. It is Trish's life, Margo. Trish's decision."

"But hospice, Claire. What message are you giving that sick woman? What are you suggesting she do?"

"I didn't make the suggestion. Dr. Webster said we should talk to hospice!"

"Did you ask Trish if she wanted to do that? Did you ask her for her permission? Or did you just give Webster the go ahead? Since when are you the mistress of life and death? Who put you in charge?"

"Watch it, Margo! Trish said she wanted to talk to hospice. Damn it, what else was I supposed to do? Walk into our best friend's room and say 'you're not allowed to die?' Stop this right now. This damned second, stop it. Stop blaming me because Trish is going to die!"

"You're abandoning your friend!"

"I'm doing no such thing! Get a grip on yourself, Margo. I'm not the enemy here. That damned disease is the enemy!"

"I could hit you, Claire. You're willing to let her be defeated by this vile disease. You're giving up on her!"

"There is no choice here, Margo! The doctor said she has very little time left. There is no influence we can use to change that fact. We cannot fucking stop this because we want to keep Trish with us. We cannot stop it at all."

The two friends stood still, panting with fear and rage, dizzy with helplessness. Words, waiting in impatient lines to be voiced, stepped back in the queue, their molten power dimmed by the intervening silence.

Claire's anger, leaving her body, left her without physical support. Abruptly she collapsed to her knees on the sidewalk, arms hugging her body, her shoulders shaking as she cried aloud in agony and grief to the indifferent sky.

Margo dropped in front of her weeping friend, and engulfed her in her arms.

"It's not our decision to make, dear Margo," Claire whispered. "She wants home. She's a sick, scared child we do not have for much longer, and we are not going to deny her what she wants because we're scared, too."

Margo wept quietly with Claire. When she could speak once more, she patted Claire's shoulder, sniffed, and each woman helped the other, stumbling, to her feet. Margo picked up and handed Claire one of the paper bags she had been carrying. "All right then," she agreed firmly with a shaking voice. "Let's go get our Dish." For a fleeting moment, the two friends, bound together in pain, touched hands in agreement, before, turning together, they walked into the building from which Trish would begin her short journey home.

Trish had a visitor when they got to her room. The visitor smiled, bounced to his feet, walked quickly to the foot of the bed and shook hands with Margo and Claire, smiling and talking. "Hi, I'm Harry. I'm a volunteer with Ann Arbor Hospice. Trish and I were just chatting and going over paperwork. Please take this chair, I'll stand, and if it's all right with Trish, we can continue the conversation."

"Harry, actually my friends hopefully brought me some clothes. I'd like to get washed up and dressed, and then, if you have time, we can talk some more later. Maybe you'd like a cup of coffee?"

"Oh, of course, I'll be back in about half an hour then?"

Trish's gaze landed on the pair still standing, the light behind her eyes veiled, like a gauze curtain in an evening window. "Let's get the mechanics out of the way first, and then I'd like to tell you both what I hope can happen in the next few..." she hesitated while she tried to elbow herself upright, kicking back the sheet and blanket with her feet, as Margo and Claire moved quickly to help. "Harry is a breast cancer survivor. Who knew men got breast cancer, too? There's a plastic tub in the bathroom. The nurse uses it for sponge baths. I don't think I can stand at the sink right now, so would you..."

Claire was already on her way back before Trish finished the sentence.

When she was washed and dressed, chin poked at her chest, arms rigid on the bed, Trish was quiet for a long space. When she finally raised her head, it took all her strength to move her chin upright. She closed her eyes slowly with great weariness, and when she sighed, it was a puff so fragile and insubstantial that Margo and Claire both rose to reach for their friend.

"There are things I want," Trish began. "I'm going to ask for these straight away, and use few words. Words and I have great need and little time. Years from now, you can talk about how rude this seemed, but as the great sage once said, 'for now, let us be brief.'" She opened her eyes to smile at Margo.

"Harry said the medical folks from hospice will let us know when the time is coming, and I would like a small party planned. Margo, you're good at this, and I'll leave the details to you. Claire, I have a will at Frasier's firm, and you don't have to talk with him, if you don't want to, you can talk to Tom Parker instead.

"I want to be cremated and buried with my grandmother. You both know where that is, and how it has to be done.

"The party should be the day I'm to move on. I want to be there. Not after, with all that maudlin nonsense, but while I'm still alive." Trish smiled at Margo and Claire. "I love you. I know how hard this is. I'm glad you're with me. Now. Let's blow this popstand."

The guests would talk about the party for months afterward; some with a chuckle and a smile, others with frowning disapproval. There were some who never spoke of it again until, many years afterward, like a realization sparkling into consciousness after a long draught of confusion, understanding begrudgingly appeared.

Harry was there. He had called them early that morning and quietly reported, "Today's the party" and Margo and Claire marshaled their troops, the ribbon-tethered balloons, their tenuous strength, and the celebration began with a quiet visit among the three friends around the hospital bed Claire and Margo had wheeled into Trish's living room. Trish was dressed in her favorite Buzz Lightyear pajamas, the white background indistinguishable from her pale hands folded on her thin chest. Harry thoughtfully left to run some errands.

"I don't know what to say, Dish," Claire admitted, rubbing Trish's nubby-haired head.

Trish, eyes still shut, smiled. "Words don't matter right now, Claire. I know what you'd want to say if you could. That's enough."

"Remember the card you sent me a couple years ago?" Margo murmured, holding Trish's hand as tightly as she dared with both of her own. "The one that read, 'If I were sitting with God on the front porch' on the outside, and on the inside 'I'd thank Him for sharing you.' Those are good words."

Trish walked the beach between the water and the land she would make her new home, unaware of the people who touched her bed or her hand, like loving postcards from the shores of the world she was leaving behind her.

Conversations ebbed, flowed, crashed into nothingness, receded like the evening tide. People arrived and left quickly, trailing good wishes and hugs in their wake.

Margo and Claire put their arms around each other in front of Trish's little Christmas tree, sparkling with light and memories. "She left the ornaments to us, Margo," said Claire. "And the stories that go with them," answered Margo. "Her grandmother will be pleased."

Triumphant, Olympian music played softly in the background. At 5:29 p.m., the theme from *Indiana Jones* vibrated the stereo's woofer as Harry, knowing the signs, turned the volume up.

Trish moved softly to the Great Beyond, or something like another state of mind, that Christmas Eve Eve at 5:30 in the afternoon. As the light left the sky, Patricia Ann Worthington, beloved sister, cherished friend, took the light's hand and went with it into the night.

Chapter 8

"Who is that?" Margo whispered into Claire's neck, seated next to her on the couch in Claire's sun room a week later, the day before New Year's Eve. The hiss of her whisper was almost lost in the wheeze from the gas stove waving cookie cutter flames at them from its stone logs.

"Who?" Claire asked, concerned hostess at this memorial gathering.

"There," Margo pointed with her thumb in a discrete gesture. "Standing alone by the mural. With the purple coat."

"I have no idea," Claire answered. "But I want some more tea. Let's go introduce ourselves."

The two women moseyed in tandem through the crowd toward the kitchen by way of the mural. Claire, kissing her husband Vik on the way through, still arrived at the purple coat woman first and extended her hand. "Thank you for coming. My name is Claire Chernikova. I'm a friend of Trish and this is my home where you're welcome. And this is Margo Sawyer, another friend."

The woman shook Claire's hand, reached to clasp Margo's next. "Hello. I'm Janine Rowlandson. I met Trish at the writers' group in Davisburg. We're all sorry about her passing. We will miss her wit and strength."

"Yes, we will. I'm on the way to the kitchen for tea. Would you like to hang up your coat, get something to drink? Come this way." Claire lead through the short hallway where they hung up the purple coat, past the front door and into the kitchen. Margo was asking about the writers' group. "We just found out recently that Trish was going out to Davisburg. It wasn't a part of her life she shared much, but there wasn't much time as it turned out."

Janine smiled, her eyes sparkling. "We didn't have her for very long, but it was a pleasure to share time with her. Such an old soul, so generous with her spirit. What a great laugh she had!" The gray-haired woman's eyes dimmed, smile fading like a light going out. "She was kind to me when I needed kindness very much."

Claire suddenly turned from the stove where she was fiddling with teabags and teapots. "Janine Rowlandson? I know that name. Let me…writers' group. Oh! You wrote *Pretty Pleas*. Did you? What a powerful book. Remember Margo? I made you read it. About 10 years ago maybe. Is that you?" Claire asked in an unusual voice for her, bordering on hero worship.

"I wrote it. More like 16 years ago now. Seems longer." Janine's voice faded, following where her smile had gone.

"There was another, wasn't there? Before or after, I don't remember." Margo watched the other woman's face, wondering about the untold story of the last 16 years.

"*The Anarchist's Toybox*. It came out the next year." Janine thanked Claire for the tea cup handed to her, and sighed, the sigh scurrying after the smile and the sparkle. "I haven't written anything since."

"How long have you been in the writers' group?" Margo asked, blowing on her tea, and the burn wound in Janine's words. "Do you meet at that sweet store still?"

"I've been going for a little over a year. My therapist sent me there, interestingly enough. Don't know how she knew about it, but I think she lived in the neighborhood. There is a core group of five or six, and others wander in and out. Trish said she found the store on a field trip with friends. Perhaps that was you?"

"Sure was," Claire answered. "We drove out one Saturday, and haven't been since. We just learned that Trish joined." Claire cast her eyes down for a moment. "Was Trish writing?"

Janine smiled. "I don't know. She didn't share anything at the group but herself and her encouragement. We'll miss her." Janine's face crumbled, its fine lines folding into grief-laden runnels, filling with tears. Claire moved quickly to put an arm around the huddled crying woman. Janine straightened and whispered, "I'm a 10 year cancer survivor and I never had the strength Trish had. She was so vibrant and alive. I can't believe she's gone."

Claire and Margo's eyes danced befuddled together in the center of the threesome. "Sorry," Janine said, extricating herself and reaching for a napkin on the counter. "I'm a mess. Trish would have something to say about all these tears." She set her unfinished tea on the countertop. "Trish and I shared water stories. I know she had a Dagger canoe." Claire and Margo nodded, unsure where this was headed. Janine fumbled in her coat pocket. "I don't think this is the time, and perhaps we might meet again one day? She left this note in my book bag a couple weeks ago - she wanted someone named Caldwell to have her Sojourn."

Margo and Claire stared at Janine. Neither reached for the note. Janine waved the note weakly. "Listen - sometimes it's easier to do this sort of thing through someone you don't know all that well. It's one way to keep the tears from drowning everyone around you, especially those you love very much. It's harder to watch a friend cry than it is to cry yourself. She just wanted this handled quickly after she was gone, is all. Doesn't mean anything about your friendship. I was honored to take the note for her. I'm sure you know there's a will that covers most of her other wishes. But I agreed to deliver this when the time came and that seems to be today."

"Caldwell's in the other room, as a matter of fact," Claire finally said. "He'd be the one to get the note."

Margo put her hand on Janine's arm. "Come on, I'll introduce you." Margo glanced over her shoulder to find Claire giving her the one-eyed Popeye look. Margo smiled. Claire smiled back, signaling with one raised eyebrow, in friend language - we'll analyze this all later, but soon, quite soon.

Margo introduced Janine to Caldwell, who had been standing talking with Dr. Amy by the fireplace, and hurried back to Claire, still in the kitchen. "What the hell?" Margo started, eyes wide. "Trish with a secret life?"

Claire tossed some more crackers on the cheese tray, moved it to the dining room table, brushed her hands in the sink, turned, crossed her arms and her legs. "If you think about it, Margo, most of Trish was a secret since the lymphoma. She lived quietly, even when she was with us. I think cancer cuts the crap between the folks who bear it. Bravery shared doesn't act like bravado among her own.

"Why do you think Dish joined the writers' group? To write? No. To share. Maybe share with Janine. It's probably the same for everyone who meets someone who carries a dreadful disease, or great grief. Remember Trish talking about trying to find a support group? She hated it; that she thought she needed one, and then she didn't like those she tried. She said if she was going to fight cancer she'd damn well do it with a sword and a sneer, not a sash and a sniff. Maybe Janine was meant to be found for Trish. For both of them. Seems likely."

"Do you remember *Pretty Pleas*, Claire?" Margo asked, eyes narrowed in concentration. "There's no way Janine Rowlandson wrote about that sort of childhood without having some experience of it. I'm going to check the library for *The Anarchist's Toybox*. I have a feeling we'll be seeing more of Janine."

Caldwell Spooner stood staring at the handwritten note the woman had given to him. "I don't understand why she's giving me her canoe. We didn't know each other well. Not yet." The flames from the fireplace danced mystically in his solemn eyes.

Janine glanced outside at the snowy land around Claire's house. "She was in a hurry to live, and to share those things she thought others would enjoy when she was gone," Janine said. She turned to smile at Caldwell. "We didn't know each other for long either, but she wanted me to deliver this note to you, I think. You must be a paddler. She hoped you'd use the Sojourn, didn't she?"

"Yes, I guess she did. Do you know the boat?"

"I borrowed one once just to try. It's too tippy for me. Trish must have been quite good to paddle that boat."

"I don't know. I only just met her a few weeks ago at the gallery where my daughter works. Claire's gallery." He made a sweeping gesture, encompassing the house as Claire's, too. "We went doubles paddling once. Trish sat in the bow, and had no difficulty there, even in her condition." He looked at the note, still extended in his hand, not having moved it since Janine explained it to him and laid it in his palm. "I'll have to think of a special trip to take it on. To thank Trish. Do you paddle?"

"Yes, I do."

Caldwell and Janine were in the sun room talking. The others milled about in small groups of two or three, quietly conversing when Margo and Claire rejoined the crowd. Dr. Amy was animatedly explaining something her listener was struggling to understand. Bob and Marion looked suspiciously close together in the corner in a decidedly non-work-related posture. Margo thought swiftly that she'd want to discuss this development with Trish right away, then clutched at her chest when she just as suddenly remembered that Trish would no longer be here to share secrets and speculations.

"Everyone?" Margo called in her strong clear voice, trained to act no matter the quaking heart. "Thank you all for being here today." She held her tea cup high. "To Patricia Ann Worthington. And a life well-lived. Näkemiin, Trish Our Dish. Soon again."

January of the first year without Trish warmly near began bleakly smudged, freezing snowy and empty. Margo's mood reflected the weather and Claire was glacially prone to cracking and biting cold. Since the night before New Year's Eve, the friends had stayed close to family, relishing the connection and the familiar, desperately trying to return the warmth to a chilly world. Claire and Margo had drifted into frigid uncharted waters, wandering bereft without their cheery captain at the helm.

Margo was as blue as the snow piled against her doorwall, the only color darting from the finches who frequented the feeder, and even the tiny flyers were dull and brown. She stared at the white world, idling one morning over her coffee and croissant. When the phone rang, Margo expected it to be one of her daughters, and was surprised to hear Claire's voice after her initial "hello?"

"Vik says I have to get out of the house," Claire confessed grumpily. "He suggested I call you about having lunch maybe."

Margo frowned. "If it's too much trouble…"

Claire growled. "That's not what I meant. I'd like to see you. We haven't talked much since the memorial brunch, and we both could use an airing, I think."

"We could. Yes. What do you think? Sushi, Thai or Indian? All right. I'll meet you at Garam at 1:00. Or do you want me to pick you up? Okay. See you there at 1:00."

Claire was the only person at a table in the tiny restaurant in Ypsilanti when Margo walked in at 12:50. Students who may have come for lunch from Eastern Michigan University were staying indoors, eating fast food. Claire was sitting at a window table with her coat still on, hands stuffed in her pockets. Her hair was in her face and Claire made no move to put it back when Margo sat down across from her, looking up at Margo through a raven veil.

"Aren't you at the gallery, Claire?" Margo was surprised at Claire's appearance.

"No, I'm not," Claire snapped, then softened. "Salinger and I had a fight. I think it's best I stay away for a little while."

"You told her you were doing that, yes?" Margo asked.

Claire practically sneered. "Yes, Margo, I called off work."

Margo stiffened. "I didn't come here to argue with you, Claire. I'd rather not. It's too hard right now."

"Don't I know that," Claire said, as she began to pull her coat off her shoulders. She occupied herself getting up, setting it on the chair back, smoothing imaginary wrinkles, then reseating herself, pulling the chair up to the table so she could set her elbows on it, head in hands.

Margo watched her from the corners of her eyes. She noticed the orchid, regally growing in a tiny pot on the windowsill, the ice lace at the corners of the windows, the white linen tablecloth, crisp ironed folds sliding under the sauce bowls and the paper-wrapped chopsticks. She noticed how slowly Claire moved, how her hands worked stiffly in tiny motions, rubbing her temples with purpose.

"Can you tell me what happened? With Salinger?"

"I happened," Claire sat back. "I spouted a lot of stuff before Christmas about how I was fine with the changes in my life. I was going to adjust to being older, to hearing 'ma'am' all the time instead of 'miss.' I would get used to my children being grown and having their own lives. The new girls at the gallery could be given more control over the art and the life of the shop, and I would content myself with doing things I always promised myself to do one day when I had the time," Claire sighed.

"What a load of crap," Claire confessed after a long pause. "It was probably hours after I'd said all that stuff that Salinger told me about the details of the spring puppet show. She'd asked about doing it, I'd said yes. I told you about it, how the new girls were getting it all organized. Salinger particularly was excited, happy with the contacts she'd made and the commitments for puppet commissions. She'd even reached a puppet theatre outfit in Africa, who had agreed to loan a couple of puppet characters. Some of what she's accomplished will be first American appearances. She's even got the PR lined up. Journalists are interested. It might be huge."

Claire hunched forward again, face cushioned in her palms.

"She was in the middle of telling me all this, simply keeping me informed, when I told her I'd changed my mind."

"Oh," Margo's comment was so unsubstantial, it disappeared before it reached Claire's ears.

Claire looked up from her study of the folds in the tablecloth, caught Margo's sympathetic look, and shrugged. "Salinger was crushed. We fought. I told her what you'd expect I would - that it was my gallery, my decisions, my choices, blah, blah, bladdy blah. I broke her heart, and then she gathered up the broken pieces and threw them at me with intent to do harm." Claire laughed abruptly. "For a fine arts-educated young lady, she sure has some salty language skills. She exploded a very blue word bomb all over my gallery."

The chopsticks Claire had picked up gestured in one sweeping motion. "She was right, Margo. I was wrong. I felt left out, like a kid who's grounded on Halloween: I did the best I could to recover some dignity, told her to continue doing what she was doing, and that I would be at home if she needed me for anything. She won't, Margo. I expect if I get any phone calls at all, it will be from the other New Girl. Whose name I still don't remember, damn it."

"You did the right thing, Claire." Margo soothed.

"But it was right after I'd done the totally wrong thing. From ego! I hurt her deliberately and maliciously. Teen-agers do that shit. Not grown women."

"Oh, yes we do," Margo disagreed. "Especially if we feel our territory is threatened, or the ground under our feet is squishy. Yes, we most certainly do. So much has changed in our lives, Claire! When we're young, change feels dramatic and seems important, but what is it really? A new house, a new job, change in styles. But now! Now. Change is profound. Careers changing, retirement, uneasy marriages, bodies weakening, children leaving home, parents ailing, menopause, finances out of whack, having to learn new life skills. Enormous changes. I don't know how we cope. Some manage better than others. Some aren't able to adjust."

"I can't just stay at home, take classes," Claire admitted.

Margo nodded. "I told Lynn I'd stay through January, since, well, since we have to replace Trish now as well. Not every day, just often enough to keep the work flowing smoothly. Maybe I was afraid to be without something to do, too."

Claire still sat, fondling the chopsticks, looking for solutions in a bit of paper, some sticks of carved wood. "Salinger's last volley before she slammed out of the shop hit home hard, Margo." Claire dropped the chopsticks abruptly, and leaned into Margo's gaze. "She said it is an older woman's obligation to help younger woman along the way. That is our duty."

"I don't know about that, Claire." Margo remarked quickly. "I just don't know what our duty is any more, what obligation must mean as we get older still. Is that what's left to us? Duty, obligation? Haven't we done all that already? Isn't it time to find the joy again? The fun? Damn duty. How is it a young woman can define duty for us?"

"I thought about what we saw at the accidental shop. Antoine and Saima, coming back to turn us around, straighten our pinafores, smack us on the butt, and send us out in the world to do what it is time for us to do. They were helping us, I think. Telling us that the future belongs to the next generation. That there is joy in letting go. It is the new girls now who will change the world, Margo."

"Margo," Claire started, then stopped. "Have you thought any more about The Artcraft Shop? Were you at all interested still in buying it? Or talking about buying it? Did Trish mention this idea of hers to you?"

Margo waited to answer, reluctant to abandon the discussion of duty, confused by the subject change and the idea of The Artcraft Shop, as they gave their orders to the owner, as their tea was delivered to the table, the cups filled, polite pleasantries exchanged. Margo held her cup in both hands, peering in it as though divining the answer to Claire's question.

"I have thought about it. Quite often since Trish insisted on us thinking about it. If we can figure out how to, and then agree to, the financing, I'm in, although I do not know what I can contribute," Margo smiled at her friend, whose face was peering at her with a small child's anticipation of a parent's nod. Margo smiled wider, raised her teacup to Claire's. "I think we'll make quite a successful team, with a little help from our friends. To adventures in retailing," and both women smiled as the teacups chimed together.

The drive home from Garam took Margo out of the Eastern Michigan University realm and close to the old neighborhood where Frasier and she had bought their first house. Margo smiled, remembering how hugely pregnant she was with Morgan, and the young couple in a big hurry to get into a new house before their first baby was born. Frasier was different then: eager, kind, looking forward to his law practice and his new family.

On a driving whim, Margo kept going straight past her turn, drove slowly down Golfside, turned on Packard and again on Hewitt. There was Ypsilanti High, where Morgan and Caroline would have gone to school if they hadn't moved when both were in junior high. She smiled at the memory of Morgan's brief anger at leaving her friends, changed into the chattering conversation about new friends when she started at the different school, happy with the adjustment she'd made in her young life.

And there was the house. Neighborhoods age as we do, thought Margo. Most of the houses on the street had belonged to newlyweds and young parents when she and Frasier had moved in. Now the folks shoveling snow were older, due to retire. The houses were harder to keep up as the years went by, until eventually the fixed income would force the elders to move out. And the young marrieds would take over once again. The houses would have facelifts and swing sets. That's one way people and houses are different, Margo mused. Houses are reborn.

Frasier and I were happy then, Margo thought suddenly as tears welled. We were in love and there was only good ahead for all of us. What changed? How did we move away from one another? Was it the pressures of career? Children? Is there a way to predict personality changes, prevent ennui from taking root in a relationship?

The man running his snow blower had stopped, and stood unabashedly watching Margo in her car. Embarrassed, she scrubbed her cheeks, put the car in gear, and moved slowly away from the past that she knew, onto the yellow brick road of the unknown future.

"You're a fraud, Janine Rowlandson."

Janine stood, head wrapped in a towel, hands on the sink edge, nose-to-nose with her reflection in the steamed bathroom mirror.

"So there. What you have always feared would come out if people knew you just has come out. You're a complete, utter, useless fraud."

Janine lowered her head from the accusing face, and caught her body, naked. After she listened to the voicemail on her cellphone, she'd dashed into the shower, befuddled by the tapes in her head, making a futile run for the exit. There's no exit, she admitted to her unflat belly and her swollen feet. No exit. She had turned the water hotter, hoping heat on her skin would jar her out of the confusion in her mind, accusations hurled from one old tape to the other, across the void that she had once identified as her higher self.

Now, dizzy from the too-hot shower, she sat abruptly on the toilet lid, slamming it shut before she landed. Head in hands, she wondered if her heart was going to stop twittering this time.

The message on the phone had been that the guys were heading home from the winter hideaway in the woods. The time for relishing being alone, and free to write was gone. She had not written enough yet. Time had fled by again, leaving Janine spinning in its swift passage, like a leaf in a whirlpool in winter water. She was ashamed of feeling regret, bitter about feeling ashamed.

She had run for the shower, wanting desperately to run far away, and knowing that there was no far away, only the tiny room that was her sacred sanctuary, around the corner in the basement space she occupied in her father's house. In the confines of the bathroom, she worked her mind like the squishy organ it was, kneading out the old labels: labels she'd taken up out of a past that supplied a rich and tainted thesaurus of names to call herself.

Selfish. Unworthy. Useless.

Janine hoped to watch the shame swirl down the drain, wielding the bath brush too hard, grinding the guilt out, knowing that even if she scrubbed her skin to scarlet, the shame would still be there, making her skin itch and burn.

Dutiful daughter, try as she might, she couldn't make herself feel better about wishing her father and brother weren't coming home just yet.

Swiftly, a movie on fast-forward, she watched the last years whiz by on the screen in her head. The jobs disappearing, the house in jeopardy of remaining in her hands, the fear and anxiety and, then moving into the basement at Dad's on his suggestion, the stunned realization of how old and frail he had become, watching her brother disappear into early-onset Alzheimer's Disease; the battle within to deny it all while submerged in it. How had Geri described it? The thrill of being able to breathe underwater and spitting out water at the same time.

I won't cry again, damn it, Janine screamed at her other self, the strong one, the face in the crowd that spoke out of her mouth when she was with other people. In her head she visualized slapping the weaker sister. Shame is a toxic emotion! Stop being stupid!

Cage fighting. Mortal combat in her head. *I have to clean the upstairs bathroom before they get back tomorrow. Is the refrigerator wiped? Will I listen to the complaints about the family who had gathered there for the holiday, and be quiet? Can I please, please not feel rage this time? Please?*

You have a right to be angry! It isn't your life that's bitter! This isn't your story!

But it was. There's the end to it. All the therapy, the work, the effort, the pain.

They'd talked about it in writers' group, early in a windy, wet spring. How hard it was to grow, how exciting and scary to examine the roots tugging tentatively at new ground in the changing geography of their middle years. How thrilling it was to find that others share your trepidation and tenuous joy, without judgment or scorn.

"Do you really want to help, or do you just want the credit? Do you send birthday cards because you want the best for the celebrant, or do you want to be remembered as the best birthday card sender ever? Do you forgive with no reservation? Was that exactly what you meant to say? Do you love with no expectation of love in return? Do you send light into the world, even when you think all around you is dark?"

"Where do you think the rest of the rainbow is?" To poke and prod and reveal hidden strengths, bright and brittle truths, because they could do that in a safe and loving environment. With friends.

Trish had spoken quietly one afternoon, sitting in the window at Higher Ground, sharing fragile, fragrant feelings. Janine remembered thinking Free Trade squared. The coffee we hold and the thoughts between new friends. Trish had been quiet for a spell, watching the sky, while the leaves danced along the sidewalk, the naked tree branches waving good-bye as the last of their older children wandered off into the world, still waiting for the next generation to be born green and tender in the spring.

In the schizoid sky, half bright blue, half thick gray wool, a barely visible sliver of rainbow played tag with the ghost moon. A cloud plume, so tall it looked like the sun was smoldering, as though a gigantic deity had tried to douse the fire, drifted toward the game to join the fun.

"Some days I cannot stand how shallow I am," Trish said softly to the window. Janine looked up from her study of the reflected world in her coffee. "My mother was so strong and brave at the end. I've thought often how I'd like to be like her, when the time comes. Quietly resolved." Trish moved on her stool, recrossed her legs, fiddled with the cup, turning it with both hands. She looked up at Janine and smiled a brief and bitter smile. "I'm not that brave. I don't have the courage. I'm a sham."

"You're not, Trish," Janine disagreed.

Trish smiled a bright, watery smile. "I'm not, huh? How about you?"

Janine frowned. "It's not the same. My life was never threatened; it wasn't a future I had to peer at too closely."

"Yes, it was, Janine," Trish shook her head. "It most certainly is. And you're facing it still this minute. Aren't you? We want desperately to believe that even if we judge ourselves harshly throughout life, at least at the end, we can pull off a victorious and elegant exit. Every single minute we survive is a triumph that we must celebrate with fierce joy. There is a word 'chantepleure' - means to sing and cry at the same time. It is what we both must do. Relentlessly, even when we stumble. We must admire and revere ourselves, even if we cannot endure."

Janine fought back the tears that wrestled to launch from her eyes. "I thought I had this licked. Four years of therapy and I was beginning to feel as though I had said good-bye to the fear, self-loathing, the survivor guilt. My mind knows what it needs to, but my subconscious doesn't play well with others."

"Circumstances change. The familiar becomes the unfamiliar. Chaos picks up the crown again." Trish shrugged. "I never studied philosophy, and know just enough to be a pain in the ass, but I think moving back with a senior parent has to be a difficult adjustment. You've been on your own for...what? 40 years?"

Janine smiled. "My dad will call out instructions for making salmon mold that I've made myself for nearly that long. Parents don't stop being parents just because their kids belong to AARP and are studying their social security report late at night."

Trish laughed. "And the kids don't stop being the 5 year olds caught stuffing the cat into their backpacks. Why don't you write about this? There are thousands, maybe millions of grown women who are either back at home caring for a parent, or doing their best from another location. You're not the only one. Maybe it will help you feel less odd and isolated?"

"I've tried," Janine admitted. "A woman who came once to writers' group, when I was talking about some of the daily stuff, and wondering about writing about it, said, 'wow, you're going to have to get rid of the rage first.'"

Trish smiled. "Nice snap judgment. No, I think the rage is the truly personal part of it. I can't imagine living with my mother, bless her beautiful brow, when she was in her 70s. She didn't live to her 80s, but gee, I can't believe her temper would have improved. No, I'd have done almost anything to avoid being in the same house for any length of time. And you do it every day!

"My point is," Trish leaned forward, shoulders hunched, palms extended flat on the table near Janine's own clasped hands. "There are women out there who feel just as guilty, just as ashamed, just as angry, and think they're crazy because they feel that way. We're all afraid, Janine. Everyone."

Trish the Dish laughed suddenly, the joyicity of it winging jubilantly into the brilliant blue world. "Margo, my friend, says 'If we cannot be fearless, let us be fleet.' You can help, Janine; you can help us all. You can ease our pain. You can remind us we are not alone."

"I cannot get out of my own way," Janine observed quietly, confessing to Trish as priestess in the sanctuary of Higher Ground. "I collect pens, paper, ink. I block myself with accoutrement and research and… *things* until I'm too exhausted to write. I'm not ready yet," Janine demurred in a tiny voice. "Some day perhaps, but not yet."

"I know," Trish said, her voice so insubstantial, Janine wondered if those were the words exactly. "We all worship at the altar of 'Some Day.'"

Janine felt a stab of selfishness. Of course, how clumsy can I be? she accused herself. Trish did not have years to be prepared for a game of interstellar tag. She was on the warm-up deck, time measured in tiny jerks, not grandiose circles. How did anyone prepare for that leap? Janine was about to murmur some words of comfort, when Trish slapped both hands emphatically back down on the table.

"Well. The smallest effort we can make is to stop playing a waiting game with a Being who has a millennium hand on Her watch. How about this, then? Let's you and I make a pact. Let's agree to be gentle with ourselves. For a day. For now. For this afternoon. We'll work on the rest of our lives another time."

Janine stood up, dropped the wet towel from her head to the floor, remembering the quiet warmth of understanding, and feeling the hot poke of knowing that Trish would not be there tomorrow; not there ever again. No more lovely conversations in the upstairs coffee shop; the blue sky outdoors and the blue sky on the ceiling at Higher Ground.

She dropped her hands to her sides, defeated again. "I hate this," she whispered to the empty bathroom. *Hate is too strong a word*, the memory of her mother's voice whispered from the walls. *You can't hate. You dislike.* "Stop it!" Janine screamed, throwing her hands over her ears. "Stop telling me how to feel!" Janine fought the ugly urge to scream and scream until she could not stop, until her voice, disappearing into the void, carried her with it.

The weary woman picked up the towel, hung it on the rack. Tomorrow would arrive, no matter how she felt about that. She would do the best she could for at least this afternoon, as she had agreed that autumn day with the blue, blue sky. Bless your memory, Trish, my friend. Tomorrow she would join the writers' group and have that precious feeling of far away for a little time, and conjure the spirit and light of Patricia Worthington. She could surround herself with people who wished her only well. Women who, even if they knew how weak and selfish she really was, might still be glad to share space and conversation with her.

She squelched her stomach's demand to heave its contents, ran the cold water hurriedly, splashed some on her face, poured water into a glass and slurped small sips, set the glass trembling back on the sink. For right now, she had another bathroom to clean.

Claire remembered Colasanti's as she passed it this Saturday early afternoon. The pond was frozen, except for a small space of open water in which ducks, geese and swans paddled in tiny circles, wing to wing. Claire tried not to think of the fowled water, and turned her attention back to the road, which wandered from clear to windswept ice in the open spaces.

Chantepleure

She'd made up her mind last minute to drive to Davisburg to meet the writers who Trish had found. Vik had listened to her fumbled explanation of where she was going with one cheek elevated to receive her good-bye kiss, happy in his garage tinkering, and anxious to have her somewhere farther out of his tool clanking realm.

Claire didn't know what she expected, but she was determined nonetheless to carry on. She turned right on Highland Road, remembering to slow down through downtown Highland, the gun shop sign expanding their offerings to include buying anything of value. Tough times, even for gun stores, thought Claire.

Ormond Road was a changed route in the leafless world of January in Michigan. Snow clung to the tree stems like blisters where it had been propelled by the plows, more picturesquely where the wind had settled a recent blizzard on the trunks. Claire tapped her brakes rapidly on the S curve she remembered as beautiful in the autumn, the orange-crowned trees now shivering, leafless, like skinny elders without their sweaters, shooing her along to return to their winter reverie.

There were no parking spaces on the street when Claire slowly drove into Davisburg proper, and she turned around to move back up the hill, parked the car, walked in the street to the store, avoiding the partially cleared sidewalk, then stomped her boots when she reached the pavement in front of Sweetgrass, took a deep breath and pushed open the wooden door.

The bell over the door tinkled.

Claire smiled, remembering the aromas from their first visit, finding the same fragrances wafting in the warmed air. Several women standing turned to the door, smiles still on their faces. "Hello," someone greeted. "Welcome," said another voice.

The crystals hanging from a display to her left twinkled a greeting in their prism language, and a white cat sauntered up to meow at Claire's feet, rubbing white fur welcomingly against her wet boots, although the feline darted away when she bent to stroke its coat. From a room beyond the counter, another woman emerged.

Janine smiled when she saw Claire at the door, and walked briskly to greet the new arrival, her hand rising in a gesture of welcome and peace. Claire took a cleansing breath, and moved forward to say hello to the women of Sweetgrass herself.

Chapter 9

Was that the garage door? thought Margo, swimming upward out of deep sleep toward the surface of awake. Swiftly alert, focused on the sound of the back door opening, she threw the covers back in an adrenaline surge that launched her to her feet, rigid with fear. God! No weapon in the bedroom. She picked up a picture that at least had sharp edges, she tiptoed to the bedroom door, flipped the light switch, simultaneously afraid to look past the door opening, and terrified to be caught in the room without an exit.

Frasier stumbled over the hassock in the dark by the doorwall, swearing softly. Margo dropped her shaking arm, poised with the picture to fling it at the intruder. "Frasier!" she expelled with her pent breath, relief and fury spinning entwined into the living room. "What the hell are you doing?"

Frasier wobbled, peering into the darkness, trying to focus on the apparition that Margo made in the light from the bedroom. He had left the doorwall open, the January wind rattling the vertical blinds like bones in a movie. Margo shivered with cold and fright retreating. "Damn it, Frasier, what are you doing?"

"You left the doorwall open, Margo. I've told you not to leave the door open when I'm not home."

"This is not your home, Frasier. What are you doing here?" Margo stopped suddenly, intent on his slurred words. "Have you been drinking? Are you drunk?"

"What do you care? Careful, Margo. That's a lot of interest from such a disinterested wife." He waved both hands floppy in the air, dismissing the interruption. "I'm tired. I need some sleep. I'm going to bed."

"You're not sleeping here, Frasier. Did you drive? Where's your car?" Margo moved, picture still clutched in one hand, to pass Frasier to slide the doorwall closed.

Frasier grabbed her arm before she was by.

"I'll sleep where I like," he said.

Margo went rigid with loathing. "And so you have done. Let go of my arm. Immediately." Frasier held her forearm tighter, teeth clenched in a cartoonish imitation of sober anger, eyes squinted at her face. Margo gasped as a wave of pain from his fingers wove up her arm. "Let go!" she yelled, and moved to pull her arm away harder, just as Frasier's other arm swung upward, palm flat and slapped her in the temple with such force, Margo saw stars.

She dropped the picture on the carpet; Frasier stumbled backward as Margo, catching the forgotten hassock with the back of both legs, fell over it and unable to get a handhold on anything at all, hit the floor backwards hard.

When she finally lifted her head to get back on her feet, Frasier was gone. Margo sat on the floor, gathering her body back in order, held her hand in front of her face and watched it bobble like a broken neck doll. She leaned toward the couch, grabbed the cushion with her nails, and dragged herself up on it, so that she could turn and sit. You're not hurt, she told herself over and over. You're fine. You're not hurt. You're fine.

She breathed deeply, herding her hammering heart like it was a small child; away from the danger toward safety. She stood tentatively, standing still for a spell, then walked slowly to the powder room, turned on the light, leaning on the doorjamb for a moment, then walked to the sink, looked in the mirror. Blue shown faintly behind the skin near her eyebrow, colorful evidence of the dull pain hovering within, preview of the purple and yellow that would undoubtedly follow.

She reached for the glass to have a drink of water, and her trembling hand knocked it to the tiled floor. Her heart fluttered like a hummingbird trapped in a pine bough. Little bubbles rose in her throat and burst, as though her heart was drowning, spitting blood into her lungs. Clutching the sink with both hands, shaking like a sapling in a high wind, her face crumpling along the tiny trails in her lined face, she wept in despair when she realized that she had wet her nightgown.

"Did you drive yourself? Is anyone with you?" the young man in the white coat asked, having been summoned immediately after Margo had told the woman behind the desk in the emergency room that she thought she was having a heart attack. He gently guided Margo to the wheelchair he had brought with him. "Please sit. We're going to get some tests done. Are you faint? Have you passed out?"

Margo was having trouble hearing. She was trapped in a surreal bubble of heart noise and lung panic, everything else paling into a background of white and white and more white. She could only hear her heart beating erratically, eyes half-closed she could see her pulse smeared in a fluttery veil over the hospital emergency room surroundings. Black, white; black, white.

"Mrs. Sawyer? Can you get on the gurney? Okay. Just lie back, that's right. We're taking you to x-ray. Can you hear me? Mrs. Sawyer?" The overhead lights whipped by in a blur of light trails. Dark, light; dark, light. Dark, dark, dark.

She was in a tunnel moving swiftly beyond reason backward away from a tiny pinpoint of light in the diminishing distance. She heard her heart slow, the metronome that dictated the speed of her life's waltz, louder and slower until it was all she knew in the blackness.

And then she heard voices. "Blood pressure coming back up, Doctor." Margo opened her eyes, blinked to clear the remaining tendrils of oblivion. A pretty young nurse smiled at her. To her immediate right, a ridiculously handsome face peered at Margo. "Wow," was all Margo could say, her voice muffled by the oxygen mask. The nurse laughed. "Yeah, I know what you mean." And she turned to adjust a knob on the machine beside her. "Mrs. Sawyer," said the young man in the white coat, the fashion model version of an emergency room resident that Margo could only think of as G.Q. Doctor.

"We don't think you've experienced a heart attack, but we're going to run further tests to be sure. We're going to admit you; you'll be transferred very soon to a room. Your blood pressure and heart rate dropped rapidly and you passed out, but again, we don't believe it was a cardiac episode. Someone will be along shortly to take you to your room. I'm going to take the oxygen mask away now. No, it's okay, let go - you don't need the oxygen now. Mrs. Sawyer, let go, please. Is there anyone we can call for you?"

The frozen evening mist was huddled around the building like cattle at a fence in a Montana blizzard. Claire hustled through the hospital parking lot an hour after the hospital called about Margo, moving as quickly as her stupid legs would allow her. She'd mentioned this newly manifested intermittent leg weakness to Viktori last month, chatting idly in companionable pillow talk, musing that she hoped it would pass soon. "It won't, Claire," Vik had pronounced as he moved her body to get his arm around his wife.

"What do you mean?"

"It's age, my love. Aging is not something you get over like a summer cold."

Claire prayed that whatever was ailing Margo was as simple as a summer cold, as she slammed through the emergency room door, cornered a nurse, and found out where they were keeping her best friend.

"Not a heart attack? What does that mean? Can these medical people figure out what it is by identifying what it is not? How long are they going to keep you before they figure out how to treat what it is?" Claire was irate, panicked at the sight of an uncoifed, pale and diminished Margo in a hospital bed with an IV stand for company. "Is that a black eye? How did you get that? Did you faint?"

"Easy, old girl," Margo cautioned. "I don't want you in the bed next to me."

"Old girl, my cellulite-riddled butt. Where did you get the black eye?" Claire asked this question with a cadence that allowed significant white space between the words; the blanks hinting at dark mayhem in store for whatever or whomever had injured her beloved Margo.

Water pooled in Margo's eyes, and she held her stomach with both hands. "I can't tell you until I get the visual of your butt out of my head." Claire was relieved Margo was laughing, not crying, but she wondered how closely behind the laughter the tears were shadowing.

"Tell me or I'll moon you," Claire threatened, as she hovered over the guest chair she had pulled up to the side of the bed, waiting for her friend to decide whether Claire would reveal the imagined body part, or park it on the seat.

"Sit. Please." Margo said softly, erasing the mock horror from her face. When Claire was seated, smiling at Margo, Margo told her how she got the black eye.

Claire was off the seat in a flash. "What? WHAT? Damn him. We'll press charges. Damn! Wait until Viktori hears this. He *hit* you! Margo!" but, seeing the plea in Margo's eyes, her hand pawing the air as though she were soothing the rage Claire spilled into the room. Claire altered her tone. "How awful for you! Is that what triggered the heart attack?"

"It wasn't a heart attack, they said it wasn't, Claire."

Claire fell back onto the seat cushion, anger spent, worry picking up the tab. "What was it then?"

"Don't know." Margo closed her eyes. "I can feel my heart beating. It's not right."

Claire jumped up once more. "Should I get someone?"

"No, I don't think so. Just stay and talk with me awhile, please, Claire. I'm sad and frightened." Claire scooted the chair forward without rising and took Margo's hand in both of hers. "I'm here, my friend. I'm here. I won't leave you."

Claire left Margo sleeping. She asked for, and found the cafeteria. There hadn't been that much time when Trish was here to go exploring for coffee. When there was food or drink, the kind nurses had brought it to Trish's room for the vigilant friends

Claire sat, coffee untouched, staring out the window, past her own tired reflection. She narrowed her eyes and focused outdoors as the bushes wiggled to shake the snow off their boughs with the wind's assistance. A snow bundle loosened and, in the split second before it fell to the ground, a sparrow, sitting on the branch, jumped into the air, and then landed again on the bare branch. If it were only that simple, Claire thought. Jump up, the cold, wet and foreign is gone, and you're right where you're supposed to be. She snorted, sighed. Making analogies from winter's hijinks. Just as she dismissed her goofy thoughts, the sparrow looked directly at her, cocked its head as though to say "why not?" and flew away into the gray morning.

Why not, indeed, thought Claire, as she flipped her phone, dialed a number and waited while it rang.

Dr. Amy moved like a broken field runner past the cafeteria tables, most empty in the predawn world of a major university hospital. Yawning men and women in University of Michigan scrubs dotted the room with dark blue. Claire watched her approach and knew that Dr. Amy came with professional intent sweeping the spaces in front of her.

"What do the doctors say?" she asked straight away as she sat next to Claire. "What's the diagnosis?"

Claire smiled, wanting oddly to hug this bristly woman on a mission of mercy. "It's not a heart attack. That's it so far," said Claire, running both hands through her hair, and then crossing her arms. You should know there was an altercation with her husband just before she started experiencing the chest pain. He hit her. I don't think he was strictly sober, and Margo doesn't seem to want to discuss it, but I wonder if that's not what triggered whatever happened."

Dr. Amy stood up, shifted the strap of her purse back on her shoulder. "I'm going to find the doctor who admitted her. I'll be back. Wait to call her daughters until we check if that's acceptable to Margo. She might want to make those calls herself later."

Claire pulled a Popeye face at Amy's back and then grinned. She'd called precisely the right person. She picked up her cold coffee, grimaced at the taste, and went to replace it with a hot, fresh brew.

There was a muffin tin sky lowering over the day when Claire walked back to her car, hours later, physically and emotionally drained. She had left Margo in the care of her daughters. Dr. Amy had left soon after returning to Claire in the cafeteria with the news that there were still no answers, but Margo was resting comfortably and had called Caroline and Morgan. Claire waited to hug the young women as they arrived, and to soothe Morgan who wanted to focus on the anger she felt. Claire wondered how much she'd been told, or if Morgan was just mad regularly lately. She hadn't seen Margo's oldest in too long. Caroline hurried up to her mother's room, but Morgan lingered, simmering for a little while longer before she too, hugged Claire good-bye and went to her mother's bedside.

Claire called her husband from the car before she drove away, the expected heat quickly starting up, engine smoothed. "Vik? How's your schedule? Can you meet me at home? She's going to be fine, it wasn't a heart attack. They're running some tests. I'm okay, honey, but I need a huge hug. Would you meet me at home? Yeah. No, I'll call Jaqueline later. Nikolas phoned? Nice. I'll see you in a little bit. I love you too, baby." She flipped the phone shut. "You're a lucky woman, Claire Chernikova," she sighed contentedly, and putting the car in gear, pulled out of the parking spot, going home to a man who would change his plans for the entire day just to give her a hug.

Claire walked hesitantly into her own gallery the following day, having unlocked the Monday closed front door. She quietly flipped the lock shut once more, and turned to find Salinger walking to the front of the shop, frowning slightly but trying to look pleased to see Claire at the door. Claire waited until she was within hearing distance, and began her prepared speech. "I came to apologize to you, Salinger. I spoke to you in a way I would not want to be addressed, and I belittled your work and disrespected your autonomy. I'm deeply sorry."

Salinger watched her for a space of time that Claire began to think of, in turn, as disrespectful, and then quickly the young woman moved forward, stuck out her hand, which Claire took, confused, until Salinger said, "Good. Apology accepted. That was hard to do, and I appreciate your effort and consideration." Salinger smiled happily. "I had some questions I didn't know whom to ask if you weren't talking to me. Would you like to discuss them now? Have you the time?"

Claire relaxed visibly, and although she knew she was being flattered, she was glad to be asked to share what she knew. They walked to the back room while Claire took off her coat, answered polite questions about her well-being and family. Claire stopped, stunned by the jammed hallway past the washroom. There was a barely-there path between cardboard boxes and unpacked flotsam. Salinger's voice hurried into the silence to explain. "Puppets have started arriving, but most of this is display material. I thought it would be interesting to suspend small lights from the ceiling with real string, leave the overhead gallery lighting off for the duration of the show, move some of the halogen feature lights onto critical pieces only. Come this way, let me show you, watch the peanuts - they jump at wool. Nothing personal. Static."

Claire listened as Salinger explained her display ideas, pushing the urge to guide and take lead back down into her belly where she kept stuff for later, to talk over with Vik in private. "The gallery will still make money without you watching the till, sweetheart," he said last night as they lay in bed talking before sleep. "This show is Salinger's baby, Claire. Let her birth it." Claire's head rested on Vik's chest; his voice rumbling basso profundo in her ear. "Find your own new baby to start." He raised his body, rolling Claire off onto the bed, and then leered over her, waggling his bushy eyebrows at close range. "I know where babies come from. Want me to show you?"

If there was new creative life left for Claire, she'd find another den to nest. She was able to put her hand on Salinger's shoulder, and say, without reservation, "Salinger, you know exactly what to put in the window. I'm not worried about your decisions. You know what you're doing and I'm darn proud of you. You must be proud of you, too. Now. Relax and enjoy all this fuss and bother. The excitement is not far behind."

Claire rumbled past Magyo with a paper bag clutched underneath a glass dish, her scarf wrapped around her face so that her eyes were all that showed, protection from the subzero wind Margo shut out when she closed the front door behind Claire.

"What in the name of all that's holy is that?" Margo asked, pointing to the glass dish Claire deposited on the kitchen counter, its contents blood red and murky.

"That, my wonderful healing friend, is Viktori's mother's borscht," Claire pronounced behind the scarf, before she unwound it and removed her mittens. "Not hers literally, of course. Her recipe. I make it once in a blue moon, and this, Margo, is absolutely a blue moon. Good medicine. Make well," Claire thumped her chest with her fist, and Margo laughed. "And," Claire turned to flourish the paper bag, "in case you're not bonzo for borscht, this is carryout from Dragontown. Also good medicine, make well."

Margo smiled tenderly and felt the flush of friendship flood her body. Claire, always a boon companion and a delight to be around, even when she was a crotchety curmudgeon, had been especially gentle and attentive for the last three weeks, as Margo dealt with, first, the shock of discovering she was now the victim of serial panic attacks, and second, the depression that accompanied the dismantling of her world as she had known it. *Past tense knowledge,* Dr. Amy said. *When what you know doesn't work for you any more.*

"Did you ever think I was clinically depressed?" Margo had asked, a little girl in unfamiliar woods in the dark night with no moon. "Did you know this, Claire?"

Margo was being released from the hospital then, due to leave the clinical green walls of her room; the memory of tiptoeing out into the hall in her backless gown, peering at the other rooms to discover by herself that she wasn't on the psych floor as she feared. The dreaded night terrors that spawned a flurry of body jerks and pings; the panicked button-pushing that brought an attendant to tell her, no, it was too soon for more medication, perhaps wiping the sweat from her night-soaked hair, perhaps not this time.

"Margo, I don't know anything about anything right now," Claire had answered her the morning of her release. "There isn't anyone else to ask. It would make some sense, I suppose, to say that, but these people don't know you; your story, your life. Don't judge yourself too much. Please don't spend time on anything but recovering for a long time. The panic attacks are the focus. How do you hope to tackle those?"

"It's so funny how life works, even without us turning the gears," Margo mused. "It was the perfect instinct to call Dr. Amy when you did." Margo looked up from her study of the clothes she had on, ready to leave the hospital and start redefining normal. "I called her this morning myself. She has agreed to help me get through this. She thinks it might be good for both of us to learn more about each other. Claire, the woman I spoke to on the phone this morning is not the woman I've talked with before." Margo nodded once ruefully. "I suppose I'm not the woman I was before either."

Claire touched Margo's knee, moved her hand to the fragile friend's elbow. "Whoever you are, let's blow this popstand," and together, they had walked into the new world beyond the hospital parking lot.

"And now here you are, bearing borscht," Margo brought herself back to her kitchen and the rosy cheeks of Claire Chernikova, trusted friend, magical healer.

"Are you still ready to do this? I can meet the man myself, Margo, if you're not up to it. He's a classic curmudgeon - it took three phone calls to get him to stop hanging up on me. I have a visual of him in my head: skinny, ancient, toothless, cranky. Not exactly what one would hope in the owner of a place called The Artcraft Shop. There's a story to be told there, for sure. I just hope he's willing to get past the nasty parts and sell the place to us. At the least, he's agreed to meet with us. We'll work on him from there."

Margo shook her head. "I can do this. I think the flutter I'm feeling today is excitement, not fear. There is a tiny little yellow light that is struggling to grow up in my stomach. If you don't mind though, you do the talking. I still can't be trusted not to start bawling without warning."

The women bundled into winter gear, dressing in solemn ceremony like warrior goddesses preparing for war, silent and formal, donning the mental armor to assure inexorable victory while pulling on big boots to repel winter's wrath.

"Margo," Claire began tentatively as she pushed the gear shift into reverse, backing her car through the froth of exhaust moisture, crystallizing in the freezing temperature. "Margo, Annie asked if she could come with us. I told her I'd ask, but if you're not comfortable with her coming, that's fine."

"Oh, absolutely. She'll add a pink light. Yes, of course, she can come along." Margo felt the little spark in her belly get brighter.

"This is so cool, Grandma!" Annie enthused, leaning forward into the tiny driver's compartment of the car, arms resting on the back of the seats. "I told Mom that when your new store is opened, I'll have two places to work. Salinger already said I could work part-time in the summer at the gallery." Claire raised her eyebrow at Margo, gave her the Popeye look, and Margo smiled widely back, winking. "Dad and Mom said I could have a car when I'm 17, if I pay my own insurance, so if I have two places to work, then I'll be able to earn enough over the summer to have a car. So exciting, isn't it, Aunt Margo?"

Claire called the shop owner to tell him they were on their way, give the old man one more chance to turn them back. "He's thinking he'll say no," Claire analyzed, as she put her phone back in her handbag. "He's mad he agreed to meet. This isn't going to be easy, but we'll get a foot in the door anyway. Anastasia, please try to keep as still as you can while we're there, it's going to be dicey as it is and really old folks don't always share your enthusiasm. All right, troops, everybody ready? We're here. Onward into battle."

The wizened man who flung open the door was even older than Claire or Margo had imagined. His thin-lipped mouth was drawn tightly across his lower jaw, the jutting chin reminding Margo of cartoon renditions of the merciless landlord, minus the swirling moustache. He was bald, the dome mottled with age spots and small abrasions. He wore a white t shirt, yellowed at the neck from long wear, egg stains dripped on the big-bellied front overlapping old coffee marks. Sweat pants couldn't hide the thinness of his legs, the pale veined feet stuffed into deerskin moccasins, the laces untied. He said nothing, made a half-hearted gesture to follow him, turned, walked to a sagging and tipped lounge chair, and dropped from upright to seated in one swift motion. His hands rested on the padded arms like an eastern potentate, regal and resolute.

Claire and Margo continued to stand, uncomfortable without further instructions, convinced now this visit was folly, not knowing how to extricate themselves without admitting instant defeat, like children caught too soon in a nighttime game of hide-and-seek by a wicked old witch.

Annie poked her head around her grandmother, sidled to the front, took one small step toward the stern oldster, and asked politely, "is it okay if we sit down please?"

Claire felt a chill, and Margo glanced quickly at Annie, confused, catching a sidelong flash of movement. The three standing stared unabashedly at the old man seated on his tattered throne. With Annie's words, his face had changed; a watercolor painting still wet and flowing, color leaking into the sunken cheeks, eyes clearing, the pale color sharpening in hue; mouth slackening, then reforming. His eyes opened wider, and leaning forward, he peered at Anastasia as though she was an exotic and compelling sea creature.

Annie stepped back into line with the older women, listing toward her grandmother, seeking contact with the familiar. The old man slumped, leant back against the chair, closed his eyes, hung his head. The women did not move. He spoke without opening his eyes. "You're not the first who wanted The Artcraft Shop. I won't sell it. I…can't sell it."

He snapped his eyes open, raising his knobby hand, pointing a long, bent knuckled finger at Anastasia. "Who are you?" Annie put her arm through her grandmother's, shrinking closer to her body, and Claire answered, "My granddaughter. Her name is Anastasia Renė." Having found her voice again, Claire kept it alive. "My granddaughter is named for my husband's mother and my own mother. She wants to work in a shop to pay for her car insurance. This is my friend, Margo. She needs to have good work in a business she owns so she can get better. She has not been well. I am Claire, and I need to learn how to step aside, proud of work well done, and let the young people in my world have their own future." Claire ran out of confidence at the same time Anastasia rediscovered hers. "We love The Artcraft Shop, sir. We think it can be born again, if someone loves it. We love it very much, sir."

The old man's lower lip trembled, his eyes misting, awash like a baby with an upset stomach, miserable and surprised. "You look like her," he whispered, tears now spilling onto his shirt to soak the egg and coffee. Annie impulsively stepped to the chair, laid her hand on his. He raised it to hold the young girl's hand. "It was my wife's dream: her gift, her work, her joy."

He smiled a weak watery smile at Annie. "You are the age she was when I first met her, and fell forever in love. I thought I'd met an angel, and I never, never once thought otherwise. 50 years we were married. I miss her so!" He wept in lonesome misery; Annie, kneeling on the floor, stroked his hand and cried in sympathy, as Claire and Margo still stood, amazed, awestruck, and holding hands.

Chapter 10

The bell over the door tinkled.

Edgar, his arms full of file folders capped with an upside-down coffee cup, got tangled in the tattered curtains on the door of The Artcraft Shop, tripped two steps forward and dropped the load on the floor, breaking the cup that scattered its remains among the papers. Caldwell, his arms equally as full, set his load quickly down on the old glass counter, and examining the mess, swiped both hands through his hair, holding clutches of it upright. Edgar was staring at the pile, transfixed.

"It's all right, Edgar," Caldwell said, clapping the younger man on the back. "At least nothing landed in the toilet. Maybe we should move that thing out of the way." Stooping and laughing, he reached to collect the pottery shards first.

Edgar said nothing. Suddenly he turned and ripped the threadbare, dirty drapery from the door. Caldwell laughed again. Edgar smiled dimly and shrugged. "Fewer obstacles might help," Edgar said as he knelt to help retrieve what he'd dropped. When they were sure all the cup pieces were gathered, the two men carefully assembled the papers and put them back in their folders. Done, Caldwell straightened his back and looked around.

"I hope those two women know what they're in for," Caldwell warned, observing the tin ceiling with the cracks exposing the second floor, the boarded windows at the front, the caked and filthy floor. "I saw Claire at the gallery the other day and she was positively cheerful. She said that when they were at the bank, signing the papers, Margo began to write her name with a purple pen. The bank person said, 'I'm sorry, but you can't use a purple pen to write a check.' Margo smiled, eyes open wide, and said, 'On the contrary. It's the only possible color to use!' And Claire laughed when she was telling the story."

Caldwell shook his head, further rearranging his disarrayed mop of hair. "Annie and that old man are best friends now, according to Claire. Annie brings him borscht, of all the awful brews to visit on a senior." Caldwell grimaced like a kid with liver on his plate for dinner.

"They'll have help with the shop," Edgar offered, his gleaming teeth suddenly revealed in a Cheshire cat grin. "From more than one dimension. Trish leaving Claire and Margo the proceeds from the sale of her house to buy this place was a gift from beyond.

"I'm not clear on all that is happening with this store, Spoon, but I can't help thinking that it will all work out in the end. I don't understand so far, but it feels interesting." He nodded as though confirming his opinion. "Yes, what it is, is exciting." He laughed out loud, one burst of jocularity.

"You know, I'm used to a physical system that speaks a language whose grammar consists of the laws of physics. Quantum mechanics. Physical systems respond to energy, force and momentum. Light and sound. Electricity and gravity." Edgar wiped his hands on his jeans, turned slowly around, taking in the surroundings. "Perhaps there are other systems that respond in a similar way. Perhaps a vision in a dream can find three dimensional life, if enough people believe. Yes, it's definitely exciting."

"You keep thinking that, Edgar. We're all going to need your enthusiasm." Caldwell gingerly scooped an armload of papers. "It's snowing again. Let's get the paper stuff in out of the weather, and then we'll tackle the furniture. Margo said she'd be here after lunch, and we're going to have to explain our lack of progress if we don't hustle."

Edgar was alone in the dusty, disheveled dim light, sitting on the dirty floor, wondering futilely how he had seen what he knew he had seen when he'd first stumbled into the shop that windy October morning. Caldwell had left with the truck to pick up another donated piece, although why they were moving things *in*, when more dirt and disorder still had to definitely go *out*, Edgar was not sure.

He wanted Monsieur Lavoisiere back. He needed to ask him more questions, to watch the merry light in his blue eyes as he talked with gentle fondness about work that healed, work to love, work a person could accomplish with joy for a lifetime. But Lavoisiere was gone, taking with him the spiderweb Edgar now would like to climb. Trish, the friend who gave joy to his new women friends, was gone as well.

"Gone is all right, I suppose, in a bad habit or a virus," Edgar thought aloud, staring at the beautiful wooden box that held Trish's ashes, reposing on the glass counter at The Artcraft Shop, awaiting the friends' trip to northern Michigan to tuck Trish in for her long rest. "Gone is not good in a best friend."

"Define 'gone,'" encouraged a paper-thin voice from Edgar's left shoulder. He spun around, leaping to his feet, momentarily disapparating the misty humanoid form before she realigned into a reasonably corporeal likeness of the living woman.

"I'm so sorry, Edgar," Trish the Dish apologized, her voice as wispy as her countenance, there, but not quite there. "I did not want to frighten you. I wanted to help you, and I'm not good at that from where I am quite yet. There's something about the whole appearing business I can't get the hang of, but," she smiled a translucent grin, "I'll catch on eventually, if I need to, although," Trish turned dreamily around, "I may not need to do this much longer. You all have been working hard, haven't you?"

Edgar collapsed against the counter, putting his hand out for support, he touched the wooden box with the ashes of the spirit talking to him. "Goodness! My word, I mean, um, this is altogether confusing. I, you, he, is all this real?"

Trish laughed a merry misty chuckle. Define 'real.' Oh, Edgar, again, I am sorry, it's a shock, I know. I remember walking into this lovely shop and seeing my grandmother sitting on that stool, as pert and pretty as she'd been before she moved on." She posed a pouty face, looking up at Edgar through lashes with color, if not substance. "It takes one by surprise to say the least."

"Sit down, Edgar," Trish said, draping herself cross-legged on the floor, and patting the scuffed smeared wood, sending another tiny tornado of ectoplasm spiraling into the room to quickly join the dust motes for a chat. "Sit here next to me. Let's talk, shall we?"

Edgar sat, arranging his heron legs into a spiky, lopsided X, poised to scuttle like a crab into the nearest corner if this conversation didn't go well.

"Edgar, dear new friend, I'm going to get right to the point. I don't know how much time I can hang around. Not even sure if it's permitted to be here yet, but I am and I will be blunt." She rearranged herself briefly, folded her hands in the empty space on her lap, and stared intently at Edgar. "Edgar. Antoine and Saima came back because they had something to do. Now I have something to do, too, and I hope you will pay close attention. Edgar." Edgar raised his eyebrows, paying closer attention. "Edgar. What you have been doing up until this moment is eating the menu instead of the food."

Edgar gaped at Trish. Blunt certainly didn't mean clear. "Huh?" bubbled out of Edgar's throat, a cartoon balloon of intelligent conversation.

Trish laughed again. "You have been so busy studying the tile work on the yellow brick road, you weren't actually going anywhere at all."

Edgar couldn't stop the next bubble from popping in the room. "What?"

"Ah, nuts, this isn't as easy as I thought. Some sort of cosmic interference. Okay, let's try again. Edgar, you have worked your whole life in a dimly-lit room. You were busy running start-up scripts in an environment with artificial air; lots of wires, all headed out of the room, delivering information and help to other closed systems. There was a gigantic humming server cranking all that great stuff out, but you were just watching it work: you weren't working yourself." Trish watched Edgar's face, static and confused, and she tried again.

"Maybe you could think of yourself as the server in this place. You are the one who will chug along, helping all of us - your wires and connections - to do what we're supposed to do, work you know in your gut we can love. Isn't that what Antoine was here to tell you? Work at what you love?

"Think about it, Edgar. I know you can make the leap. You're the computer science version of a shaman. You know it, you just have to find the knowledge in that big ol' heart of yours." Trish stood, dusted off her nonexistent rear, leaned and kissed Edgar an ephemeral kiss on the cheek. "Be the you you were born to be, young man."

Edgar had closed his eyes, dizzy with the clash of real and unreal, and when he opened his eyes once more, she was gone.

The bell over the door tinkled.

Edgar still sat, blinking slowly, a bullfrog on an enormous filthy wooden lily pad.

"Excuse me? Excuse me? Do you work here?"

The bell tinkling followed by a voice talking penetrated Edgar's addled receptor neurons. He turned his head toward the door, seeing another figure silhouetted against the striated light streaming through the front door. Oh, dear, thought Edgar. Not again.

"I said, *excuse* me? I'm looking for my mother."

Edgar tried to stand, could not untangle his legs, used both hands on the floor to shuffle his lanky frame sideways before he could elevate to wobbly height. He peered at the figure in the doorway, making out just a shimmer of dark gold hair around the edges. The figure moved a handbag strap that had fallen back onto her shoulder with an impatient snap. "My mother?" she said with more impatience.

"Um. Mother, ahem. Mother, yes. Is she living?" Edgar inquired politely.

"What? Of course she's living. Say, are you supposed to be here? Where is Margo Sawyer?" real urgency brought the figure two steps closer to Edgar, and now Edgar saw the woman who had been the silhouette.

What little articulation had been loitering around Edgar's tongue took off for more eloquent parts in a snap, and Edgar was confronted with a brain that denied ever having the ability to form words.

The woman was stunning, lithe; a willowy druid, with golden skin and almond eyes the color of pine boughs. Her hair was autumn wheat, flashing with gold as the sun teased the air into tickling the thick strands into motion. A warrior queen, confident and unflattered by Edgar's regard, her pose demanding she have the answers she sought.

"Where is Margo Sawyer?" the vision actually stomped her foot, sending yet another dust mote storm system into the stratosphere of the shop.

Edgar shuffled synapses like a card deck, desperately searching for vocal motor skills. "I. She. I." He cleared his throat loudly, stomped his own foot. "She's not here. Not now. That is, she was, but not now. Back soon."

The bell over the door tinkled, but Edgar beat the sound to the door. He almost bowled Margo over, held her elbow and dragged her and the packages she was carrying forward to present her, sputtering, to the younger woman. "Here!" he said in dual triumph, words and mother found. "Here is your mother."

Margo laughed. "Edgar, she knows I'm her mother. Honestly." she widened her eyes at Morgan briefly, still laughing as she gently untucked her arm from Edgar's hand, and took a step to hug her daughter with the freed arm. "Hi, honey. I see you've met Edgar. Or have you? Morgan, this is Edgar Pavelka; Edgar, my daughter, Morgan Valentina. Edgar, you and Morgan actually have something in common. Morgan is a paper rep. Well, maybe not so much in common, but she's in the world of words in a way, too.

What are you doing here, Morgan?"

Morgan was still eyeing Edgar, leery of any more sudden moves and odd behavior. "I wondered what was going on here. Aunt Claire said you're buying this place with her." Morgan gave Edgar another eye command *stay!* and giving her head a shake, she turned to look at the shop. "Oh, mom. What in the world?"

Margo grinned. "Isn't it something? Did you see the Celtic knot plaster work on the façade?" Margo turned slowly once herself. "This is going to be something."

"It's something now, Mom. What, I don't know. But something, definitely."

The bell over the door didn't tinkle. Margo stopped still, coming in the doorway, spun and stared at the doorframe over the stack of boxes topped with a paper bag in her arms.

"What in the world?" she accused the empty space where the bell should have been.

"I took it down to clean it," Caldwell said, coming forward from the back, scrubbing his hands on his jean legs, then bouncing the fabric to shake off the loose dirt. "It was filthy, not surprisingly. Let me help you with those."

"I brought some lunch from next door. You know what the name of that restaurant is? I'd forgotten. It's The Constant Velocity Joint."

Caldwell laughed, "That's a car part." He laughed harder, "A part that makes a car go. And a good name for a coffee shop with caffeine-addled clients. The owner stopped in a little while ago to find out what was going on here. She said the baker down the street - I think his name's Joseph - wants to know what happened to the old man who came to work here early mornings. Do you know who she's talking about?"

Margo looked up briefly, got busy unpacking sandwiches and cardboard coffee cups. "Maybe," was her short answer. "Can you set these over there? Thanks." She took a wool blanket from the stool, and fanning it like a bullfighter, settled it on the newly polished floor. "Is this all right?"

"Sure," Caldwell said, setting himself on the wood, putting a cup and paper plate in front of the space next to him for Margo.

"There's a spring wrap, and ah nuts, a spring wrap. I thought I ordered tuna." Margo briefly panicked, and Caldwell, seeing her concern, shrugged it off quickly. "Spring wrap is perfect," eyeing Margo surreptitiously again to see if she was okay.

Margo noticed the glance, and picked up a spring mix wrap quickly, wishing for the damn day when she found her old self again.

"I wouldn't count on that, Margo," Dr. Amy had said. "You will get used to your new self, even enjoy the transition one day quite soon."

Maybe today, thought Margo. Maybe today I'll enjoy. She practiced her Living in the Now mantra. Be. Be.

"Do I make you nervous?" asked Caldwell gently, a soft father's voice soothing his frightened child.

A baby blanket of a voice, Margo mused. If I could suck my thumb, I would. Unconsciously she rocked herself imperceptibly.

"No. You don't make me nervous. I'm...adjusting," Margo stated, coddled into truth telling. "I don't have my land legs yet. From the breakdown. Everything seems new and...unfamiliar. Dr. Amy said it's similar to learning to walk again. Mental legs just don't work like they used to. It will get better." She moved to pick up her coffee.

"Caldwell, tell me about your work," she said, changing the uncomfortable subject. "Trish said you are a what? Something to do with ancient manuscripts."

"Paleographer. Old paper, yes. I teach the study of handwriting. In brief, it involves one human working to understand the communication style of another, with centuries and societal changes in between the writing and the studying. Writing is an art as well as a means to discover history." He barked a brief laugh. "Edgar has gotten much better at explaining what I do than I can. It's changed over the years. I've changed over the years. Like you, what used to work well for me doesn't have the same usefulness.

"I thought I was a scientist. Maybe I still am, but I think I used to be a time traveler, too. What I am rediscovering is what I loved about the work I chose early in my career. There are the manuscripts still, sure. The history that can be gleaned from papyri and iron gall ink. But now I remember that it is storytelling, too. That people wrote the stories of lives; their masters' or their own, real or imagined.

"I'm remembering how it felt to imagine myself scraping the hide, drying the skins, mixing the ink. Devoted for a lifetime to putting words and pictures on paper. The visions of inking and coloring books in the magical city of Istanbul during the reign of Suleiman I, the Magnificent, the Law Giver." Caldwell stopped a moment to drink.

"You studied literature, Margo," he began again. "Can you imagine the life of a respected, well-paid and honored artisan in the Topkapi Palace? How would Suleiman write to his love, the exquisite empress of his harem? To his beloved, who the bedazzled European court observers called Roxelana? Would he write her a love poem himself? Or dictate it to a scribe from the atelier, even though he was a trained goldsmith and a skilled artisan in his own right? What tools would he use to write his passion? Who would be chosen to illuminate the Sultan's words? Would it be me?"

He glanced at Margo, returning to the wool blanket and her company from his magic carpet ride to the past; secret life exposed, he smiled sheepishly.

"The Golden Age of the Ottoman Empire and my soul was there, tending its heart with papyri and styli by candle wax light." Caldwell harrumphed, dismissing his dreamy thoughts. "Sorry."

"Don't be," said Margo, touching Caldwell's hand briefly, like a butterfly's wing, then snatching it back to herself. "We're all trying to get reacquainted with real life."

"We are, I suppose," Caldwell stated flatly. "I've lived in the past for so long. Not my own past, the past I enjoyed more than the one I was living. Not that it was a bad life. I just didn't pay attention. My wife left me because I forgot she was here. Woody Allen said that 90 percent of life is just showing up. I guess I didn't show up for a lot of life. A life unattended." He sighed.

"One day you wake up and you're 60 years old and you don't know how the hell that happened. And you might be bitter about it, or you might decide to fill up all the spaces you have left."

Margo nodded. "Trish had a word she used – chantepleure. Sing and cry simultaneously. Seems to suit these golden years."

"It does indeed. Well," Caldwell summed up, smacking his thigh, hoisting his paper cup. "Here's to both of us finally showing up."

The day of the February Chocolate & Champagne dinner dance dawned frozen solid with ice. Margo stood at the doorwall, watching the finches, wondering how they didn't get frostbite on their feet, clutching ice sculpture the rungs of the bird feeder had become. The phone rang, startling Margo into jostling coffee onto her robe. Damn! "Hello," she glared into the phone. "Mother, Mom!" Morgan announced. "Did you see the ice? Must have had freezing rain during the night. Mom, I don't have any shoes to wear! I'm not going shoe shopping in this. Can I borrow your bronze Valentina Rangoni sandals?"

Having promised to bring them along and meet Morgan at the door at 7:15 p.m. sharp, Margo smiled happily, remembering her feisty firstborn, helping at the shop one weekend, wearing holey blue jeans, a ratty cut-off t-shirt, and sequined mules; cleaning the toilet. That's my girl, thought Margo, feeling the best she had in weeks. Goodness, is that true? She examined all the corners of her well-being for mushy spots, poking in familiar dark places she knew, and found none. Picking up the phone again, she speed dialed the first number.

"Amy? I'm sorry to call you so early, but I could not wait to tell you I feel just fine right now." Tears momentarily watered the view of the finches, giving the ice multicolored auras that sashayed in the sun. "Thank you, Amy, bless you, Amy. Yes. I will do that. I look forward to hugging you, too. See you tonight."

"Viktori Alexandros! Aren't you the handsome devil!" Claire laughed at her tuxedoed husband, emerging from their bathroom, still tying his bowtie.

"What a contrivance this is!" Vik grumbled. "$250 to be tortured with clothing. Ackh, can you work this thing, Claire?" Claire got up from her dressing table, tied a perfect knot, knowing that before the night was over, the cloth would be off his neck and in his pocket. "Come in, sweetie," she called over her shoulder, answering the knock, and Annie peeked around the door. "Mom and Dad are here, Grandma. Wow, Grandpa, you look nice!" Vik growled.

Downstairs at the front door, Jaqueline hugged her mother, whistled at her father, and said "all right" to her husband as he reminded the family they were going to be late. Vik had disappeared. "Viktori, let's roll!" Claire shouted. Vik returned, putting something in his coat pocket. "What is that?" Claire accused suspiciously. "Duct tape," her husband barked, jabbing a thick thumb toward his granddaughter's strapless dress. "In the event of a wardrobe malfunction. Better safe than sorry."

Margo stood from the center of the hall, waving one hand royally as Claire and company arrived under the arch. "We have these two tables, Claire. You are beautiful," she beamed, hugging Claire in her beaded gown. "Hello, Annie, what a lovely dress! Jaqueline, it's wonderful to see you. Vik, leave your tie alone."

The others wandered off to check coats and get settled, and the two old friends had a moment to speak quietly together. "It's nice to just be able to relax and enjoy tonight," acknowledged Margo out of the blue. Claire cast a swift glance at her friend. "Really?"

"Really," Margo admitted. "Look at Bob. He's fitting into the leadership role better than I thought. It was brilliant to pick Marion as his second-in-command. I can't help thinking Trish orchestrated that succession from the next dimension. Amazing she can tweak Lynn's nose from the Great Beyond."

"Or another state of mind," both women said together.

"Margo," Claire began, and shook her head softly twice. "We're living in our next dimension already, aren't we?" Margo smiled, settled an arm around Claire's waist, as the two friends admired the softly lit space from their new perspective.

Salinger had donated the decorations, and supervised the installation for the dinner dance. She had chosen to discard the classic Valentine reds and whites, and the hall was a baroque fugue of velvet umber and satin crème de la creme. Transparent globes, suspended with invisible jewelry line, floated like champagne bubbles around the ceiling, above the tables cloaked in mocha linen, overlaid with cream brocade napkins. Table centerpieces were champagne glasses, full of colorful foiled dark chocolates.

"It's perfect. Salinger said the red dresses sure to show will add the brilliance to the room instead of clashing with it." Claire said sheepishly. "And the men won't feel hostile without the girly, frilly Valentine crap." Margo squeezed her friend a hug that brought Claire back from the comparison she was contemplating. Claire smiled, hugged Margo back. "How many new girls will it take to change the world, Margo?" Claire asked.

"All of them," Margo replied immediately.

Hours later, Margo plopped into the chair next to Claire, who was talking with Edgar, Caldwell and Morgan. "I never thought I'd say this in life, but I can't wait to get these shoes off," Margo groaned, rubbing the back of her foot where the strap Enzo Angiolini designed wound around her ankle.

"We were talking about that very subject," Caldwell volunteered.

"Shoes?"

"No, change."

"Caroline mentioned that Ezekiel is starting to crawl, and commented that life as you know it changes fast when you're a parent," Morgan explained. "Caldwell said life changes forever when your children leave home. Uncle Vik said life changes forever when you retire. Edgar said life as we know it changes every nanosecond." Morgan smiled at Edgar, who was gleaming back at Morgan in a way that Margo wanted to ask somebody to explain.

"I remember Trish talking about the change cancer causes," Janine mused quietly, comfortable in the company. "She said choices become critical. What tools do you reach for? A bottle? A Bible? A brick? I suppose those are the decisions we make every day."

Salinger put her hand on Caldwell's shoulder, leaned in to kiss his offered cheek, as he placed his own hand on hers. "You bedazzled once more, honey," the proud father said, as seconds of support made a wave around the table. Salinger said her good nights, and Claire rose to hug the surprised woman when it was her turn. "Congratulations, Salinger. This is your time and you shine more every hour."

"Good night, Bianca," Claire hugged the next woman who had put out her hand to shake Claire's, surprise blinking in her eyes, as Margo, watching, smiled.

"New girl?" Margo asked Claire, as the still shocked young woman walked away, whispering to her companion and glancing over her shoulder at the fondly smiling Claire.

"Bianca," said Claire with pride. "I remembered her name."

"How many new girls does it take to change the world?" whispered Margo.

"All of them," answered Claire emphatically, signaling the nodding and tieless Viktori it was time to go.

Chapter 11

"I don't understand what is happening," Margo said softly.

Claire and Margo had just moved the music cabinet to the spot they knew it belonged, in the back corner of The Artcraft Shop. Claire stood up straight, looking at Margo without answering, waiting for her friend to share what was difficult to grasp.

Margo looked slowly around the space that was revealing itself in its new form. The front windows still wore the tape the installers had not removed from its transparent surface. Light from the chandelier, soft and glowing, rather than illuminating, drifted to the floor, pooling in pale shadows. The glass countertops wavered as the wind moved the wreaths on the light poles outside, joining the dance the reflection from the little fireplace had choreographed.

"It wakes me up at night. Just as I'm drifting into sleep. It's then that my mind decides I need to be reminded that this can't be happening. That this cannot be real. None of it."

Claire busied herself tying her long, dark hair into a knot at the back of her head, waiting.

Margo sat on the floor, pulled her headscarf off, dropped her hands into her lap, the ability to hold them up lost.

"I'm scared, Claire," Margo confessed.

Claire joined Margo on the floor, "I know," Claire agreed.

"We're chasing ghosts, Claire," Margo said softly. "Everything I've ever known keeps bashing up against what is going on in my life now. You've known me for decades. When have I ever acted on a whim? I don't think I've ever paid any attention to what my gut was telling me." Margo sighed, clutched her stomach. "Did we see what we thought we saw? "

"We did, Margo," Claire said with heat. "No good can come of denying it."

"It doesn't fit," Margo shrugged, hands out in need.

"There isn't an explanation that we have experience with."

"Edgar tried to explain something like it when I first met him. But I didn't understand altogether what he was saying." Margo stood, walked to the doorway to the back room, peering at the fireplace, and the boxes stacked on top of the old work table. "He grabbed his head like he wanted to shake out the words he needed. That's how I feel now."

Claire came to Margo, walked into the firelit room, put her arm on the mantel. "Do you remember Trish talking about the possibility of time travel, Margo?"

Margo laughed. "I sure do. I thought she'd had too much wine."

Claire smiled, "Me, too, but Trish thought she was on to something. A string pulled taut between two hands. An ant on the finger. How the distance could be shortened by just looping the string; bringing the fingers together so the ant just stepped across."

"Maybe that's what is going on here, you think?"

"I think thinking doesn't have a lot to do here. Our string has been looped. Margo, we honestly don't have any idea how many other women have experienced this. This group hallucination, or awakening or whatever. I don't know what to call it. It's not as though we have anyone we could ask. I wouldn't know where to start. My experience has been that anyone who talked like we're talking, or saw what we saw, or claimed any connection to anything that wasn't in the newspaper, was wrong first, and desperately confused, second."

"And we put money into this delusion."

"No. If there's one thing I do know, it's not a delusion. A dream maybe. A guided dream. Anastasia has no trouble with this. She saw what we saw, believed it was possible and is confoundedly blasé about it.

She made up her mind that snowy day she would work in the shop, never faltered when she stepped in here with her buckets and mops, and really saw what the place was like. She just rolled up her sleeves and dug in. She believed. We can too, Margo."

Margo smiled, put her headscarf back on her hair, tied it with determination at the back of her head. "Trish used to say something - what was it? To accomplish the impossible you first have to plant both feet firmly in the absurd." Margo widened her grin. "All we can do is shuffle our rickety selves forward."

"Little steps, Margo. That's how we start."

"Has anyone seen Trish?" asked Margo, as the draperies she had come through waved back into position, guarding the inner sanctum from the public floor of The Artcraft Shop. One hour from now, the bell over the door would tinkle on the new life of the store. When the door opened, crabapple blossoms would swirl on the brightly polished wood floor, vortexes of pink and white joining the other uninvited petals in merry conversation with guests, patrons and the accidental visitor on this sunny May Day, the shop's new birthday.

Dr. Amy paused in mid-sentence in front of the flickering fireplace, squinting her eyes to open her professional third eye, examining her patient and friend for clinical creases. "Trish's urn is not on the counter," Margo explained.

"She's right here," Caldwell said, patting the oak box that was keeping company with the Czechoslovakian golden pheasant teapot on the fireplace mantel. "Janine moved her in here. She said she'd be happier to share some quiet time with her friends."

"Oh, good," Margo fussed, smoothing her suit skirt nervously, smiling at Janine, leaning against the oak work table, and Janine smiled softly, too. "I'm glad she's here."

"Indeed," laughed Edgar, and laughed harder when all eyes turned to him; Dr. Amy speedily switching the crosshairs of her third eye to sight on the chuckling young man.

Morgan moved from Edgar's side, gracefully passing the Queen Anne wing chair and its companion table, to look closely at the teapot on the mantel. "Mom, don't you have some of this pattern? Is this teapot yours?"

"No, it's not," Margo said, coming to join Morgan at the fireplace. "I have some dessert plates. Antoine - that is - a friend told me it's a fairly common pattern. I don't know where the plates at the house came from. There are some in the cabin, too."

"I do," said Morgan. "I know where they came from. These are from Dad's great-grandmother's good china set. I have some dinner plates and the soup tureen. You remember, Mom? Oh, that's right. You aren't very good at family history. Dad's great-grandmother was from Czechoslovakia. Slobovoda was her family name. A distant relative taught at the university in Prague in the first part of the last century, I think. Franz maybe. Yes, Professor Franz Slobovoda. He taught paleography."

It was Caldwell's laugh that focused the group's attention next. "The old greets the new," he chuckled, taking Margo's hand. "Slobovoda wrote some of the papers in Lavoisiere's collection of Czechoslovakian history. Edgar? You recall the name?"

"I do," said Edgar softly, taking Margo's daughter's hand, remembering vividly Antoine's story of his mother, the fragile and peach-cheeked Irina Slobovoda. "Remarkable, really. Divine chaos. Circles within circles."

Dr. Amy interrupted the reverie. "Do I need to be concerned here?" she asked in a good imitation of the voice of reason in a world

291

gone mad. Janine, standing next to her by the desk, laughed merrily. Dr. Amy stopped short of whipping out her appointment book, an item always with her since she opened her private practice in April, specializing in the issues of older women making the transition from warrior to elder. She had begun that sacred labyrinth walk herself with the help of the women in this warm and glowing room.

"Like an onion," Annie said. She startled at the sudden attention, as all eyes turned to her. "I mean the new from the old. Like the layers. Peeling the layers."

"Revealing the center," Margo said, squeezing Caldwell's hand. "The new from the old. Isn't it amazing? Art imitating life. That's what we chose for the shop. Art imitating life. Shadow puppets made of patinaed metal, abandoned and lost on railway bridges and roadsides. Candle holders from broken glass. Journals from discarded mother boards. Sheet music of scores by young composers restoring old film soundtracks. Antique paper with gothic letterform words inked. Reborn. What do you call it, Claire?"

"Repurposed," Claire rose from the second wing chair, and touching the letterform desk gently on her way toward the draperies and the front of the store, she thought reverently, *Thank you, Uncle Antoine, thank you Saima Aaltonen, thank you Trish Beloved Dish.* Claire took Anastasia's hand, entwining her knobby fingers lovingly with the smooth, pink flesh of Annie's own.

Chantepleure

On this rebirthing day for The Artcraft Shop, the grandmother and granddaughter together took one each of the mottled and shaking hands of the old man who had been sitting quietly smiling in the other wing chair, awed he had lived to see his wife's dream come to life once more, content to feel his own life rekindled, for however long.

"Come," beckoned Margo, still holding Caldwell's hand. "Let's open for business. Let the bell tinkle and see what happens next. Shall we?"

Epilogue

Early Summer, One Year Later, Idaho Wilderness

"Sorry!" Dr. Amy said to Annie, sparks from the log Amy toppled onto the glowing fire sending the young girl jumping back. Claire laughed. "Miss Michigan Outdoors will have one more story of dire peril to tell her friends when we get back. Right after the fire-breathing mosquitoes and 20-feet tall whitewater waves." Annie stuck her tongue out at her grandmother, and Claire roared with mock insult. Annie smiled, sat next to Claire, who put an arm around her and grabbing her head, gave her a knuckle rub.

"Last year you would have called my mother to come pick me up," Annie said, a little surprised.

"Last year I wasn't the same person I am now," Claire nodded at Margo, who smiled sleepily at her old friend.

The friends were camped on the fifth night of their second annual Patricia Worthington Memorial Adventure. On the autumn equinox last September, those present had traveled with Trish to the Upper Peninsula island she loved, and following her strict instructions, at midnight, shovels in hand, they all had illegally buried Trish the Dish's ashes at the foot of her grandmother's grave. Then, building a fire, crying and laughing, the friends had toasted the lives of all women who had gone on to their new adventures.

It was last year in the midnight cemetery when Edgar had shared the story quietly that he had seen and bid farewell to Trish and Saima on that first day of The Artcraft Shop, as the two women had smiled, turned and disappeared into the cubbies that held the old manuscripts from Antoine Lavoisiere's life.

They all had vowed to continue with a trip a year, a memoriam and a celebration.

Caldwell sat back down from a foray into the Ponderosa Pines of Idaho, on the banks of the Salmon River, and put his arm around Margo, who resettled against his side. "I wish Janine had been able to come," Caldwell observed.

"I'd like to have her reason not to be here though. Imagine! A book signing tour after all those years without words. She's put her heart

into the words in the new book. Good thing hearts can be reborn, too."
Claire's soft smile was shining straight at Margo.

Amy laughed raucously. "Words. Words and our Annie here,
startled out of her shoes by that big orange cat that wandered into the
shop last summer."

Claire hugged Annie tighter. "That old kitty would have been
pissed to get hit with that fistful of letterforms you picked up to throw.
That old cat's happy you put the words back."

"Edgar's started writing," Morgan said softly. All eyes turned to
Edgar's sheepish smile. "Just a little history," he demurred. "Just a small
history from the books and manuscripts Antoine left. Spoon is doing the
hefty lifting with the research, and the cataloguing and the outlining."

"Pshaw, Edgar, the book will have both our names on it, side by
side, in the same sized font. I want the window seat in the limo on the
book tour though." Caldwell joked.

"Who's minding the store, Margo, Claire?" Amy asked,
contentedly stifling a lazy yawn.

"New girl."

Margo laughed as Claire shot her the Popeye look.

Annie sat up and yelled, "How many new girls does it take to
change the world?"

"All of them!" shouted the friends.

Made in the USA
Columbia, SC
19 April 2022

59171694R00183